C000104460

ELLIE FRUMPP
PEE AITCH DEE

Phie Robertson

Badinerie Books

I am well aware that funding bodies and universities are full of incredibly bright people doing amazing work. This book has been written only to amuse and entertain. It is a work of fiction, and I must stress that the story, names, characters, institutions, businesses, publications, events, inventions and incidents portrayed are made-up. The only exceptions to this are obvious references (geographical, historical, literary, musical, film, commercial etc.) that help give context to the storyline. No identification with actual persons (living or deceased) is intended or should be inferred.

Copyright © 2019 Phie Robertson
All rights reserved.
ISBN-13: 978-1-5272-2503-9

Contents

1

DEAD ON ARRIVAL

I am She: I am the Mad Woman in the rear view mirror. Today, *The Best of James Bond* is playing on my tape deck, and I am singing along, slaughtering semi-tones. You can spot me in the queue next to the industrial estate, amid the drifting exhaust fumes. The smell of fried onions is seeping into the car from the burger van parked next to the tyre shop nearby. The traffic lights are unremittingly red. My love-life is non-existent. Do I care? No. I am soaring over a vast volcanic crater in the Far East; *I can feel the heat.*

Now, I admit that it *is* incongruous, literally chugging along in my decrepit brown Volvo to that unforgettable melody from Monty Norman. I realise that tossing my head seductively at the small, gap-toothed gentleman driving the Reliant Robin in the next lane is not necessarily to be recommended (although he ignores me anyway – I think he is appalled). Granted, as my virtual Aston Martin speeds its way down a hill in Monte Carlo, I can't help noticing the sign to Middle Waddling out of the corner of my eye. But it is worth it, isn't it? This mobile fantasy slot is my form of catharsis; a vent for my anal retention. Where else can I express myself? Here, I can say what I like, be who I like, and say 'fuck' without offending anyone.

I was to start a new job. The interview had gone well, but as I ambled back to the station that day, I felt empty and unexcited. I had yet to find out what I wanted to be in life, and was merely continuing along the line of least resistance. How is it that some people *know* what they want to be? There must be advantages to having a murky trajectory – a misty, unplanned future: a less intense feeling of disappointment in later life, perhaps? In retrospect, I should have considered a year off. I could have toured the world as a waitress (starting in the Virgin Islands, appropriately enough); but I am naturally conscientious and guilty and felt I should do something 'worthwhile' (I am not very waitress-y either, in all fairness).

On the day of the interview, I remember noting a rather doleful girl sitting on a green plastic chair in Harry's Greasy Spoon Café near the station. She was eating a large doughnut. In fact, it was such a large doughnut, I could hardly see her face, and it seemed to me as if she were hiding behind it. Hiding from the World Behind a Large Doughnut – a decent enough strategy, especially if it is fresh and jammy (what is the point of a doughnut with a hole?). For a moment, I thought how *nice* it would be to retire having 'done' this

2

career thing[1]. But my Auntie Ruby said you should never wish your life away and I think she was probably right. Still, there was something ineluctable in the way the job was offered and accepted. The people seemed 'nice' enough, the objectives 'worthy' enough, the location 'pleasant' enough. A place called Hardnox – a rather small university town nowhere near anything in particular (well, apart from Middle Waddling).

It had taken me a couple of weeks to find somewhere to live: the usual soul-destroying experience. Traipsing round an unfamiliar urban landscape, ringing from dicky telephone booths, clutching a local paper creased and blotched with hopeful red circles.

"I'm sorry, dear, you really will have to be quicker if you want to get accommodation in Hardnox at this time of year – the students, you know."

And then there are these awful letting agents who, with seemingly non-existent senses, show you around the most noxious places, at the most inflated prices. Smooth young men: too much aftershave.

"As you see, we have quite a spacious bed-sitting-kitchen-dining room here," said Mr Fixit from Smallholdings Inc., squeezing past the cooker (bathed in sausage fat) next to the bed.

At least driving back and forth from home enabled me to indulge my fantasies regularly, but the duality of my existence meant an inevitable let-down. Each time I reached another destination ('a bijou flat with all mod cons' or 'a character garden studio in desirable area'), I had to make that painful transition from 'Bond girl' to

---

[1] One of my old college friends has a great definition of a 'career'; he said 'I thought that meant going downhill rapidly out of control'. Need I say more?

Miss Jo Bloggs; from Hilton to hovel. Reality was inevitably an aching anticlimax ('a dirty, minute room with peeling wallpaper and a Baby Belling'; 'a dirty, minute room with peeling wallpaper and a Baby Belling with a dense *Cupressus leylandii* pressing against the only window').

I finally found a room in a three-storey house of bedsits not far from one of the rare green spaces in town. The landlady, a wiry, well-spoken, well-dressed woman of about fifty, was highly predictable.

"Oh yes, this is a *delightful* bedsit, in fact, my niece used to live here when she was a student. I *would* appreciate it if you could pay the deposit with cash. We're off to the Seychelles next week, and cash is *so* much more reliable. As you see, there is a splendidly trendy bed." She pointed to a sponge strip in the corner of the room. "Very à la mode, don't you think? Go on, try it out, go on," she urged with mock enthusiasm. I got onto the floor and lay on the 'bed'. A puff of mould spores and assorted mite-related debris squirted out of a small hole in the cover, and I sneezed. "Splendid, splendid!" cried the landlady, whose name was Mrs Nibbly.

"Plenty of cupboard space," she continued, gaily opening an elderly door with chipped paint. A flurry of friendly moths greeted her. "You wouldn't believe it, but we actually have a problem with space in our seventeenth century home in the country. The cooker's over here." She guided me to (yes it was) a Baby Belling behind a screen. "It's got a grill and everything, oh."

Whoops, the professional landlady act slipped a bit as even she was genuinely appalled at the charred remains in the grill pan: a mixture of gnawed bones of uncertain provenance, and discarded tomato skins dusted delicately with a haze of *Penicillium*. Her composure was quickly restored, however.

"Oh, naughty Mr Tailor," she simpered, "he did *promise* me that he'd make the room fresh as a daisy! Still, that won't take long to tidy. And you have a lovely big window. We are having a new conservatory put on our house. Had a devil of a row with the planning people: listed building," she continued in a chummy, confiding sort of way, moving her eyebrows up as if to say 'pity me'. "You don't dye your hair, do you?" she added dubiously.

I was pleased to see Mrs Nibbly leave, weighed down as she was by the substantial wad of money I had given her. She had snatched the cash from my fingers in a most undignified manner that smacked of greed, or desperation. Frankly, I had seen enough. I was reaching that weary, 'out-of-will-power' stage which had allowed my standards to drop. But at least this hovel was in a nice street with a deli at one end, and a paper shop round the corner.

I had duly spent many hours tidying the place up, and was attempting to make it homely, building on what meagre vestiges of potential I could find. The aforementioned window was certainly an asset. Although there were risks involved in its operation (*Madame La Guillotine* would have been proud), it ensured that one's gaze was automatically directed to something green and alive. Yes, there was indeed a *leylandii* nestling nearby – its dark intimacy intrusive, but its foliage fragrant – a refreshing contrast to the stale interior of my new home. I had to hire a carpet shampooing machine, which, whilst initially 'keen to clean' (as the slogan assured me it was), soon flagged with decades of accumulated dirt. The end result was a mixed blessing. Although it did a reasonable job within its own limits (Mr Tailor or one of his forebears had clearly decoked their motorbike in the middle of the room), it brightened the already shocking pattern, creating a fascinating ophthalmic assault with mildly nauseous consequences.

The shared bathroom, in faded avocado, was stained but tolerably hygienic. The calcified cold taps hung with incipient stalactites, especially on the bath, where geological time was marked by a dripping 'tick tock'. A glossy red and blue cardboard tube of cleaning powder, its base beginning rust, had left a series of ignoble Olympic rings on the bath-side. The main shortcoming, however, was the sink which, when drained, sucked the water from the U-bend in the shower. The strangulated sound it emitted was quite awful. It was worse at night, when, cloaked in the quiet oblivion of half-wakefulness, trips to the bathroom culminated in a fear-fuelled adrenalin-rush. For long seconds, I would be convinced that I was to be a midnight feast for the monster behind the shower curtain. The dreadful noise was always followed by an insidious seeping of smells from the sewers of Hardnox, a miasma worthy of 19th century London. Constant manual topping up of the shower U-bend was required and often forgotten about until the stench prompted action from someone.

I had just got round to dabbing at a sporulating colony of *Aspergillus* in the fridge, when I heard a knock at the door.

"Come in," I said, "door's open." After a brief pause, the door creaked, and in peered a small, earnest face.

"Oh, hello," it said, "I just thought I would pop in and welcome you. Er, my name's Jemima, I live in the room opposite."

"Hello," I said. "Very pleased to meet you. My name is Ellie, Ellie Frumpp[2]. I would shake you by the hand but, yuk!"

"Are you all right?" Jemima took a few cautious steps forward. "Have you hurt yourself?"

"No, no – no problem. Roving mould, I'm afraid. That's all." The *Aspergillus*, now evicted from its long-term ecological niche, took revenge by becoming globular and revolting, and sliding onto my thumb. "Come in and have a cup of tea."

"Oh I would but I, er, do you have any camomile?" she said timidly.

"Well, yes, as a matter of fact, I have."

"Oh good." Jemima came in and sat on a battle-scarred armchair, a scratched and stained veteran in dire need of a truss.

"Be careful of that chair, I think one of the rubber thingies has snapped," I cautioned.

"Rubber thingies?" Jemima looked a bit alarmed. "Oh, rubber thingies," she repeated, the concern draining from her face as she located the flaccid strap dangling beneath the bulge that was her backside. She made a stevedore's adjustment of position to ensure an even keel.

"Well, you're doing a good job," she said, looking at my smudged face and dish-pan hands, "it was a little bit

---

[2] Yes, my name is Frumpp; Frumpp by name, frump by nature, I've heard it all before. Yes, and people have made the connection between me and the largest land mammal on Earth.

of a mess in here, wasn't it? I don't think Mr Tailor was a very good tenant, was he?"

"That's a bit of an understatement," I said, smiling.

"Hmm," said Jemima, giggling. There was something a little restrained about my guest. Her compact prettiness shone defiantly through her apparent attempts to remain plain. Wisps of bouncy blonde hair rebelliously propelled themselves from a bunch held together with a band decorated with two large green plastic blobs of the primary school variety. Although clad in a bright turquoise knitted top with woolly appendages[3] matched with a basically brown, long, floral, corduroy skirt, she could not conceal an admirably female form. Her bulbous black shoes completed the picture which, despite lacking much in the way of harmony, was charming and innocent.

"What do you think to the Nibbly, then?" I said, as my trusty kettle sighed into action.

"Who? Oh, *Mrs* Nibbly," said Jemima, with a bit too much respect. "Well, she's all right really."

"Have you seen my 'splendidly trendy' bed? I'm wondering whether to get pest control in for the weekend."

"*Really?*" queried Jemima, a little alarm flickering over her face again.

"No, not really," I said, beginning to feel a certain lack of rapport.

As Jemima took the proffered mug, I detected a hint of politely constrained disapproval as she read the slogan on the side.

---

[3] Frumpp's Fashion Tip Number 1: woolly appendages are to be studiously avoided.

"Bit of a studenty mug I'm afraid," I said, slightly embarrassed.

"*Really*, you're a student," said Jemima, eagerly.

"Well, no, not anymore," I said, "I've got a job up at the university – research sort of thing."

"Oh, how *nice*," said Jemima, with more enthusiasm than I had ever managed to muster. "I work at the university too. I'm a secretary at the Department of Biochemistry."

"Do you enjoy it?"

"Oh, *yes*," said Jemima, "I wouldn't want to do *anything* else. I work for a really nice professor." We sipped our drinks in silence. I could tell that Jemima was working up to something. She fidgeted with her mug, and her lips kept opening and then shutting again, as if she was about to speak. Finally, she said, "Er, I thought you might like to come to our church. We meet every Thursday and Sunday. It's great fun."

I'm ungrateful, I know. Although such invitations are always well motivated, they somehow disappoint. One is lulled into a sense that someone may like you, only to find that the friendliness on offer is a means to another end.

"Oh, well, you know, I'm not really into that at the moment. I'm not sure I believe in God. I like to think I believe in *good* though. I sometimes think the other 'o' must have got lost somewhere in religious history."

"That's *so* interesting," said Jemima, sounding unconvinced. I had this feeling I would have to watch that she was not on the kerb the next time I said 'fuck' in my car. She smiled uncertainly and finished her drink in silence.

"Well, I must be off – work to do." She looked earnest and sweet again. "Thanks for the tea. I'll see you soon."

"Yes, thanks. It was very nice of you to pop in." And it was. Despite the attempt at recruitment, I could see that Jemima was fundamentally a good soul, and the first sign of amiability I had encountered in the town.

I went back to the scrubbing, removing the last of the mould from the freezer box. Do you remember Dr No? He set Bond a test of human endurance that required crawling through a long expanse of tubing filled with tarantulas. I wondered whether a better task would have been to clean my bedsit: positively Herculean.

The day after was my first at work. The concrete campus was just outside the city and I was planning to get the bus. It was one of those blank September days, the sky uniformly white, offering no hint of sun or rain. I was up and out early enough to detect that rather depressing sense that summer is over. My poor old Volvo was all dewy. On closer inspection, I noticed a sticker on the windscreen. 'This vehicle is parked illegally, and will be towed away. Recovery fine £100'. Welcome to Hardnox, I thought.

I was later to learn that you had to be on your guard in Hardnox. A second over your designated time and the pick-up lorry would magically materialise. Cars would be prised, creaking and squeaking from their comfy roadside slots, leaving pregnant shoppers and toddlers stranded, and tourists bemused at the disappearance of their rental vehicles.

I imagined a big black tow truck appearing like some beastly alien to feast upon my metal friend and quickly got to work on the sticker which was intentionally placed to obscure the driver's view. Its removal, with the application of hot soapy water, did little for my punctuality and appearance. Still, the need to drive to work was a good excuse for a quick fix of fantasy: Lulu's forceful 'Man with the Golden Gun'. The gleam returned to my eye. There was something very wicked about Bond at this time in the morning: it was a bit like having a gin with your breakfast. Unfortunately, I got lost in the over-complex one-way system, and had to turn the music off to concentrate[4].

I finally made it to the Department of Administrative Studies (DoA, as it was fondly called). I was due to meet Professor Ronald Tweezer, one of the people who had interviewed me, at 9.30. I was already about ten minutes late. Windscreen sticker aside, the jobsworth in the car park was most reluctant to let me use any of the parking spaces. As a result, I was a little hassled, my heel got stuck in a crack in the pavement, and I laddered my tights.

Now, I don't look good in women's clothes. I've always looked bulgy in skirts, rubbery in dresses, and I cannot cope with things of a stocking-y nature. The latter merely enhance the thickness and hairiness of my legs and wrinkle generously around the ankle. This lack of feminine grace is not a new thing: I used to have difficulties with school uniform as well. How good you look in school uniform is a major predictor of future fashion sense. It sorts out the sheep from the goats: I am a goat through and through. My schoolday memories consist of ill-fitting skirts, clumsy, over-the-knee socks

---

[4] Fantasy slot or no, you must never compromise the safety of your driving or your ability to navigate.

and thick knickers in winter. Those on the other side of the great divide (yes, you sheep) managed to look like something that had just sauntered off a catwalk. Granted, your clothes were subtly tacked and tweaked, but you looked glamorous and pouting; little time bombs of womanly potential.

Grown up academic garb is, however, a different thing altogether. I one-hundred percent approve of this. At my graduation ceremony, I was obliged to wear a large black sack-like gown which covered me from shoulder to well below the knee (a dream come true!), a very jolly hood and a mortar board (handy for a game of Frisbee). I could have done with this attire as I stood poised outside Professor Tweezer's office. I was acutely conscious that the slit designed for the back of my skirt was now at the front. As a result, I was exposing an unattractive piece of leg, adorned with the ladder eagerly wending its way down towards my shoe.

I hastily adjusted what I could, and knocked at the door.

"Come," came the peremptory response. "Ah, Dr Flop." Professor Tweezer was leaning forward, peering at me over his half-moon glasses. He was a large, indelicate man with a big white beard and a Liberty's bow tie. Our paths had crossed once or twice at assorted conferences as well as at the interview, but there was rarely any indication that he recognised me (or, indeed my name).

"Frumpp, er … Dr Frumpp," I corrected him. "I'm so sorry I'm late, Professor, I had problems with parking the car." I was more than a little flustered, which I hate.

I can feel myself blushing and my throat goes all blotchy[5].

"Ah, you're living out of town then, eh?"

"Well, no, not exactly, I haven't got a parking permit yet ..."

"Well then, they'll tow you away, aha, aha," laughed Tweezer with glee. "Never mind, never mind," he said, "I'm sure that Boffin of the car parks helped you out."

"Well, no, not exactly ..."

"Excellent, excellent," continued the Professor, "welcome to the department!"

"Thank you very much."

"I've arranged for Miss Whimbrel to show you round. We've squeezed you into one of the postgraduate rooms for now. It was either that or the Annex, aha, aha."

"Thanks, I ..."

"Excellent, excellent," said the Professor. "I'll call Miss Whimbrel now." He reached for his telephone, and I could hear a ringing next door. "Good morning Miss Whimbrel, Flop is here, and wants to see the department. Can you deal with her?" There was a slight muttering at the other end of the telephone. "Excellent, excellent, as you say, Miss Whimbrel. Has to sort out the post first," said Professor Tweezer, putting the telephone down, "she'll be in in a moment. Settled in all right? Where are you living?"

"I'm the other side of town, not far from the Common."

"Excellent," said Tweezer, "very nice; you've got yourself a flat then?"

---

[5] Frumpp's Fashion Tip Number 2: wear polo necks or similar if you are likely to be under pressure in public.

"Well, a bedsit. Flats are very dear."

"So they are, so they are," said the Professor, "all mod cons?"

"A Baby Belling."

"Aha, aha, aha," the Professor thought this very funny.

I was saved from further questioning by the appearance of Miss Whimbrel, a middle-aged woman, with a benign but anxious face.

"Dr Flop?" she said, rather formally.

"Frumpp," I replied. She looked a little taken aback, and adjusted her jacket. "Dr Frumpp, not Flop," I added hastily, "and do call me Ellie."

"Ah, of course, I beg your pardon. Frumpp, Professor, not Flop," she said, as if she were explaining something to a child.

"Yes, yes, of course!" said the Professor, "Frumpp, not Flop, as you say, Miss Whimbrel."

"This way, Dr Frumpp, I'll show you round. Professor Spigot sends his apologies – he's attending a meeting of the Amenities Committee this morning and has to be in London this afternoon. I know he's keen to welcome you." Professor Terry Spigot was an investigator on the project on which I was to work. I knew him by repute, and had briefly spoken to him on the telephone prior to my interview. He had been unable to sit on the panel himself, having an important Government quango meeting on the same day. A very fashionable and rather young head of department, he had apparently dazzled the Appointments Committee by his dynamism and vision.

Miss Whimbrel led me out of Professor Tweezer's room, and into a grim corridor that smelt of stale coffee on old carpet. Its military grey walls were pocked here and there by bullet-like holes: a historical record of a decade of posters and shelves.

"We are quite a small department at present but with Professor Spigot at the helm, we are expecting to expand. You are part of his grand plan! Now, this is the post and photocopying room. You have a pigeon-hole here, er, oh, I told Christian to print out a label for you, but he hasn't yet. I'm so sorry. Now, you have to get a photocopying card from me. Unfortunately, I've run out at the moment, but the order's in for a new box. I'll let you know as soon as I have one in for you. I ordered them six weeks ago, but, you know, university administration, slow moving process." She was a little defensive and a bit upset. I could see from her appearance that she was a neat and organised woman: a lack of order would cause her stress.

"Thanks, I know how it is," I said, trying to console her.

"We're a very friendly department, of course," said Miss Whimbrel, regaining her composure, "ah, here's the computer room. Now where's Christian? Christian!" she called out.

"One minute, I'm on the phone," came an impatient reply. We walked round a filing cabinet to reveal a spotty young man with shoulder-length hair, and a piece of sticky tape holding his glasses together. I also noted his rather aggressive trousers[6].

"Anyway," said Christian into the telephone, "this is hilarious, listen to this. There was this guy, see, he was

---

[6] Frumpp's Fashion Tip Number 3: aggressive trousers can make the younger generation disagreeable and the older generation nervous.

demonstrating this new software – quite complicated stuff. He kept saying 'yeah, well this runs on your bog standard PC, on Windows, easy as pie', you know. Anyway he keeps saying this, you know, that it will run on a bog standard PC. Anyway, he's doing all these tricks, really smooth, really fast, right, and then someone at the sales meeting asks what spec. his machine is, and he looks a bit taken aback and says, well, actually it's the latest Pentium Pro with 64 megabytes of RAM. Can you believe it! Absolute scream! Yeah ... yeah ... great, see you tonight, yeah? Down The Pig and Trough, great, bye then." Christian put down the telephone, and turned to face us.

"Christian, this is Dr Frumpp."

"Oh, hello," he replied, in an off-hand way. "I suppose you'll be needing my expertise at some stage."

"Well, I think there is some computing in the job, but hopefully I can manage most of it on my own."

"Yeah, well, we'll see about that. I'm a busy man, though, in demand."

"Well, I'll try not to be a burden," I said, with a smile.

"Yeah, well, you're a woman aren't you."

"Now, now Christian, we women are more competent than you think," chided Miss Whimbrel.

"Yeah, you didn't give me that impression when your terminal was upside-down and you couldn't understand why everything you typed was the wrong way up."

"That was a long while ago, Christian. I daresay you'll never let me forget it."

"Ab-so-lute-ly not!" said Christian emphatically. "Birds and technology, huh!"

Miss Whimbrel was not taking this very well – understandably, I thought. She blushed, and said, "I expect we'll see you at coffee."

"In your dreams," said Christian, in a surly way. We left.

"Doesn't quite live up to his name, does he?" I said, smiling.

"He was a little out of order. He's a very easy young man to upset. But don't you worry, we're all friends around here really!" Miss Whimbrel continued breezily. "Now, this is where we're putting you for the time being. Oh dear, the desk hasn't been cleared yet."

"Well, if you remember, Dr Spatchcock said Jenny was not to clear it," replied a young woman, peering from behind a computer.

"Oh Rosy, hello. This is Dr Frumpp. As you know, we were rather hoping she could have Jennifer's desk. Dr Frumpp, this is Rosy – third year postgrad."

"She's welcome to the desk, but there's a bit of rubble to get through."

"Oh, that will be fine, I'm sure," I said. I'd already spent the last 48 hours clearing up someone else's rubbish, so this was par for the course.

"Well," said Miss Whimbrel, "I'm sure Rosy can show you the ropes around here. We generally have coffee at 10.30. I'll see you later, Dr Frumpp."

"Ellie, do call me Ellie."

Miss Whimbrel smiled, and left the room.

"Well, what do you think of it so far?" asked Rosy, pulling a face.

"Well, it's fine I guess," I replied with resignation. Rosy was only a little younger than me. She had dark, short, curly hair, an impish expression, and, I suspected, a mean sense of humour. She was wearing a red sweatshirt with a logo declaiming 'The Biggest Peaks Charity Climb' on her left breast[7]. She seemed robust and sporty.

"It's not bad here, when you get used to it. It's got quite a good reputation one way or another. My supervisor is Dr Mike Sweeble. He's pretty cool. I've been doing some stuff at Hardnox Council. I'm giving a seminar in a few weeks, so you'll have to come along and give your opinion."

"I'll do that," I said. "Now what shall I do with all this?"

"Oh, just bung it in there," said Rosy, indicating a large cardboard box on the floor. "I'm quite sure Jenny won't be back." That sounded a little ominous. In fact, it sounded so ominous, I enquired no further as to the circumstances of the departure of Jennifer. My main concern was that it had something to do with Dr Irene Spatchcock, another member of my project team.

It took me the best part of the morning to sort out my desk. It was clear that Jennifer was either highly disorganised, or had left in a fury – a litter of brutally ripped papers and broken office equipment on and around the desk.

In order to make myself at home, I considered hanging a large James Bond film poster on my wall, which I had had at college. I concluded, however, that I had not yet gauged the mood of this new department sufficiently to know whether I would get away with such excesses. I therefore contented myself with a small,

---

[7] Frumpp's Fashion Tip Number 4: this is not to be advised, it draws attention to your assets, or, in my case, lack of assets.

politically incorrect, postcard of Mr Connery, peering cruelly over his gun.

It transpired that Dr Spatchcock could fit me in for a 'briefing' just before tea time that afternoon. I had met Irene Spatchcock at the interview and she had seemed a very charming person, although I confess that I had been unnerved by her suit, which was impressively shoulder-padded and tailored[8]. I went upstairs to her room, only to find someone already there. It was Professor Tweezer.

"Ah, excellent, excellent," he said, and then with, "Ah Flop – your turn now!" marched down the corridor.

"Bit of a character, isn't he?" said Dr Spatchcock, appearing at the door. "You get used to him after five years or so. Come on in, Ellinora[9]."

"Well, Ellinora," said Dr Spatchcock when I had taken a seat, "we were all very impressed by you at your interview. Professor Tweezer was adamant that you should be appointed."

"Thank you," I said. "Do call me Ellie."

Irene Spatchcock was an attractive woman in her mid to late thirties. She was in possession of a truly elegant figure, of height and proportions that would inspire envy in the majority of her sex. At first glance, her face projected a vulnerability, which many members of the male species would surely find irresistible, but there was an edge of steely self-sufficiency. She had an oval face, verging on the elfin, with gentle cheekbones, and a small, sweet nose that turned up just a little too much at

---

[8] Frumpp's Fashion Tip Number 5: 1990s power dressing aims to intimidate. It is clearly influenced by Romulan attire.

[9] I know, it's a mouthful. I cannot recommend a four syllable Christian name.

the end. Her mouth was wide but her lips somewhat ungenerous. She spoke deliberately and precisely with a quiet emphasis which resulted in the minor snowballing of spittle in her mouth. Her pale blue eyes, which she fixed mercilessly on any conversational partner, had an uncanny depth, producing an unnerving, knowing look, made a little cruel by a pair of finely plucked and slightly sarcastic eyebrows. Her hair was blonde and layered into an efficient and fashionable bob that framed her face to perfection.

"You know, of course, that this latest study is a grant that Professor Terry Spigot and myself share. To be honest, I am the 'mover and shaker' behind it – academic politics alas – a professor always helps to enhance a grant application." Spatchcock smiled, and wrinkled her nose in mock resignation. "Still, if my collaborations with Max – Dr Snoode – continue to go well, I might be so bold as to suggest that I may get a chair of my own in the not too distant future, and then we can leave poor Terry alone. Anyway, the great advantage for you, of course, is that I'm really in charge, so if you have any problems, you can always come to me – you may find that a little easier. Terry is always at a meeting. I am sure that we will make a good team. I hope that this will be very much a two-way process. Whilst we can draw upon your expertise, we hope that the project can also offer you something in the way of personal development," she paused and smiled knowingly. "The first thing we need to consider, of course, is this conference."

"Conference?" I enquired.

"Yes, I want us to submit an abstract about our work to the International Workplace and Productivity Meeting in Vancouver next May. It's a biennial conference run by Amity Action in Canada – they fund this study, as you may remember. Do you think you could write a paragraph about the project?"

"Well, yes, I'm sure, but I will need to get to grips with it first."

"A useful hint," said Spatchcock, raising her finger with tutorial magnanimity, "and the first rule of academe: write first, think later. Here, this should help." She passed me a thick folder containing the research proposal, along with a rather glossy flyer for the conference. "Have a look at this today and tomorrow, and see what you can sketch out for me. Now, come and have a cup of something."

Dr Spatchcock stood up decisively. She led me back down the stairs, and into a dim room, lit only by one small frosted window set behind a malodorous sink.

"The postgrads. and admin. staff tend to use this room. There's another one upstairs, but this will be more convenient for you. I'm sure we can find you a cup in here." She rummaged for a while in a cupboard, emerging a few seconds later with a large, stained mug with a china frog in the bottom of it. "I think this is one of Hermann's, but I'm sure you can use it. Tea or coffee?"

"Oh, tea please," I said.

Dr Spatchcock flicked the switch on a vintage kettle with a long, glossy and perfectly formed fingernail[10]. She was still looking threateningly smart. I glanced at my tights to see how the ladder was progressing.

---

[10] How do you pick your nose safely when you have long fingernails?

"There you go," said Dr Spatchcock, handing me a coffee. "We're a very friendly department," she said, as various other people meandered into the room, including Christian and Miss Whimbrel.

"Hi," I said.

"Make way – genius needs caffeine," said Christian, and barged past me. I added a coffee stain to my jacket. Dr Spatchcock laughed.

"Oh, he is a tease! Now, I can't stay – I've got a very important meeting now – but do make yourself at home. Sally, *darling*, could you get that letter off to Max by four?" she said to Miss Whimbrel, and left, leaving the scent of expensive perfume[11] in the air. Sally Whimbrel put her mug back in the cupboard, and followed her out.

I spent the rest of the day trying to understand what the study was all about. It was entitled 'The Hardnox Work Improvement Initiative: working for a happy workplace by the year 2000 (*WImpI-2000*)'. The project was one of several that used the 'Spigot Sympathetic Interrogation Technique' or 'SpIT' (random intercapping being popular). The idea was to take in body language and visual cues whilst interviewing people or facilitating groups. This enabled a better understanding of people's feelings, and consequently a sensitive adjustment of the conversation to maximise truthful information exchange. Because of its success in eliciting experience and opinion, the technique was a useful research tool. Irene Spatchcock and Max Snoode had undertaken a series of focus groups with workers in different environments; I was to transcribe the

---

[11] Frumpp's Fashion Tip Number 6: probably worth the investment. Whilst smelling of deodorant is inexpensive, it is not very classy.

recordings, code and analyse the data, then develop a work satisfaction questionnaire and do a survey.

I felt completely exhausted when 5.30 came around. As I left the department in search of my car, I noticed that I received a few disapproving looks from one or two members, as if leaving on time was something of a faux pas. My car had been clamped by the helpful Mr Boffin who took great pleasure in extracting £25.00 from me, tipping my feelings of how the first day had gone from 'tolerable' to 'dissatisfied'.

2

MINUTES, MEETING, DEPARTMENT OF ADMINISTRATIVE STUDIES, UNIVERSITY OF HARDNOX, JUNE 6TH, 1995

Present: Professor Terrence Spigot (chair), Emeritus Professor Ronald Tweezer, Dr Mike Sweeble, Dr Irene Spatchcock, Ms Rosy Cloudberry, Ms Jennifer Biffing, Miss Sally Whimbrel (minutes), Mr Christian Wynde-Ryder, Mr Cornelius Boffin (Car Parks and Amenities)

Apologies: Dr Hermann Peewit

1. Notes from previous minutes

Professor Spigot congratulated Miss Whimbrel on her excellent minutes of the last meeting, but pointed out that 'Tarmac', whilst often not spelt with a capital 'T', should be spelt with a capital 'T' as it was originally a trade name.

2. Matters arising

Professor Spigot updated the group on his negotiations with Mr Wulfric Ramsbottom, the gardener, to replace the mugwert against the eastern side of the department with an assortment of geraniums and busy lizzies. According to Mr Ramsbottom, the replacement of the mugwert, which is a perennial, with the aforementioned annuals, would require additional labour both in autumn and spring, but if the department would like to suggest a more colourful perennial, he might be able to comply.

Action: Colourful perennial suggestions to SW.

3. Bollarded parking

Professor Spigot introduced Mr Cornelius Boffin (Car Parks and Amenities) to the meeting. He had been invited to further discuss Professor Spigot's request for personal bollarded parking space on the university campus. Mr Boffin informed Professor Spigot that according to current university environmental policy, car parking spaces have to be limited and that the provision of personal space, whilst allowed for visiting dignitaries, was not usually afforded to members of the university under the rank of dean. Professor Spigot showed Mr Boffin University Statute 103/1899, which states quite categorically that 'Fellows and members of the *Collegium Hardnoxii* resident more than 50 furlongs from Hardnox

Tower are permitted a space in the stables for their horses, and the services of a groom'. Mr Boffin said that the statute in question was out of date, referring to the original university building in the town, and had been superseded by the aforementioned environmental policy in 1960. Professor Spigot contended that there was no formal withdrawal of the statute and until there was, he should be entitled to a parking space with retractable bollard. Mr Boffin said that this was not possible, but that Professor Spigot was welcome to take up the issue with the Vice Chancellor should he so wish.

Action: TS to talk to VC about personal bollarded car parking.

3. Stationery cupboard

Miss Whimbrel requested that staff inform her when they remove items from the stationery cupboard. Recently she has been caught short by the lack of availability of a number of items when requested, in particular, paper clips and staples. As it takes on average six weeks to obtain stationery items via the University's Central Leasing and Ordering Group (UCLOG), she would appreciate it if staff could fill in the booklet attached to the stationery cupboard by a piece of string whenever they remove goods from it. She can then ensure that items are available on request.

Action: All to use booklet on string attached to stationery cupboard.

4. Newsround

(a) Appointment of Dr Ellinora Frumpp

Dr Spatchcock informed the meeting that Dr Ellinora Frumpp had been appointed to *WImpI-2000*, the project for which she, Professor Spigot and Dr Max Snoode from the Department of Sociology had received funding from Amity Action in Canada. The first phase of the study, involving a series of focus groups, is nearly complete and Dr Frumpp's role will be to analyse the focus group material using the LOOFAH software package to inform the production of a quantitative work satisfaction questionnaire. She will then undertake a national survey of workplace satisfaction. Dr Frumpp has just completed a PhD in qualitative research at the University of Swinbrooke, and appears well qualified to do the job. Miss Whimbrel pointed out that the departmental software licence for LOOFAH expired in 1994 and has not been renewed. Dr Spatchcock asked Miss Whimbrel if she would renew the licence as soon as possible. Miss Whimbrel said she would, but that due to UCLOG, this could take up to three months. Dr Spatchcock said she was unsure as yet where Dr Frumpp would be sited, but that it was likely that she would have to share an office with Dr Peewit in the Annex. Dr Sweeble remarked that this might be unwise as once staff were sent to the Annex, they were rarely, if ever, seen again.

Action: SW to arrange LOOFAH licence.

(b) Update on Ms Biffing's study

Dr Spatchcock was interested to know what progress had been made on Miss Biffing's PhD, since she and Professor Spigot undertook their review in March. Ms Biffing reported that as she had seen neither Dr Spatchcock nor Professor Spigot for a supervision since March, she was transferring her PhD studies to Dr Stenworthy at the University of Oxford. Dr Spatchcock suggested that this would not be possible as the grant was attached to the DoA at Hardnox. Ms Biffing replied that she would not be taking the grant with her, as she had obtained an independent scholarship from the Management and Organisational Research Council (MORC). Dr Stenworthy had been impressed by Ms Biffing's research progress despite 'very poor support' at Hardnox. She would be re-starting her PhD in September, which she expected to be a success, as she now had 'a genuinely interested and helpful mentor'. Ms Biffing said she had no regrets, and that she had not enjoyed her time at Hardnox. Professor Spigot expressed regret at Ms Biffing's decision. Dr Spatchcock said that whilst these things happen, she felt obliged, for the record, to say she was disappointed by Ms Biffing's lack of loyalty. In the circumstances, she felt that it might be better all round if Ms Biffing were to leave the premises immediately, since Dr Stenworthy was to all intents and purposes an academic rival. She said that some good would come out of the move. It would mean that Dr Frumpp could have Ms Biffing's desk. Ms Biffing said that Dr Frumpp was welcome to it. Dr Sweeble suggested that before Ms Biffing left, there should be some reflection on what had happened to avoid future problems of this nature. Dr Spatchcock felt that this was unnecessary.

Action: Ms Biffing to leave the premises.

(c) Publications

Professor Spigot was pleased to announce the following publications:

Spigot, T. Spatchcock, I. and Snoode, M. (1995) Making performance review pleasurable: the use of the Spigot Sympathetic Interrogation Technique in City appraisals, *Society in Flux*, volume 3(4): 27-41.

Spigot, T. and Spatchcock, I. (1995) How to make top down change appear bottom up. *Annals of Social Dynamics*, 861: 714-758.

Spatchcock, I. (Ed.) (1995) *Facilitating Happiness in the Workplace*, Hardnox University Press (including a chapter by Professor Spigot entitled 'Innocenti's Dream').

6. Academic Research Review

Professor Spigot said that as the Academic Research Review (ARR) was due within two years, members of staff should attempt to increase their research outputs. Whilst he was pleased that he and Dr Spatchcock had formed a good collaborative alliance with the Department of Sociology, and in particular, the prolific Dr Snoode, it was important that staff continue to obtain grants and publish. He noted that whilst Dr Sweeble should be congratulated on his involvement with teaching and supervision, this should not be a priority.

7. Departmental barbecue

Miss Whimbrel reminded staff that it was the departmental barbecue on Saturday week on Hardnox Common. She had agreed to provide a variety of salads but would be grateful if other members of staff could also contribute. Dr Spatchcock wondered if the barbecue was really necessary. Professor Spigot suggested that everyone should bring a bottle of wine, beer or soft drink, as unfortunately this year his entertainments allowance had been reduced. However, Professor Tweezer volunteered to provide alcohol. Dr Sweeble said he would be happy to provide sausages and beefburgers. He could also bring his own barbecue equipment. Miss Cloudberry said she would bring in two puddings. Miss Whimbrel suggested that Dr Spatchcock might be able to bring in cake and Mr Wynde-Ryder could provide a quiche. Mr Wynde-Ryder said he did not want to bring in quiche, but might be able to bring something 'less girly'.

Actions: as specified above.

8. AOB

Next meeting: First Tuesday in December.

3

MR TRAMANE

Grace Lefavarie sat typing at her polished wooden desk in the Amity Action building. Her head remained still, her eyes intent, as her fingers flicked lightly over the keyboard of her computer: a rustle of furtive activity amid quiet concentration. Out of the large window, framed by Virginia creeper, she could see English Bay, shimmering and restless in the late afternoon sun. Tankers hummed, silhouetted and motionless; brooding but benign. The room glowed with reflected light and water. Grace paused, and glanced over her last page of work; a quick spell-check.

As research co-ordinator, Grace was directly accountable to Jack D'Oretz, head of the organisation. Her responsibilities included assessing and commissioning projects, a task she shared with Jack.

WImpI-2000 was one of many projects that had fallen under her scrutiny. The lack of detail and excess of jargon had ensured that it was rapidly consigned to her 'reject' pile, but Jack had wanted it otherwise. He said the project had potential, that Terrence Spigot had a reputation, and that a link with the prestigious University of Hardnox would be an asset to the programme. Grace had accepted Jack's decision with only a little resistance. Perhaps his understanding of the strategic value of the work was superior to hers. She still had a lot to learn, after all.

Grace's work for the next eight months would be dominated by the organisation of the International Workplace and Productivity Meeting which would be held the following year. Flyers had been sent out several months previously, and abstracts were piling up. The deadline was imminent: only a week to go.

Over the last three years, Amity Action had been doing exceptionally well. This was thanks largely to the dogged networking of D'Oretz. He now seemed to spend most of the year darting from business to business, sweet-talking millionaires into parting with money to fund projects. These, in the long term, promised to improve the working environment and business relations worldwide.

Grace looked at her watch. She had to work this evening. D'Oretz was entertaining a potential donor and she was often called upon to escort him on these occasions, his wife unwilling or unable to fulfil the role (and indeed, why should she feel obliged to get involved with her husband's work?). In this respect, Grace was an incredible asset. She was tall, elegant and well-spoken; her face was open and symmetrical; her hair was straight, long, blonde; her eyes, a striking blue; attractive in every sense of the word. Her presence was definitely to give the clientele something to admire. She had initially entered into the spirit of these occasions with enthusiasm, keen to impress Jack and do well. But now, even though she convinced herself that the end justified the means, it was beginning to pall. Jack seemed to take it for granted that she would lead on the charm offensive, leaving him to execute the business deal. She was acutely aware of her ornamental role, and uncomfortable with it. If she was to get on in the job, which was what she wanted, she should be leading on these meetings from a business perspective, not providing a pretty side show.

Grace was due to pick up Mr Tramane downtown at his hotel and had booked a table for three at the Rain City Restaurant. Twenty past five. She had to get back to her apartment and change, then get to the hotel. That would take an hour and a half. She saved the file she was working on, logged out and left. Five thirty.

The walk from the office to Grace's apartment was brief, but beautiful. English Bay was mesmerising. There was always a great temptation to pause and watch the changing colours and patterns on the water – but not tonight.

Vancouver was where Grace wanted to be. It was a wonderful place – a World City, unique, with unclaustrophobic, urban sophistication counterbalanced by accessible wilderness. Here in British Columbia she could go easily to Vancouver Island: Clayoquot Sound and the temperate rainforest. The turbulent Pacific was a therapeutic contrast to the unbalanced perspectives born of metropolitan life. Inland, she could visit the raw and spiky Rockies: the Icelands Parkway with its stupendous glaciers and brightly coloured lakes. She had been in Vancouver now for five years; she was well paid, and lived accordingly. She had no plans to move on. It was a refreshing contrast to her childhood. Grace came from London: London, Ontario. Whilst she could claim an intimacy with the River Thames and Oxford Street, the Thames she knew disappeared into a vast complex of lakes; and the street name, whilst providing comfort to brave but homesick pioneers, was emptied of its meaning, and deprived of its sense of direction. Her memories were of flatness and aestival temperature oppositions as air conditioning clashed with walls of hot, moist air.

Grace's apartment was on the tenth floor of a block overlooking the bay. She rented it at some expense, but it was worth it. Although it was not large, through careful and tasteful decoration she had given the flat a sense of space. Inside, Grace went to her bedroom and opened the wardrobe. Jack had said he wanted her in something to impress an Englishman. She sighed. She knew that a twinset and pearls were not what he had in mind. There would have to be silk – perhaps the red dress she had bought one summer when she was in Europe. It had not been worn since she tried it on in the small boutique in Milan.

The most difficult decision of the evening dealt with, Grace got herself a drink out of the refrigerator in the small kitchen, ordered a taxi, and had a shower. At twenty to seven she left the apartment. The taxi was waiting outside. It was only a couple of kilometres to the city centre but she wasn't dressed for a hike.

The Fraser River Hotel was not a mediocre affair. When she had heard that this was where Mr Tramane was staying she knew he could be very valuable to Amity. However she felt, things would have to go well tonight. Grace went to the reception desk. She had to wait while the woman in front of her was attended to. Looking up, she could see the concentric rings of rooms running round and round and up and up to a restaurant bar that looked out over Vancouver. The lady in front was fussing. The man at the counter cast Grace an apologetic glance.

"Be with you in a moment, Madam." A key card had been lost: the world was at an end. The lady, an over-fed, grey-haired American tourist, was in the process of winding herself up into a frenzy, the wattle hanging from her neck flapping in disgruntlement.

"But I had it a minute ago. Jules, did I give it to you?" She looked up at her husband whose eyes were blank with conjugal passivity, immunised by a ruby wedding's worth of verbal assault and battery. He touched the brown leather satchel he was carrying; a token gesture and all he could manage.

"Madam, I assure you that we can supply you with a replacement," said the young man, with patient professionalism.

"But that's not good enough, can't you see," shouted the lady, angrily. "It means that someone may have my key card; someone could get into my suite!"

"Would this be what you are looking for?" A cultured voice interrupted her incessant flow: an English, cultured voice.

"Why ... why yes, that's it. Where did you find it?"

"On the floor," said the man, "by your bags."

"Well thank goodness for that," said the lady. "Come on Jules," she snapped, and shuffled over to the elevator, "bring my bags!" Her husband shrugged, and with a barely perceptible rolling of the eyes, picked up five bags of shopping and followed.

"And thank you madam," said the man, amused at the lack of gratitude.

"Thank you, Mr Tramane," said the receptionist, unruffled but relieved.

"Are you Mr Tramane of Amatheia Exports, London?" said Grace, "Grace Lefavarie. I'm here to pick you up on behalf of Amity Action."

The man turned to her.

"Well, I would be happy to be picked up by you any day, I'm sure," he said, his eyes shamelessly running down her body. He was tall, lean, firm, and exuded an indolent self-confidence. His hair, parted to one side and cut short, was a rich dark brown. His face was handsome, tanned, with pale, grey-green eyes; his mouth, tickled by the recent exchange, was relaxed with a slight sardonic twist.

"I'm very pleased to meet you," he said. "Tramane; Alec Tramane." He held out a hand, looking at her intently. She shook it briefly, and detected the inevitable, but subtle, squeeze. She ignored his gaze, and said, in a business-like way,

"I've booked a table at the Rain City Restaurant; it's not far. We can walk, or catch a cab if you'd rather."

"I'd be quite happy to walk," said Tramane, still watching her.

The warm day had ceded to a fresh evening, and it was a pleasant ten minute stroll to the restaurant. Tramane ambled along the sidewalk, a contrast to the purposeful rush of commuters around him. He chatted amiably about Vancouver, his flight, and the economy in the UK. Grace responded as was expected, with polite small talk. Tramane made it easy, though. At least he was good-looking and intelligent. By the time they reached the restaurant, Tramane's easy manner had engaged her in a genuine debate about the pros and cons of city life. Had this been a year ago, Grace would have relished the opportunity to captivate him, to lubricate the business deal Jack had in store; but not this evening. She wanted to be taken seriously; flirtation was off the agenda.

At the Rain City Restaurant, they were relieved of their coats, and Grace looked around briefly for Jack D'Oretz. She couldn't see him. They were early – they must be – Jack was never late for a potential donor. Grace explained to the head waiter that they were expecting company, and he waved them formally to a cosy corner with soft, comfortable chairs.

"May I buy you a drink?" asked Grace, stopping at the bar on the way.

"A whisky and soda please," replied Tramane, "on the rocks."

Grace ordered the drinks, a glass of white wine for herself.

"How long have you been working at Amity Action?" asked Tramane, settling himself at right angles to Grace, his long legs stretched out a few centimetres from hers.

"Eighteen months now," Grace replied.

"And is it your job to charm money out of people? I'm sure you're very good at it."

"Is that how you see it?" laughed Grace, raising her eyebrows slightly. He was no push-over then.

"Actually, I'm very happy to be charmed," said Tramane, smiling, adjusting his legs and gently touching hers in the process. "Why don't you start by giving me the low-down on Amity Action?"

"You mean you haven't done your research?" said Grace, feigning surprise and crossing her legs so his no longer rested against them. The physical contact had rekindled her sense of rebellion. In other circumstances she might have enjoyed it, but tonight she would work to rule: business is business after all, even if Jack wanted a little more from her.

"Oh, I've certainly done my research," said Tramane. "I just want to hear it straight from the horse's mouth."

"Are you calling me a horse?" said Grace. She laughed, instinctively tipping back her head, exposing her beautiful neck, and then regretting it. This was an old routine. "Well, according to this horse," she continued, bringing up her hand to cover her throat, "we are an independent organisation which aims to promote harmony and happiness in the workplace – the idea being that a contented workforce is a productive one. We raise money, largely through donations, partly through consultancy work, and we fund projects worldwide which evaluate or promote good, honest working relations. I'm sure you've seen our brochures."

"Very glossy," said Tramane, with a hint of sarcasm.

"They may be glossy, Mr Tramane, but not superficial. We take our work very seriously."

A moment later, Jack D'Oretz joined them.

"Mr Tramane," he said, shaking hands and taking a seat. "Jack D'Oretz; I'm glad to see that you're being well looked after."

"I couldn't have wished for better company," said Tramane. Grace smiled on cue, and felt only a little sick.

"Thank you, Mr Tramane," she said. "Now, shall we find our table?"

The food was excellent, the wine old and costly. Alec Tramane was a man of class, and very particular about which vintage he would drink. Maybe he was playing the game too: the bill would be big. His business was import–export but he was a little vague. A good year had produced profits they wished to ostentatiously donate to a good cause. They wanted to raise their profile amongst potential clients. Donating to Amity Action was one option, and obviously they were seriously considering it.

The evening appeared to be going fairly predictably. The low lighting and warmth of the restaurant created an easy ambiance that removed the edge from what was essentially business talk. Jack seemed pleased. Grace sat patiently beside them as they talked about Amity's work. She was occasionally tempted to say something but the two of them were facing each other and the only time they turned to her was to discuss their starter and main course choices. She was the hostess after all, thought Grace crossly. For the rest of the evening, Jack's elbow was firmly planted on the table in front of her – a non-verbal 'no entry' sign. She felt excluded and irritable. She could close this deal herself with no difficulty; Jack should give her the chance. But she couldn't help noting her flimsy Italian dress and the ridiculous clutch bag she had next to her: hardly a suit and briefcase. She was a decoration – she was there to be admired, and that was it.

And Alec Tramane did admire her. Even as he talked intently to Jack his eyes would wander in her direction.

He kept moving his legs around under the table and Grace could not decide whether he was genuinely uncomfortable or simply misbehaving.

When at last the dessert menu arrived, Jack finally removed his elbow in order to take it from the waiter.

"Alec, may I tempt you?" he said.

"You certainly can," replied Tramane, catching Grace's eye, "but Grace, we've been ignoring you. Perhaps you could tell us what we should have for dessert?" His foot moved gently on top of hers and the knowing look on his face confirmed that the whole evening had indeed been an elaborate game of footsie.

Perhaps Grace had had a little too much wine to drink – after all, there'd been nothing better to do all evening. She removed her foot from under his, and placed her stiletto heel on top of his shoe. Tramane looked momentarily pleased.

"It's a difficult choice, I know," she said, "and I can see that I am the obvious expert on puddings here, but you will have to manage this decision without me, as I need to go to the washroom. At the end of the day, they are *just desserts*, and you will find them all good in this restaurant. Please excuse me," and she stood with her full weight on Tramane's foot. She noticed his sharp intake of breath, before heading for the washroom.

Grace looked at herself in the mirror and shook her head. She had gone too far. She was always being told how lucky she was with her looks. And yes, there had been times when she had used them to her advantage – it had always been easy, but it was rarely done without a cost to herself – mainly in terms of dignity and self-respect. Now she wanted recognition for her character and it was proving so much more difficult. Her anger subsiding, she began to think more rationally about the possible consequences of her actions. Jack would be furious – he might even sack her; Tramane would probably withdraw his interest in Amity.

"Oh fuck!" she whispered to herself, "I'd better go and deal with it!"

When she approached the table, she was surprised to see that Jack and Tramane seemed quite happy. Jack was eating some sorbet, and Tramane had a lovely looking tiramisu in front of him. He looked up with a smile, and one eyebrow lifted in amusement.

"I took the liberty of ordering you a lemon tart," he said. "Personally, I like a little sourness with my sweet."

"That is very kind of you, Mr Tramane," replied Grace. "How is the tiramisu? Surely no sourness there?"

"No – but a little alcohol adds piquancy, don't you think?"

"I suppose it gives it an edge."

"It makes it *much* more interesting," said Tramane, "a little wickedness concealed in a deceptively innocent package." Grace did not reply. Jack seemed oblivious to her impulsive lapse and she knew that she should be grateful to Tramane, but she would not be drawn into this badinage. She was not in the mood.

"Now I think we have been neglecting you," said Tramane, looking more serious, "and I would like to ask you a few things about your role in Amity Action." He then quizzed her on her job, asking questions about the projects they supported and demonstrating considerable understanding of the issues. There was no hint of a foot under the table and he was at last treating her like a colleague. The punishment had worked and disaster had been averted. Grace couldn't help feeling a little pleased with herself. Tramane had got the message and now he was giving her what she wanted: a conversation about the business.

Jack ordered some coffee and tried to get Tramane to tell them a little more about his company, but the Englishman kept the conversation general. Then, without much preamble, he said rather pointedly,

"Of course, being in the import–export business, we are often asked by the Government to keep an eye on all sorts of odd transactions. They are always on the look-out for the next global conspiracy," he paused and looked at D'Oretz, "you look tired, Jack." Grace thought this highly unlikely, and turned, smiling, to Jack, about to crack a joke about his amazing capacity to work all hours. But she was surprised to see that his demeanour had changed. He did not look *tired* exactly, more shocked.

"To be honest, I'm a little worn out myself," continued Tramane. "I'm a bit jet-lagged. Maybe we should call it a day."

"I'll get the check," said Jack quickly, motioning to the waiter.

They parted in the street, D'Oretz shaking hands hurriedly with Tramane before taking a cab. Grace accompanied Alec back to the hotel. As they walked along he smiled and said,

"Well, you've certainly left your mark on me tonight. I'll have a bruise to remember you by."

"I'm sorry about your foot," said Grace, looking contrite, but relieved that he was being good-humoured about it. "I should have restrained myself. I'm immensely grateful that you said nothing to Jack."

"I daresay I deserved it. I guess I forgot we were at a business meeting. But can you really blame me? You are a very attractive woman, and that dress of yours does nothing to conceal that fact."

"Well yes, I do blame you," she said, "but I also blame myself. I know that Jack expects me to host these events, and I do take on a certain role – but I hate being excluded from the business side of things. I'm actually rather good at it."

"I can believe that. Jack has a real asset in you, Grace – you are beautiful and intelligent. He'd better watch out, or he might lose you."

Grace was amazed at how frank she was being and, feeling suddenly treacherous, felt the need to defend D'Oretz.

"He is much better in the office," she said quickly, "he really does appreciate my intellectual input there. It's just this sort of thing really."

"Well, you are a convincing team, and I'm definitely interested in you." Was there a double meaning in that? Grace was on her guard again. This man was quite annoying. One minute he was being inclusive and understanding; the next he was setting off little alarm bells in her head.

"I'm sure you know that I wouldn't have travelled half-way round the world if I wasn't seriously interested in you." Bugger, there it was again. But how would she feel if this were a Saturday night and he were her date? He was a very handsome man – but she stopped herself – a very handsome man who had played footsie with her all evening. That made him a creep.

"Would you care for another drink?" They had reached the hotel. Grace was a little surprised at his offer, but she should have been prepared for it. It was nothing out of the ordinary.

"I, er I have a busy day tomorrow."

"You mean you have to wash your hair?" he laughed and Grace couldn't help smiling at her feeble excuse. "Look," said Tramane, "we've talked a lot of business this evening and things were decidedly more interesting once you were included – and by that I mean Jack gave me a lot of company-speak but when I finally got round to talking with you – well – you told me how it was on the ground. I would love to have some more intelligent talk – perhaps about other things," he paused. They were in the lobby now, and he touched her shoulder gently and she liked it. 'Creep', she reminded herself, 'he's a creep'.

"Intelligent talk?" she repeated, raising her eyebrows.

"Intelligent talk," he said, "anything you like."

Grace paused. Was this a genuine offer? 'No' she concluded, 'wishful thinking. This man wants a bit of feminine company for the night'.

"Not tonight," she said, smiling. "Remember – you're jet-lagged. I'll see you tomorrow."

"I'll look forward to it," said Tramane, leaning forward and kissing her cheek. "Goodnight, Grace."

"Goodnight," she replied, thinking that he would have shaken her by the hand if she'd been short and fat.

4

BURIED UNDER A PILE OF THE PROVERBIAL

After about a month in the DoA, I found myself in the red. My cash machine had flatly refused to deliver the goods to the mixed amusement and irritation of a lively Saturday evening queue in Hardnox. On investigation, it appeared that I had not been paid.

"Oh, Dr Frumpp," declared Sally, the following Monday, "Dr Spatchcock can't have got you onto the payroll in time. I'm so sorry!" She promptly rang the Finance Office where an officious gentleman informed her that I had not been put 'on the system'. It was now too late to get me onto the next month's payroll as well. Sally generously approached Irene on my behalf, and was informed that the appropriate paperwork had been left in Sally's in-tray weeks before. Sally then felt immensely guilty, and began sorting through the backlog on her desk. By tea time, the poor woman was close to tears. I had managed to cleave her from her office, with the suggestion that a cup of tea might clear her mind, when Irene intercepted her in the corridor, brandishing a manila folder.

"Dear Sally," she began, "look what I've found! Silly me! You'd better see to these immediately; we don't want Ellinora on the street." It was clear by the dust and autumnal curling of the cardboard that the folder had been sitting neglected in Irene's office for some time. Sally had immediately taken the forms to the man in the Finance Office, who said that it would take at least a week to set up, and that I would still not be paid for the next month. His iron will was melted only when Sally sat in his office, moaning, with her head in her hands. This embarrassment had enabled him to set everything up immediately. I was to receive two months' salary next month, but would have to live in debt until then.

I spent half the following day with my bank manager, an unsympathetic fellow, who was not entirely convinced by my story. He said he would arrange a temporary overdraft. I would, however, have to pay assorted bank charges. In a brave moment, I asked Irene if I could claim these back from the university, but she laughed, saying there was no heading in the grant for 'bailing out employees'.

I had dutifully stored Jennifer's bits and pieces in the large cardboard box. There were assorted documents and personal items: the historical record of an uncompleted PhD. Flicking through one of her notebooks, I couldn't help but notice the increasingly violent doodles and deteriorating language. On the last page was scrawled 'FUCK YOU SPATCHCOCK!!!!'

The room I shared with Rosy was very small, and the only place to put the box was under my wobbly desk. This meant that I had to lean uncomfortably forward to use my keyboard. I now had a nagging backache, not helped by the rather elderly wooden chair supplied for my use. I broached the subject with Sally Whimbrel, finding her behind her customary pile, nursing her wrist.

"RSI," she explained, wincing, "goes with the job."

"I've got a few ergonomic problems of my own," I said, stooping slightly. "Is there any chance of storing Jenny's stuff somewhere other than next to my knees?"

"Oh, Dr Frumpp!" she exclaimed. "I only wish there was, but there's not an ounce of storage space in the whole building. I have asked Professor Spigot whether we could rent some space, but he is terribly busy, and Professor Tweezer is so impractical." I could see that the subject was upsetting Sally, so let it rest.

Professor Tweezer's 'impracticality' was something of a feature. I was learning rapidly that despite his generally amiable nature, he was naturally muddled. Luckily, being an Emeritus, his administrative role was largely non-existent. His relationship with Sally was a mother–son thing and he needed an awful lot of attention. He would ring Sally every ten minutes or so, even though his office adjoined hers. This meant that Sally frequently ignored the telephone altogether.

I had pored over the project brief at length, and having considered the time-scale available to us, had composed a brief abstract covering what I hoped to have achieved by the time the Vancouver conference took place. Irene was rarely in the DoA, but I finally managed to pin her down during one of her brief visits.

She scanned the A4 sheet I presented for about two seconds and said,

"This is a very good start, Ellinora, but I think you should mention some results."

"But we don't have results yet," I protested. "I do say that we are about to undertake the analysis and that we should have a broad idea of the questionnaire content by May."

"Sadly, the abstract won't be accepted unless there is something more concrete. Talk in more general terms, Ellinora. Second rule of academe," she again raised her finger and crinkled her face with encouragement, "if in doubt, be vague, and use your imagination. Let's make use of that doctorate of yours – I'm sure you can be creative."

I left my second attempt in Irene's pigeon-hole that afternoon. Being an honest soul, I erred on the side of nebulosity, rather than imagination. I was not wholly confident of what I had done. To make matters worse, I had odd socks on[12].

I met with Irene in the 'academic staff' tea room, a sunny spot on the first floor, the morning of our first project meeting. She was in good spirits.

"Thank you for the abstract, Ellinora. It gave me some material to work with. Would you like a cup of coffee?"

"Tea would be nice," I replied.

"Have you settled into your flat?"

"Bedsit," I corrected her, "yes thanks."

---

[12] Frumpp's Fashion Tip Number 7: always hang matching socks together to dry.

"I was wondering whether we should have a project meal or something. You know, to officially start the work, welcome you to Hardnox and so on. We've been a bit discouraged about such things since Dr Sweeble blew up the barbecue in the summer. The rain didn't help either. Perhaps we should sort one out at the project meeting today."

"Great," I said, taking the mug of coffee Irene handed me.

We'd booked the seminar room for the meeting that afternoon – a small, dark construction, in a dank, colonic basement. Here, amongst belching pipes and salted brickwork, a set of plastic chairs surrounded an old, heavy table upon which sat an overhead projector – the indigestible remnants of a grander, under-funded plan for a DoA audio-visual facility. Irene and I arrived to find Christian already sitting down, picking at a piece of wooden veneer that was curling in a bid for freedom from the table-top.

"Any sign of Terry?" asked Irene.

"Haven't seen him," said Christian, giving a final tug to the hapless piece of veneer, which broke off in his hand.

A moment later, the uneasy silence that had fallen upon the room was broken by the entrance of a man in a fashionable blue suit. Professor Terry Spigot was a man of average build, forty-ish, with foppish, coiffed light hair (in which I detected highlights), an incipient paunch, and a pair of glasses, with miniscule and surely vestigial lenses surrounded by thick black frames[13]. His

---

[13] Frumpp's Fashion Tip Number 8: we all know small lenses look trendy, but remember – you'll look very silly when you walk into things.

eyes were set a little too far apart, creating a fish-like visage and vacuous expression. He sported a sunburn which was particularly pronounced on his bulbous, unrefined nose. What was most striking, however, was his overpowering scent, which might have been attractive at a lesser concentration or a greater distance.[14]

"Greetings team!" said Spigot, enthusiastically, "so glad to see you all – and hello Ellinora, pleased to meet you at last. I would apologise for not saying 'hi' sooner, but I'm not sorry to have caught up on a bit of annual leave. Too many committees makes Terry a dull boy. In need of a bit of R and R. But now I'm back on board: ready to rock." Spigot proffered his hand, which I attempted to shake, but it slipped strangely from my grasp: a docking malfunction that left me feeling slightly clumsy.

"Do call me Ellie," I said.

"Max is on his way – saw him over by the Biochemistry Block," continued Spigot, taking a seat at the table. "So, how's *WImpI*? We're quite proud of *WImpI*, Ellinora; brought a nice wad into the department. Still, we deserved it, eh, 'Rene. All those late nights in Sociology paid off. A small price to pay, I suppose, for a pot of gold." Irene looked across the table with slight disgust. "Yes, Terry, Max and I put a great deal of time into the proposal."

"Still needed a bit of the old Spigot magic to get it through round two though, eh? It's the language that's important, you see, Ellinora, got to get the jargon right.

---

[14] Frumpp's Fashion Tip Number 9: potent aftershaves are to be discouraged.

And I'm on top of all that – I'm a lexiconographic legend."

"Did Max say how long he'd be?" said Irene, looking a little impatient.

"No," said Terry, "dark horse, that one. Why don't we start without him?"

"OK then," said Irene. "Sally should be along in a minute for tea and coffee orders, and I've written a brief agenda." She passed round copies.

"Ah, Sally," said Irene, looking up, as Sally Whimbrel appeared, "I'll have a coffee."

As I always find being waited on a little disconcerting, when you're not leaving a tip, I offered to help.

"Oh no, Ellinora," said Irene, "I think we need you here. Sally is more than capable, I'm sure." Sally smiled kindly and left the room.

"Now, item number one: the research plan. I'm sure we're all happy with that. No problems or queries concerning what we're doing, and what we have so far?" Irene cast a hopeful look about the room.

"There are a couple of things I'd like to query," I said. Irene looked surprised, but indulgent.

"OK, Ellinora, I'm sure we'd be interested to hear them," said Professor Spigot, "it's important that we all get to express our views." He turned, leant very deliberately towards me and looked me straight in the eye. I have a friend who went into sales, and he tells me that this method of communication is known as the 'half-buttock technique'. It is designed to make your potential client feel that he has your full attention.

"Well," I began, a little unnerved by Spigot's steady gaze. He seemed to be homing in on my chin, which I found rather embarrassing – a spot had been brewing there for a day or so. "I'm obviously very impressed with the material that we have, but I was a little concerned about the timetable. There are thirty focus groups to transcribe and analyse. This is a large number for a qualitative study, and I think you have only allowed eight weeks. I'm not sure that this is possible."

"Yes," replied Terry, furrowing his forehead, "I can see where you are coming from. We had lots of groups because we covered very diverse workplaces; and the time-scale we based on some pilot work that I undertook last year. It was hard work, but I managed it. Do you remember, 'Rene, how tired I was?"

"Yes, Ellinora," said Irene, looking at me, with a secretive smirk and nod in Terry's direction. "I think if Terry can do it, I'm sure that you can."

"Um, er, I was hoping to have another eight weeks or so, but I, er ..."

"Regrettably, that's out of the question," said Irene, her mouth assuming a business-like tautness. "We have a meeting of the steering committee soon, and I would expect you to have a broad idea of the emerging themes for the postal questionnaire by then."

"I see – I'm not sure that ..."

"And your other concern?" said Terry, fixing me again with his 'trust me, I'm a salesman' stare.

"I, er, I have noticed, from my preliminary work, that there are a few internal inconsistencies in parts of the data."

"One would, of course, expect varied responses," said Spigot, tilting his head in a truly psychotherapeutic way. "What is the issue?"

"Well, I've listened to all the recordings and on the ten occasions when Dr Snoode has worked with a group, whilst the first half of the discussion is what one might expect, the second half appears, well – different. It's almost as if the focus group has changed in some way. They are much more forthright. It's just a bit odd, that's all. Irene's are all pretty normal."

"Dr Snoode is a very experienced facilitator ..." said Irene.

"... and I'm also very good at getting people to tell me how it really is ..." Dr Max Snoode laughed as he came into the seminar room. It was a controlled chortle, short and lacking in sincerity. "I was clearly on good form!"

Snoode was not a large man, but what there was of him was tight and well-formed. He had an attractive, balanced face, and an expression of indifference that bordered on contempt. He had small pointy sideburns like Captain James T. Kirk, and dark hair tied in a bunch that tugged at his subtly receding hairline. Irene looked up excitedly.

"Oh Max, there you are. I hope you don't mind – we started without you."

"Not at all. Got held up – my apologies. Dr Frumpp," said Max, turning to me, "good to see you again." He looked me up and down briefly, and finding nothing to arrest his attention, took a seat at the table.

"So, you have a problem with my facilitation skills," he said, the amiability in his voice not entirely reflected in the metallic frigidity of his eyes, which had the pale, grey, intelligent self-assurance of a wolf.

"Not a problem exactly," I said, hastily, "it's just that yours are, well, a bit unusual – inconsistent, I guess. It's not that the material is not useful. In fact, in some ways it is very informative ..."

53

"Well, there we are then," said Irene dismissively, "it's simply a combination of SpIT and Max's aura. Max is a very sympathetic man. Undoubtedly as the focus group progresses he is encouraging them to get to the heart of the issue successfully. Do you remember, Max, that group of admin. assistants in Solihull ...?" Irene gave Dr Snoode a very sickly smile.

"Oh, yes, yes," replied Snoode, grandly, "they thought I was a god!"

Irene and Max laughed lightly at their humorous mutual memory. There was then a pause, after which Irene said, wrinkling her nose,

"I'm sure that as you get down to the nitty-gritty you will find common themes coming out of all of the groups. Why don't you wait until you've done the formal thematic analysis? What do you think, Terry?"

"We are all individuals," contributed Spigot, formatting his face to 'helpful'. "Focus groups can be quite distinctive – it depends on their composition. SpIT, in addition, is a very novel method – one in which I think, Ellinora, you have little experience. You're probably not used to seeing what it produces yet – you're expecting to see the products of a more conventional group dynamical paradigm. You'll find that SpIT will broaden your horizons no end, once you get the hang of it."

"Yes, Ellinora, you'll be surprised at how it will change your worldview," said Irene, "you're probably just seeing things from one angle – it's OK, we would expect that at this stage. With a bit more experience, we'll get you out of your cerebral rut – we've all been there! It makes me wince to remember my pre-SpIT days. Believe me, it's a developmental thing." I agreed to hold judgement until I had undertaken some more formal analyses, and pondered my 'cerebral rut'.

"Right, moving on to item two. Christian," said Irene.

"What?" replied Christian. Having rolled the veneer like a bogey, he had been about to flick it at the fluorescent tube above our heads. He was annoyed at being interrupted.

"I believe you've agreed to help Ellinora with some of the computing. She may need your help with the ethnographic package."

"Impossible," said Christian.

"What do you mean?" asked Irene, laughing.

"Got no LOOFAH licence," said Christian with some satisfaction.

"But I thought that Sally was sorting that out. Sally, what happened to the LOOFAH licence?" Sally had just reappeared with a tray of drinks.

"Oh Dr Spatchcock," she said, "it's UCLOG, you see. I said it might take a while. They are trying to negotiate a whole site licence and don't want us getting one of our own at vast expense."

"But we've got work to do, Sally," said Irene, "what are we supposed to do?"

"I'll chase it up, Dr Spatchcock." She handed out the last of the drinks.

"Oh, I'll have a coffee, black, no sugar," said Snoode, as Sally was leaving.

"Well, if we don't get the licence soon, Ellinora, it could be back to cutting and pasting. OK, third item: the conference in Vancouver. I've sorted out an abstract to send off. Ellinora has been giving me a hand. Here it is." She circulated another piece of paper. It bore no resemblance to the version I had handed her earlier.

"I think, in fairness, we should include Ellinora on the abstract," said Spigot.

"But yes, of course!" said Irene, "I'm so sorry Ellinora, I'll add your name. I'll get Sally to edit and fax it today. Item four," she continued, hurriedly, "project dinner!"

"Splendid idea," said Spigot, at once salivating. It transpired that we were all free that evening, with the exception of Christian, who insisted we go without him. He had arranged to have beers with a friend of his. The meeting broke up and Irene suggested that she should give me a lift and return me to the car park later, as the restaurant of choice, well Terry Spigot's choice, appeared to be outside the town. This was just as well, as I had been clamped again, and the 'helpful' Mr Boffin said it would be a few hours before the men came round.

I met Irene in the car park at six o'clock. She had a small, shiny red convertible with endearing wing mirrors and soft, fawn seats.

"Do you have a boyfriend?" she asked boldly, catching my eye, as I strapped myself in next to her. She began to drive out of the car park. "I only ask because we should have asked him to come along if you do."

"No," I said, "not at the moment." I didn't feel like going into details. I never seemed to get very far with men, I think largely due to the aforementioned problems with tights and the like.

"Have you had one recently?" she persisted, trying to get more matey. The car growled excitedly as Irene put her foot down on the accelerator.

"Well, not really," I said, jerking forward as the car lurched into action.

"Have you ever had one?" she laughed, looking at me instead of the road.

"Well, I …"

"You haven't, have you? Nothing serious anyway. I can tell!" She was pleased at her perceived discovery.

"Don't you worry. Hardnox is full of handsome young men," she continued. This interrogation was not helping me to relax, the subject being one rather close to my heart. People often find it incomprehensible that a woman of twenty-five can have had little in the way of sexual experience these days. Woman, woman, woman – it's a good word, isn't it? Laden with ripeness and sensuality. I sometimes look at myself in the mirror and say 'I am a woman', because it helps to remind me that despite a certain lack of the more obvious womanly traits, I do possess all that the word conveys. It's just that the equipment is a bit under-utilised, and under-advertised. I am something of a dingy billboard.

"Do you have a man?" – a parry to change the focus of this rather uncomfortable personal conversation.

"Ahh, well, there is a gentleman in my life, I must admit," Irene said coyly, but did not elaborate. Not satisfied that the chinwag was over, and finding their way blocked by this reluctance to disclose, the words spun back in my direction.

"So why are you unattached?" Irene asked, changing up a gear.

"Well, I don't know really – I've never met the right man, I suppose." The standard response. I was expecting a continuation of this girly chat, but Irene changed the conversation rather suddenly.

"Ellinora, thank you for the points you raised today. I don't think you need worry about getting the work done.

Believe me, if Terry can manage it, you can. You just have to up your game a little. Now you're out in the real world, we have deadlines to meet, and sponsors to please. Sometimes we just have to get on with it. Third rule of academe: don't pay too much attention to the detail. As for Max's groups – well, Max does have a way with people. Hopefully, as you work with us, you will learn to think a little more laterally – and SpIT will help you to do that. Don't think I'm criticising you at all, Ellinora, but you have obviously been trained in a traditional way. I've an idea," she continued, her spittle boule getting a little excited on her lower lip. "We could think about sending you on one of our SpIT training programmes!"

Her enthusiasm found its way to her foot, and we powered into a new reckless speed. Emotionally prepared to defend my personal life, my professional shields were down. This unreadiness, combined with the heightened G force, left me speechless.

"At the end of the day," Irene persisted, "it will probably enhance your personal life as well as your methodological armoury. You'd be amazed at how SpIT nutures one's relationships with others. It may even help you get a man! Here we are!" she concluded, gaily. We had drawn into the courtyard of The Riverweed Restaurant, which seemed to be full of BMWs. "And ah, there's Max and Terry." She brought the car to an undignified halt, and got out, leaving me slightly stunned, and struggling with the safety belt.

The bill came to forty pounds a head, which we each had to pay and which did not help my overdraft. Irene dropped me back at the university car park and drove off into the night. I spent the next half-hour scraping the YOU HAVE BEEN CLAMPED sticker off my windscreen with my otherwise useless cashpoint card.

5

KEEPING A PROFESSIONAL DISTANCE?

Grace did not sleep well that night. Perhaps it was the alcohol; perhaps it was because she could not readily rid her mind of Alec Tramane. In any event, she awoke early, and refreshed herself with a long shower and plenty of coffee.

Grace had to go downtown again to pick up Mr Tramane and take him to the office. She was determined to keep the day focused on business; there would be no confusion, no mixed messages. She wore her grey suit and sensible shoes. At eight o'clock she walked down to the Fraser River Hotel, taking in the bustle and breakfasty smells of the streets. She found Tramane in the sunlit dining room, finishing off a croissant with a crumb-less and grease-free elegance that only comes with much practice. She couldn't help noticing how good he looked in a dark suit and white shirt.

"Good morning," he said, his English accent immediately conveying an unverified gallantry. "Will you join me?"

"I've had some breakfast already, but I'll have another coffee if it's on offer."

"It certainly is." Tramane motioned a bouncy middle-aged waitress over to the table, who took the order. Within a minute she returned, handing Grace a black coffee with a rather weary, insincere 'enjoy'.

"How is your foot?" ventured Grace.

"Colourful," he replied, "and salutary."

"Sorry," she said.

"That's OK. I get to think of you when I put on my socks." Grace smiled, and stopped herself making a reflexive, flirtatious riposte. Tramane chatted amiably on. "How long have you been in Vancouver?"

"I've been here for five years. I used to study at UBC. I did a Masters there, and some research. I almost did a doctorate, but then I came to my senses."

"I don't see you as a blue-stocking," laughed Tramane.

"Well, academe's changed nowadays, hasn't it? I think the public have this view of eccentric professors in ivory towers fiddling with their bow ties."

"And it's not like that today?" asked Tramane ironically.

"No – not at all – it's very competitive and quite insecure. Not my sort of thing."

"You struck me as a practical girl from the start," said Tramane, appraising her. The smile disappeared from

Grace's face. She was immediately reminded of the previous day, and this man's irksome sexism.

"I haven't been a 'girl' for a while," she said coolly.

"I'm sorry," said Tramane. "I can see that I've touched a nerve."

"Not particularly," replied Grace. She knew, for the sake of Amity Action, that she should watch what she said. It was unlikely that Tramane would give her another chance after yesterday's performance.

"Well, personally I like a pretty *woman* with strong opinions," continued Tramane, cruelly, because it was amusing him. "It makes life a lot more interesting. Perhaps we should change the subject, though, or I might end up with two bruised feet."

"No, let's not change the subject!" exclaimed Grace, losing patience. "Listen – times have changed. Women have been educated. As far as I'm concerned, in the working environment, we are equals. Using words like 'girl', and referring to our appearance all the time is outdated, it's passé. I don't look at you and say 'What a pretty boy', do I? It sounds stupid, doesn't it?"

"Put like that, yes. But don't you think all this 'political correctness' can go too far?"

"I'm not talking about political correctness," said Grace firmly. "I'm talking about respect. You call me a 'girl': it's diminishing, it shows a lack of respect for who I am."

"So calling you a 'pretty woman' *is* all right?" Tramane remained annoyingly unflustered.

"It depends on the context. If we were thinking of dating it might be OK, but right now, we are within a professional context, and so it's inappropriate – rather like your roving feet yesterday."

"So, we're not thinking of dating?" Tramane persisted. Grace did not answer.

"Look, I'm sorry," she said, after a brief pause. "This is hardly a good start to the day."

"On the contrary, I'm enjoying it – this is precisely the sort of intelligent talk I was hoping for yesterday. Perhaps we could discuss these issues in more detail later – over dinner."

"It's nine o'clock," said Grace, ignoring his invitation and finishing her coffee. "We should be going to the office." Tramane got up with relaxed ease.

"You'll forgive me if I don't help you out of your chair," he said wryly.

"I certainly will," replied Grace, flushed. They took a taxi from outside the hotel. Grace said nothing. She had to pull herself together. This man was getting to her. She'd be failing in her job if she alienated him before she'd even got him to the office. Tramane was irritatingly nonchalant. Every so often he looked at Grace, amused at her discomfiture.

The Amity Action building was an early twentieth century block, modernised, institutionally clean, aesthetically green, with plants externally nurtured by a company paid to water, prune, and occasionally remove. The Research Department was the largest and the one that Jack personally headed up, along with his overall leadership role. There were various other units, mainly concerned with fund-raising activities and the processing of donations. Grace had done a little work in these before Jack had spotted her real talent. She had considerable experience in research. Her Masters had been in research methods, and she had been involved with a number of studies before deciding to take another qualification in business and administration. This had made her a good candidate for the job of research co-ordinator. Grace not only understood the business side of Amity Action, she knew what a good research proposal should look like. She also had invaluable experience in dealing with academic foibles.

Grace and Jack had predicted that Tramane would want to see the Amity outfit – donors usually did, so the tour had been pre-arranged.

"You'll start today with Mr Janus – he's the chief accountant," said Grace as they sat in her office. "He'll be able to give you an idea of how the organisation operates as a whole – figures for monies raised, and grants given etc.. At ten forty-five, I'll take you to the staff café for coffee." She wished she hadn't put that on the programme now. "At eleven, you've got a meeting for an hour with Jack. He wanted to chat to you personally about how we operate. He didn't go into much detail yesterday – wanted to keep it informal. I think he will probably take you to lunch with one or two of the other unit heads. Then it's an afternoon with Mr Wickes and Dr Howe. They are more to do with fund raising. Then at four-thirty, you're back with me, to talk about the research we do – the practicalities etc.. Does that sound OK?"

"It sounds great – I'm most appreciative," said Tramane courteously. After escorting him to his first meeting, Grace came back down to her office with a sigh of relief. At least she was free from him for an hour or so.

At the risk of getting high on caffeine, Grace helped herself to yet another cup of coffee. She had just taken the first sip when Jack came into the office.

"Hi," said Grace, slightly surprised – Jack usually knocked.

"Good morning Grace, did you get home OK?"

"Sure. I didn't sleep too well, though, I think maybe I drank too much. Jack, I'm sorry if I was a little out of sorts last night. You see, I was feeling left out – and I have to say that I find our friend Mr Tramane a bit sexist."

"You don't like him?" For some reason Jack seemed to like this. "I think he likes you."

"Well if he does, I'm not sure his interest is entirely in my degrees and certificates."

"Quite so," replied Jack. He seemed worried, a little on edge.

"Is something wrong?" asked Grace.

"I don't think so," said Jack, with little conviction. "I would like to ask you a favour, Grace. There are some things I'm not sure about with regard to Alec Tramane. I wouldn't like to accept a donation from anyone dubious. If you get the opportunity, get to know him a little better – see what he lets slip."

"What exactly are you asking me to do? You know I don't mind entertaining clients a little, but to be perfectly honest I'm getting fed up of being ogled for the sake of Amity."

"Look, Grace, I'd be really grateful. Just get him to talk a bit more about himself and drill into some of the specifics of his workplace. His company looks legitimate, but – well, some things just don't quite add up."

"This all sounds very conspiratorial. Don't we vet our donors? I thought there was a set procedure. What do you think he is anyway? A money launderer?"

"I don't know," said Jack, contemplatively. "I just find him a little too smooth."

"Well, so do I," said Grace, bolshily.

"Look, I won't ask you to do this again. Just take him out to dinner or something. Please. He expects to be wined and dined while he is here. Don't let him overstep the mark – keep him at a professional distance. You know I wouldn't want it any other way."

"Hmm," said Grace sceptically, "if you insist, but we both know the routine, Jack, and you've cast me as eye candy for clients for too long. I know you respect me as a business colleague in the office, but these donor evenings are really getting to me. Yesterday you totally excluded me from the conversation until the end. It was fine a year or so ago – I was learning the ropes and I wanted to help Amity because I believe in what we do, but now I'm keen to get on and it's become humiliating for me. Ask yourself whether you'd be so keen to use me this way if I wasn't a willowy blonde." A thick pair of glasses, thought Grace – perhaps some persistent acne: that would do the trick. "So here are my terms," she continued. "I'll do this for you, but the next potential donor we entertain, I will lead on the business side. Do you agree?"

"It's a deal – and I'm sorry about last night. You are right of course – and you're ready. The next one is yours."

Jack left her to some paperwork. She had been negotiating with a couple of hotels about accommodation for the conference, and had whittled it down to two. The Fraser River was her favourite, and her recent visits there had reminded her of how impressive it was. The only problem was its expense, but she knew that a lot of delegates would be from industry. She was reluctant to use cheaper university accommodation. She didn't want shabby seminar rooms, and student residences were potentially dodgy with their suspicious stains and pock-marked walls.

She was just looking through the two hotel packages when there was a knock at the door and Alec Tramane poked his head into her room.

"Hello," he said cheerily. "I'm up to here with facts and figures." He indicated his brow. "You promised me a coffee."

"If I have another coffee, I'll become hyper, but I'll take you to our café and watch you drink one. It'll give you a feel for the place. You know, happy employees etc.." She smiled.

"Am I forgiven?" asked Tramane.

"I didn't say *that*," replied Grace archly. "I've written you off as a creature from the Cretaceous." She would try and get the balance right – just enough banter to get what Jack wanted, but no more.

"Hmm," replied Tramane, "I'll just have to hope you find palaeontology interesting. I promise not to roar and gnash my teeth."

"Good," said Grace, "that's a relief. Now – back to the business in hand …" She moved towards the door but Tramane remained in the doorway.

"After you," he said with a smile and bow. Grace rolled her eyes in fake amusement. She had to brush past him to get out of the office and was immediately cross with herself because it was not unpleasant.

"The café's on the ground floor," she said. "I'm feeling lazy: we'll take the elevator." She pressed the call button in the hallway next to her office. Tramane was looking at her again. If only she was nondescript; frumpy, even. Instead she was acutely conscious of how smart and possibly sexy she looked in her short jacket and efficient, executive skirt. She would have to invest in some trousers at least.

"I promise I'll behave myself while I'm in this building, but please, let me buy you dinner tonight, and then we can be less formal about things," said Tramane.

"OK," said Grace simply, "it's only right that Amity entertains you while you are here." She might as well get it over with. The elevator arrived with a ping and the doors glided open. They stepped in together. In the confined space, Grace noted that he smelt good, and there was something quite remarkable about his eyes. 'He's a creep,' she reminded herself.

The café was a light, airy room, with large windows. There was a mixture of stainless steel and glass tables with black, stylish chairs, and soft, black leather sofas with coffee tables. These were interspersed with the ubiquitous plant life. Grace bought Alec a black coffee, and helped herself to a chocolate fudge brownie – she needed some fortification. They sat by one of the windows which, like her office, looked over the bay.

"Tell me," said Alec, after a minute's silence, "have you ever heard of a Dr Zuserain Nexus?"

"No," said Grace, "why do you ask?"

"Oh, he's just a name I've come across during business. I had a feeling Nexus was connected to Amity Action somehow."

"The name's not familiar, but I'll have a look on my database if you like – see if there is anything I can share with you."

"Yes, that would be useful. I've heard that his company runs some system that might be useful in exports. It would be good to contact him."

"Tell me more about the work you do," said Grace politely.

"Well, it's not that interesting really. We negotiate transport, customs, that sort of thing. We have a range of clients – industry, Government, university. We're based in London, as you know."

"It must be great to work in London – the 'proper' London that is. I come from London, Ontario. I loved your London when I visited it. Rather more than the conference I was attending. It was my first paper abroad. The slide projector broke down, and it took twenty minutes to find a technician. And the chairperson – Professor Ronald Tweezer no less, of the University of Hardnox – had fallen asleep. It was a complete fiasco. I can laugh now, but it was a nightmare. So you see, I had other reasons for not wishing to stay in academe."

"I wish I'd been there," said Tramane.

"That would have made me even more nervous," she laughed, "those cold, critical eyes of yours ..."

"I believe you just commented on *my* appearance!"

"So I did – how very unfair! I'm so sorry!" 'Damn!' thought Grace, 'that was a bit of a slip. Get a grip!'

"Accepted – but I am sorry you think my eyes are cold."

Grace glanced at her watch.

"Goodness, is that the time? You're supposed to have met with Jack five minutes ago!"

Once she had delivered Tramane safely to Jack D'Oretz, Grace went back to her office. She went straight to the computer and looked through the database. She couldn't find anything on a Zuserain Nexus. Maybe Jack would know about him.

That afternoon, Jack's PA appeared with a new pile of faxes for Grace – another batch of abstracts for the conference. There were about twenty, from all over the world. One was headed 'University of Hardnox' and Grace gave an audible sigh. 'Oh no,' she murmured to herself, 'the dreaded Spigot'. Perhaps the most frustrating thing about SpIT was that Grace was sure it had nothing to do with Terry Spigot. Whilst he promoted himself quite shamelessly as its inventor, Grace had found a paper by a doctoral student in some conference proceedings reporting much the same methodology, way before Spigot published any papers on the subject.

The fax was the expected waffle: short on detail, long on jargon. There was some implication that results were available, but since Grace had known when Jack authorised the study, she considered that pretty unlikely. She could not understand why Jack was so bent on supporting this group.

Jack D'Oretz was a strange fellow. He was in his early fifties, small and pale with greying hair beginning to thin, but what he lacked in stature and appearance, he more than made up for with energy, which he channelled relentlessly into his job. Whilst overtly sociable, he was fiercely private about his home life. Grace knew he was married, had two children, and lived in Kitsilano – but that was about it. She had been to his home only once, and that was to deliver an urgent document. She had never met his wife. He was incredibly conscientious, and spent much time travelling. Grace worried about his apparent devotion to work – he rarely took his annual leave. She wondered if he was avoiding something at home. It had to be said, though, Jack's unbalanced life was to Amity's advantage: its research income had nearly trebled in the last few years.

She was tempted to bin the abstract from Hardnox but decided that she had better let Jack see it. Spatchcock, Snoode, Frumpp and Spigot: they sounded like a bunch of Dickensian solicitors.

At four-thirty, Alec Tramane reappeared at her door. She asked how his day had been, and he pronounced it 'most informative'. She told him of her lack of success regarding Dr Nexus and said that she would check the next day with Jack.

"I don't think there's any need for that now," Tramane said. "I had a good chat with him over lunch."

"Did he recognise the name?"

"In a manner of speaking," replied Tramane cryptically. "You look as if you have been hard at work," he looked at the mound of papers on her desk.

"A new batch of abstracts for the conference next May: the International Workplace and Productivity Meeting. I expect Jack told you all about it."

"Sounds like a lot of hard work for you."

"Certainly is," said Grace, patting the faxes. "I thought I would show you a few of the studies we've funded over the last year. I've picked a cross-section."

Tramane picked up Spatchcock et al. from the desk.

"What's this one?" he said. "The Spigot Sympathetic Interrogation Technique," he read dubiously. "Sounds a bit oxymoronic."

"Oh, er, that's … Well, to be honest it's not one of my favourite projects – I was against funding it in the first place, but Jack liked it for some reason."

"You don't always agree then?" asked Tramane, interested.

"Not always – less so recently for some reason ..." she checked herself. Tramane did not need to know of her occasional disagreements with Jack, but now the observation had sneaked into the open, it stuck in her mind. She shook her head slightly: Jack *did* take her seriously at the office. "Jack is a strategic thinker – he sometimes sees things I don't. We always get it right in the end. Anyway," she said quickly, "I can show you better ones than that!"

Grace took Tramane through some of the other studies they were funding. He was well versed in the field, understood the problems faced by institutions and displayed an impressive familiarity with the complexities of research design.

When she had finished, Tramane picked up a brochure.

"What's this? It looks interesting."

"Oh that," said Grace, "yes, that's a new initiative. Jack's thinking of setting up some training. There are so many different techniques around, he would like to run courses which concentrate on methodologies that are approved by Amity. In fact, he was telling me only a few days ago that he's got his first clients. They have a facility on Vancouver Island and he wants to run the training there – should be fun!"

"Who are the clients?"

"Praefortica – they develop health and fitness foods – you know – drinks, nutritional supplements. They are great to their employees, and we love what they do in the workplace. They're based mainly in Banff which is such a fabulous place to be. At the moment, all their employees have to go on a course run in-house. They've always used a lot of our material and they now want to expand the training and out-source it to us."

"Sounds like good business – but now it's six o'clock," said Tramane, changing the subject, "and you promised me dinner. Where do you recommend we go?" Grace thought for a moment.

"There's a lovely fish restaurant in Stanley Park; we could walk round there. Perhaps you'd like a drink first?"

Tramane and Grace walked a block to a corner bar. It was nothing special, but its smallness created an intimate atmosphere and it was one of Grace's favourite haunts. There were a few booths replete with colourful cushions, and a row of stools next to a thin table running along the window, looking out into the street.

"Another whisky and soda?" she enquired as they stood at the bar.

"These ones are on me," he said, "I will have another, and for you?"

"White wine spritzer please."

"And now, where were we?" asked Tramane, making himself comfortable in one of the booths. "I think we had decided I was a sexist pig with dinosaurian attitudes."

"Yes, that's right," said Grace smiling, "and that you are politically incorrect."

"It is a bit like walking in a minefield," said Tramane, "when you first get to know a woman. Some like doors to be held open; some don't. I think I'm a bit old-fashioned. I like to hold doors open."

"Do you slam doors shut in men's faces?" asked Grace.

"No."

"Then there's nothing wrong with holding a door open for a woman, is there?"

"But don't you find it difficult to treat men and women exactly the same? I mean, it's old hat I suppose, but with women, there are always other possibilities."

"There are with men, if you are gay; and there might not be with some women, if they don't like men."

"Do you like men?" he asked, a little apprehensively.

"Now you're getting personal!" Grace said. "You are right up to a point I suppose – men and women are different, but at most levels, they are similarly capable, and I think if we want to be fair, we have to treat each other the same at work."

"But you can't deny that sex creeps into the workplace. I mean, with all due respect, I am sure you know what you are doing when you wear a revealing silk dress to a business-related event?"

"That's true," said Grace, "but you already know I'm not particularly proud of that. In fact I've had words with Jack and it's strictly business wear from now on."

"But even your 'business' skirt is very short."

"Do you think we should all wear trousers, shirt and tie?"

"No, but I imagine that you would think that."

"Maybe. But I wonder whether we dress in a particular way just to feel confident professionally."

"So are you saying that a woman can only feel confident if she is wearing clothes that are attractive to men? *That* doesn't feel politically correct."

"Feeling confident does not necessarily equate to being attractive to men, if by that you mean 'sexy'."

"Doesn't it? Your skirt *is* sexy, and I know many women who pop on lipstick or a pair of black leather boots to feel professionally confident. Believe me, lipstick and 'power' boots *are* attractive to men."

"Maybe it's the only way to get noticed in a man's world? Or perhaps it is your problem – and an uncomfortable truth for us. I doubt that men are better anyway. A nicely tailored suit will go down very well with most of us, I can assure you. As I said this morning, I think it all boils down to respect. However we dress, we should try and treat each other politely, equally and respectfully at work."

"What about outside of work?"

"What's not to like about courtesy, equality and respect? Same rules apply; but the content of any exchanges would fit the context. For example, if I were dating a man, I would hope for a mixture of things."

"A mixture?"

"A mixture of respect for my intellect, brackets 'I have a brain', and polite admiration, brackets 'I have a body'. But I'd only want the latter and any sequelae, if I give an obvious cue. I don't like wolf-whistles and I don't like pushy suitors."

"I guess my foot under the table means I qualify as a 'pushy suitor'. It was unwelcome because you'd given me no cues – apart from that rather lovely dress."

"I'm going to burn it!"

"Please don't. It was my fault. The context was wrong. But now I'm thoroughly confused because I don't know what the context is *here*. I am guessing we are supposed to be professional, but this *feels* like a date. In fact I have no idea how to proceed so I'll stop talking until you clarify." Tramane leant back in his seat and crossed his arms. Grace sat looking at him for a moment. Why was she letting the conversation wander in this direction? She was being lured into flirtation. She blamed herself – she was, after all, enjoying it.

"It's still business," she said, "but I suppose it might evolve."

"That's not tremendously helpful," laughed Tramane. "OK – so when this becomes a date, will I get an 'obvious cue'?" He wiggled his forefingers to indicate the quote.

"*If* this becomes a date," said Grace, correcting him, "I promise that you will know, but don't hold your breath! There are plenty of blind alleys in evolution."

"I'll have to hope that Natural Selection is on my side then – assuming I have no immediate competitors? But while it's determining my survival as a potential beau, let's go and find this restaurant of yours."

Moving on from the bar, they strolled around the path in Stanley Park, avoiding the roller-bladers. Glancing back towards the bay, the sky was turning red.

"Why don't we wait here for a few minutes," said Grace, "you'll get to see one of our famous Pacific sunsets." The bay was still, the ships quiet – in suspended animation. Strips of cloud had formed in the west and these were turning gold. Grace could feel Tramane's body next to hers even though they stood apart. His desire for her was obvious; and her desire for him? He had been so very irritating the day before, but she liked him so much more this evening. He may have been a little personal, a little suggestive, but nothing she would not have expected from a man interested in her. Maybe he had just been winding her up before. Perhaps he really just liked a good debate?

Getting to know someone is a lengthy process, and Grace was quite aware that she never had the patience to do it properly. Discovering a person was like walking gently down a mountain, she mused. To her it always took too long. She knew she should walk the full distance and then make a decision based on complete disclosure, but she habitually leapt before she knew enough, and then the leap became a fall, and boy, that could hurt! She was not blind to the biological imperative that drove her but she could not resist its disguise: passion, romance. And she was vulnerable because she was beautiful, and everywhere she turned were promises from men who wanted her; men who would say anything to have her. And she often leapt off way above the tree line. Each time she tumbled, she made a promise to herself that she would learn from her latest mistake – a lesson quickly forgotten in the tsunami of the next infatuation. And here she was again in the half-light, feeling her change of heart towards this unknown man, whose superficial charm prickled her provocatively; whose passionate allure she felt radiating into her. Her attraction for him was sneaking up on her, and as the sun disappeared beyond the horizon, leaving a wash of pink and grey in the gloaming, she was already contemplating his probable competence as a lover.

Grace was conscious that Tramane had moved closer to her, and she was reluctant to move away, but she knew she had to break the moment, for her own sake.

"What do you think of Jack?" she asked, stripping away the magnetic field that had descended around them and walking on deliberately.

""'Type A', I expect," said Tramane, catching her up, "but very efficient, very driven. He's a damn good talker – a convincing salesman."

"Yes he is 'Type A'," said Grace. "I wish he'd go away on holiday for a change."

"Maybe he gets fed up with travelling – he seems to do a lot of it," observed Tramane.

"Yes, he goes all over the world. I wish he'd stay at home then. I'm surprised he has any time for his family."

"He didn't strike me as a family man."

"Oh yes, they live across the bay from here – very nice house."

The restaurant in Stanley Park was bright and busy, but they procured a table next to a wall, away from the flight path of the super-efficient waiting staff. As before, Alec Tramane exhibited his refinement in matters of food and wine, delighting in the fish and commenting on its presentation and taste with the fastidiousness of a gourmet. Grace tried to refocus and find out more about his occupation, but he was deftly evasive and kept the conversation away from the subject. He seemed to be trying less hard to flatter her now. Everything he said was interesting, lively and challenging. Between them, their characters met on an edge; he would let her get away with nothing. Her words were scrutinised and dissected and it led to a pacey, exciting conversation. Grace had been used to being on top of discussions with men – they were usually too keen to win her approval. Alec Tramane was different.

"The question is," said Tramane as he finished his coffee, "should I offer to pay the bill? It's been worrying me all night."

"I suppose, given the grilling you've had from me, we should go Dutch," said Grace, laughing.

"Only if you insist."

"I will insist – this time. Maybe you'll give me the chance to be hypocritical another day."

"I hope so," said Tramane. They left the restaurant and wandered in the direction of Grace's apartment. It was dark, and pleasantly fresh. Street lighting punctuated the path and people moved between light and dark, their progress lacking continuity, like a badly edited, old-fashioned movie.

"I've really enjoyed this evening," said Grace, "but I probably shouldn't offer you a nightcap. No doubt you would take it as an 'obvious cue'."

"No doubt at all," said Tramane, stopping and turning towards her.

"Better not then," said Grace, playfully pushing him away and walking on. Tramane caught hold of her hand and she stood still, allowing him to hold it for a moment. He moved his thumb gently over her fingers.

"I'm going to stay a few days," he said. "I thought I might go out to Vancouver Island. Perhaps you could join me there at the weekend? I could do with a good guide."

"I don't know," said Grace, shocked at the effect of his touch, but leaving her hand in his. "I'm not sure it would be a good idea."

"I'm going tomorrow evening. Please come with me. I'll be on my best behaviour, honestly."

"I do love the place," said Grace, not looking at him. "It's got so much atmosphere." They had arrived at her apartment block. "My flat's just here, overlooking the bay." She pointed up. As she turned, their faces met, and he kissed her on the lips. She returned the kiss, feeling a ripple of excitement in her body and limbs. He kissed her again, holding her close. She smelt his scent and the roughness of his face and held him tightly. They parted for a moment. Grace gasped, conflicted. His attraction was overwhelming, but whilst she felt an intense hunger for him, there was an intrusive undercurrent of nagging annoyance with herself. How could she have let this happen?

"Was that a 'obvious cue'?" he asked. She smiled uncertainly and he took advantage of her inaction and kissed her again.

"Was it?" he pressed. Seized by a rationality which surprised her, she said,

"I've only known you a day." He gently released her, and they parted slightly. She should put a stop to this, but could not bring herself to. She would delay the decision. Maybe she would come to her senses in the morning. "Give me a ring at the office from your hotel on Vancouver Island. I guess you'll be staying outside the national park. There are plenty of places in Tofino."

"I will," he said. "Goodnight, Ms Lefavarie." Their lips touched again briefly. "I've had a great time. I can only think of one thing that could have made it better. But don't worry, I'll see if I can find myself a velociraptor for a bit of rough and tumble."

"Be careful," said Grace. "I've heard they're the worst."

6

SPANDEX AND STEERING COMMITTEES

On arriving at the University of Hardnox, I had felt obliged to dress smartly for work. After a few weeks, I sensed I had reached a stage whereby I could give up this pretence. As I believe I have mentioned, I feel disoriented by the complexities of female clothing. It has always confused my thinking[15], but now my budget was also thrown off balance. In the space of a month, I had got through ten pairs of tights. These strange garments usually laddered in the Ladies'. Not, I might add, through a slip of some pointy and finely manicured nail, but due to my misjudgement of the speed by which they could be pulled up. And what about women's shirts, eh? Delightful a material as linen

---

[15] Frumpp's Fashion Tip Number 10: Admit it, high heels have their uses. They make you feel more brazen. But to what end?

is, it needs constant attention. Some people look splendid in a crumpled shirt, but me – well, I just look crumpled. And then there is the lack of pockets ... I could go on for some time. I had accordingly reverted to my usual sober but comforting attire, namely a pair of trousers and a jumper. This had worked well for a few days, until Sally Whimbrel pointed out that my jumper had become home to a number of small, voracious larvae. My reluctance to squash the moths (generally, I am a respecter of life) had come back to haunt me. I'm glad it was she who spotted it; Christian would have had a field day.

I was not looking forward to Monday morning. A meeting had been arranged of the steering committee of the study, a concoction of professors and an English representative of Amity Action. This placed me in a dilemma: what should be worn? I find it constantly perplexing that at times when one is supposed to emanate the maximum confidence, one has to wear clothing that in fact minimises it. The steering committee would require a skirt of some sort; and a maggoty sweater was certainly out of the question.

I supposed that at some stage Irene would expect me to update the committee on my progress. Since the project meeting, I had listened to all the focus group recordings again. By really acquainting myself with the data, I hoped to get an idea of the main issues. I was now frantically transcribing, but anyone who has ever undertaken qualitative analysis will know that it is mighty time-consuming. The situation was intensified by the non-appearance of the elusive LOOFAH, whose licence UCLOG was still 'negotiating', and a dearth of basic stationery. Paper clips are an important organisational asset when dealing with large quantities of written material (each focus group produced around fifty pages of script) and none had been sighted in the department for at least three weeks. I had only managed to transcribe about half of the thirty meetings despite working at home in the evenings – it was lucky, I suppose, that my social life was meagre.

I would take a break only to watch my favourite soap, *Reality Crescent*. This way I could vicariously experience a plethora of assorted excitements and traumas which more than compensated for my flat existence. Last night, for example, Marjorie's budgerigar, Twinkletoes, stole Lady Honoria Twiglet's diamond, and deposited it in Derek's toothmug. The police, tipped off by Derek's estranged cousin, Paolo, were about to raid the house with batons at the ready as the closing credits appeared on the screen.

So, despite my very best efforts, I was horribly behind schedule. In addition, my worries about the inconsistencies in some of the data had not gone away. I was therefore dreading the meeting. I knew that it would involve that uncomfortable mix of politics and science, the latter probably subservient to the former.

I had seen very little of Professor Spigot in the weeks since our project meeting, and Irene had been working on another grant application with Dr Snoode. I had bumped into Professor Tweezer a couple of times, as he tended to drink his tea in the postgrad. and admin. tea room. This was usually when Sally had vacated her office, and he felt obliged to track her down. On both occasions, he had asked how the project was progressing, but on the first, he dozed off when I replied, having had half a pint of stout with his lunch.

On the second, he insisted on wandering around the room trying to squash a fly between his forefingers. I had raised the transcript problem with him and suggested that perhaps using the twenty more normal groups would be sensible. He had simply said,

"Anything you say, Flop – you are in charge of the analysis."

Irene Spatchcock finally popped her head round the door the Friday before the meeting and asked whether I would prepare an agenda. I did what I was told, and in a fit of confidence, brought on I think by a new Spandex top[16], I placed 'logistics' and 'focus group data' as the top two topics.

Now, Spandex is a curious material. It is stretchy and designed to fit snugly around an attractive shape. Needless to say, I always buy extra-large Spandex clothing. Being portly (but not XL), this latter size enables me to pretend that I am wearing something designed for sylphs. This is, however, an abuse of Spandex, as it conceals rather than reveals. This brings me to the question: what is the true purpose of extra-large Spandex? Is it designed for brave extra-large spherical women who wear their bumps and rolls with pride (and for whom I have great admiration), or is it simply oxymoronic – a stretchy garment to be worn loose and baggy?

I was sitting in my office at half past nine on Monday, awaiting the arrival of the steering committee with some trepidation. Looking over the agenda I had prepared, doubts were rising within me. Having spilt some boil-in-the-bag-fish-in-butter-sauce down the front of my new

---

[16] Frumpp's Fashion Tip Number 11: Spandex is moth resistant.

top the day before, the agenda now seemed reckless and provocative. I was just rubbing my bruised knees, and contemplating a re-write, when Irene sailed into the room, looking smart.

"Hello, Ellinora, how are you? Did you prepare an agenda?" she asked before I could answer her initial pleasantry.

"Yes," I said, "here." I handed her, with reluctance, the sheet which I had typed out and photocopied. She cast her eye over it.

"I can see your point of view, Ellinora, but this is not really what I had in mind. As you know, it is important to present a professional image here. Fourth rule of academe: presentation is everything! I feel this agenda is rather backward-looking. Leave it to me," she said, competently. "I'll jot down something more appropriate."

At ten o'clock we all shifted into the seminar room where the meeting was to be held. Its darkness and mustiness had intensified since my last visit, probably due to the damp spell of weather we were having. It was also clear that Christian had attended several meetings since I was last in the room, as a large patch of veneer had now disappeared from the table, and the fluorescent tube above had acquired a tick. There were five people on the committee, including the woman from Amity Action, and four academics (three men; one woman) who had supposedly done these sorts of studies before. Dr Snoode was sitting at the back of the room. He was dressed in a trendy leather jacket, and his lupine eyes leered impassively over his new-grown designer stubble. Terry Spigot arrived with his usual olfactory assault.

"Hello one and all," he said cheerily. "Thank you so much for coming. Irene, I believe you have sorted out an agenda." Irene duly distributed her revised document. She then turned to me.

"Now, Ellinora, I believe you are taking the minutes today." I blushed slightly, unsure whether this was a compliment or an insult, and reached for my pad of paper.

"Agenda item number one is an overview of project progress. I thought I would start off with this, and Professor Spigot, who you all know, will take over from me." Irene flicked the switch of the overhead projector. Nothing happened.

"Oh dear, bulb's blown," she cooed with annoyance. "Ellinora – could you pop out and tell Christian? He knows about these things. I'm so sorry everyone," continued Irene, completely unflustered, "and perhaps while you're doing that, you could help Sally make some drinks." I left the room with a request for five coffees and four teas. As usual, I found Sally behind a large pile of typing in her office. She looked overwrought.

"I, er," I said.

"Yes?" she said peering over her pile.

"I, er, Irene wants some teas and coffees. But, er you look a bit snowed under."

"Oh, Dr Frumpp, I'm so sorry, but Professor Tweezer has asked me to get these papers off by eleven o'clock and I have no idea how I'm going to do it, and Dr Spatchcock insisted that her grant proposal be typed up and sent off to research services today as well. She always leaves things to the last minute; and Christian wants me to put an order through for his new Pentium ..."

"It's OK," I said, "I'll do it. Do you know where Christian is?"

"I think he's in his room. He's not in a very good mood though." I went to the postgrad. and admin. tea room and put the kettle on, arranging nine mugs in a row, and then walked to the computer room. Christian was crouching over his computer, intent on the goings-on of the screen.

"Hi Christian," I said, amiably. "Listen, Irene's got a problem in the seminar room – it's important – she's got a roomful of people waiting for a presentation, and the OHP's blown. Can you give me a hand?" Christian said nothing.

"Christian?" I took a step forward. Nothing ... then a resentful muttering; then an outburst.

"Just because you've got a bloody PhD doesn't mean you can tell me what to do all the time!" He said 'PhD' with emphatic, phonetic contempt – 'Pee Aitch Dee' – it sounded more like a disease than an academic qualification. I was somewhat taken aback, and paused to summon an appropriate response – no time for chastisement: perhaps charm ...

"Well, perhaps you could just tell me what to do?" Nothing. "Look, it's not really for me anyway – it's for Irene."

"I see it's *Irene* nowadays," he said sarcastically, "all chummy with the boss eh?"

"Well, Dr Spatchcock then," I said.

"Oh no, it's *Irene*, you said it was *Irene*. In any case, I'm busy." I could hear the soft murmur of some space fight, and by the rapid clicking Christian was making on his mouse, I guessed he had probably just succeeded in slaughtering a giant intergalactic nautilus, and was making warp progress to the Beta Quadrant.

"Please, Christian, Professor Spigot is there too, it's a very important meeting."

"Oh, don't you mean 'Terry', Terry and *Irene*?"

"Look, what's got into you, for goodness sake!"

"Oh there you are, Ellinora, chatting away," said Irene, in a sing-song voice, and still remarkably cool. She had clearly tired of waiting for me. "Fifth rule of academe: don't keep the punters waiting! Come on, Christian, don't let Ellinora distract you – we've a room full of people waiting for this presentation." I sighed and went back to the tea room to sort out the drinks. The slit in my skirt was round the front again.

When I re-entered the seminar room, Irene was just drawing to a close. The group were nodding their approval. I passed round the drinks and sat in the semi-darkness as she finished, drawing some comfort from my cup of tea.

"And so that's *WImpI* to date," she concluded, casting a smile about the room. "Now, I would like to pass you over to Terry." She motioned to Professor Spigot, who sat at her right hand. He stood up.

"I am sure you are all familiar with the works of the 15th century Italian poet and clockmaker, Virago Innocenti. He said: 'We are two realms: one is a limp and unsprung coil; it is oblivion! To reach the second we must climb, insensible, the gripless face, through mainspring, verge and foliot. With good grace, a mechanism and a bell, we make dream reality.'" The room was silent.

"And the mechanism, as I'm sure you are all aware," said Spigot, casting his eyes sincerely round the room, "is the Spigot Sympathetic Interrogation Technique, or SpIT for short." Irene nodded in agreement. "As Irene has outlined, we visualise the process of eliciting worker opinion as a shared experience. Through SpIT we are able to hear what workers really want us to hear in a sensitive and non-threatening way. The development of this project has stimulated Delphic personal growth for all those concerned," – he paused for dramatic effect – "not just the focus group participants." He smiled modestly. "I think you will find that if you talk to anyone who has had the fortune to share a 'SpIT' experience, you will find that they never feel quite the same again. We encourage reflection and contemplation as part of the process, you see." Terry Spigot looked around the room briefly, before continuing. "A scoping analysis of the focus groups has shown a number of promising areas for inclusion in our questionnaire ..."

And so he continued for twenty minutes as the dim light levels slowly vanquished most of the steering committee who, leaning on elbows and slumped forward in varying degrees of consciousness, were subjected to a lot of very pretty overhead slides and analogies. I was baffled at what I saw. Professor Spigot had not spoken to me properly since the first project meeting, and I could not comprehend how he had come up with the proposed themes. The matters he suggested were, at most, tangential to the main thrust of the groups' concerns arising from my preliminary work.

At the end of the presentation, Irene switched the lights on. There was a jump-start from the audience, apart from one gentleman who was snoring, and then a rustle as papers were self-consciously fiddled with, and covert yawns and stretches were made.

"Well, thank you so much, Terry," said Irene, exuding charm, "for that exciting presentation. Now, do we have any questions?" She raised her perfectly plucked eyebrows.

"Yes," I said, "there are a couple of issues ..."

"Thank you Ellinora," said Irene, in a slightly chiding voice. "I know what you want to say but I can assure you that I covered those concerns while you were out of the room. Ellinora is a little bit of a worrier, you understand," she continued, addressing the audience. "She gets a bit bogged down in details and logistics."

"I think details are very important; as they say, 'the devil is in the detail'," said the woman academic, who had thick glasses a bit like mine. The group tittered lightly.

"It's just that firstly I do feel ..."

"I know what you're thinking, Ellinora," said Irene indulgently, "but we really do need to move on." She produced the conference abstract which the group looked at blankly. None of them had much to say about it. It was vague and unclear.

Is the fierceness of academic peer review inversely proportional to beauty? I'm sure there's a study in there somewhere. It always seems grossly unfair to me that whenever I present a paper, a tirade of finely sharpened criticisms find and pierce my vulnerable under-belly,[17] and yet other more aesthetically pleasing colleagues get away with a far less painful joust. The options are unpleasant to ponder: I am either incompetent or ugly (or, I suspect, both). I remember my first conference paper, in London. There was some twitchy young

---

[17] A not insubstantial task, given its size.

lecturer at the back who kept interrupting and putting me off. I had timed the presentation to perfection but was gaily handed a 'one minute left' sign by the chairperson when I was only half way through the results section. All the interruptions were attempts to make me look silly. I was told I handled it all very well, but the paper was not the great oration I had planned, and the structure of the talk was ruined. Still, I guess that was better than the poor woman in the next room where the slide projector broke down and chairperson Tweezer nodded off.

The meeting finished for lunch. I felt pretty thwarted, and retired to the Ladies' for a slight eye-dabbing session[18], my customary composure having deserted me. It all felt like a fine opportunity wasted. Unfortunately, I was caught by the woman academic from the steering committee who came in to 'powder her nose'.

"Are you OK?" she asked.

"Oh, yes, yes," I said wearily.

"Do you think it went well?" she asked.

"I think the presentations went well," I said.

"Professor Spigot can be a little impatient, I know – but his enthusiasm usually pays off. Details are important, of course; logistics sometimes get horribly neglected." I did wonder why she hadn't pursued her comment in support of the poor neglected logistics a little more vigorously whilst in the meeting. As if in answer to my thought-wave, she said, "It's very tricky in these situations, you see, one has to be rather political. Terry and Irene have quite a reputation. They review a

---

[18] Frumpp's Fashion Tip Number 12: always carry a handkerchief; loo roll may not always be readily available.

lot of papers and grant proposals themselves. Irene never forgets a name." She smiled and left.

My mood was one of resignation as I returned to my room, and even the appearance of a box of quite exquisite pink paper clips on my desk, presumably left by Sally, could not alleviate it. They are strange, aren't they, brightly coloured paper clips – a stoic attempt to liven up the dullest of documents; a little ray of jolliness in the grey world of administration.

7

DR FLOP

The large Suzuki motorcycle draws up on the pale brown gravel outside the Department of Administrative Studies. A slim, attractive woman dismounts, leaving a stunningly perfect man in his early thirties astride the machine, glistening in his leather wear. Professor Terry Spigot is twitching in the doorway, clasping and un-clasping his hands. There are a few beads of sweat on his brow that are about to make their way down his pale, plumpish cheeks and his usually kempt hair is fiercely out of control in the spring breeze.

"Dr Flop," he says, in a faltering voice, "can't we discuss this? Please." He is in earnest, but from the woman's pose, one can tell she really couldn't care less.

"I'm sorry, Professor Spigot, but I've come to the end of the road. I quit. I've found a better way to earn my money. I'm through with your pathetic salary scales and short-term contracts." Dr Flop walks up to Spigot, and looks him in the eye. "Now, let's talk business. Have you got those files I asked for over the phone?"

"But ..." he pauses, he knows it is no good. "I'll go and get them," he says nervously, looking over towards the man on the bike. No doubt his sense of inadequacy is highlighted by catching his paunched reflection in the mirrored sunglasses perched imperiously on the biker's nose. Dr Flop gets out a cigarette and flicks it alive with a silver lighter. Somehow it is easy to tell that the lighter comes from some exotic location: Las Vegas, perhaps, or the West Coast.

"Well, get a move on then. I've not got all day." Nearby, a curtain twitches. It is Spatchcock. Flop knows this without having to look. She is probably eyeing up the man on the bike again. At least she won't try it on a second time. After the departmental barbecue, her ego can't take another rejection. Despite her evident allure, he had told her to take a walk.

Professor Spigot re-appears.

"They're here," he says, "all of them, like you asked. All that valuable work! Will it come to nothing?" He pauses. "You will acknowledge me as a co-author when you write it up, won't you?" It had taken a lot of courage to say that. Dr Flop laughs.

"What's it worth, Spigot?" she says scornfully, puffing a mouthful of smoke in his face. "A pay rise?" She takes the files from his moist and pudgy hand.

"Yes, yes!" Spigot says emphatically. "Name your price! Please stay on! Finish what you've started!" The woman laughs again,

"What a sad person you are," she says. "I'll tell you what it's worth." She opens up the first brown manila file. It is marked *WImpl-2000*, and with another flick of her wrist, she sets it aflame with the lighter. She twists the file around; the fire catches and spreads like a snake through the sheaf of paper within. She drops the file at Spigot's feet. As it turns to carbon, she crunches it with her stiletto boots. The professor turns a deathly pale.

"But you can't," he cries. "You can't do that!" He is shaking now.

"Try and stop me," says Dr Flop, reaching for the second file. He takes a step forward, and the man on the bike obligingly dismounts. Professor Spigot stops in his tracks. By now a small gathering of staff has appeared at the door. A mixture of expressions from delight to horror play upon their faces. Dr Flop can feel Spatchcock's gaze from above and glancing up she can see her expression – it is one of *awe*.

The files are burnt one by one. The little pieces of ash are taken away in the wind, and float up towards the large monkey puzzle to the left of the department.

"I'm sure your vanity will find another vent," says Dr Flop, with a pretence of sympathy. The professor casts his face down.

"But, where, where are you going now?" he asks meekly.

"Oh, I've been head-hunted by the British Secret Service, so as you see, there's no way you can compete. I guess this is goodbye, Prof.," she says. "Here, have my cigarette butt." She presses the glowing stub into his jazzy acrylic tie, which melts, obligingly. "Think of me when you wear it," she says, and leaning over, she gives him a kiss, on the lips, before turning away. He stands with a smear of red on his mouth, his pupils dilating.

"*Au revoir*, Prof.," says Dr Flop, mounting the bike. The two riders leave with a roar and a wheelie in the middle of the car park. Spigot remains standing, amid the hubbub of voices behind him.

"No," he says, under his breath. "You can't go, you can't, please!"

I was awoken by a knock at the door of my bedsit. It took a few minutes for me to realise what was going on. Actually, it was a bit embarrassing; glancing at my watch, I saw it was five past one, on Saturday afternoon. I had, unusually, fallen asleep during a quiz show on the radio, and my ear drums were now being caressed by a gently accented newsreader.

The knock came again.

"I, er ... hang on a minute ..." I glanced in the mirror, but everything was fuzzy, so I reached for my glasses. As I stumbled to the door, it opened slightly. I knew I should have locked it, but it was only Jemima. She peered into the room, in her inimitable way.

"I, oh I'm sorry," she detected my lack of co-ordination, "did I disturb you?"

"I was just day-dreaming," I said. "Come in. Would you like some camomile?"

"Ooh, yes please," she said, "if that's OK."

"Of course it's OK. Sit down." Jemima cast her eyes around the room, and sat on the floor next to the chair with the dodgy rubbery thing. I put the kettle on. As I did so, I gently pushed a box of tampons out of sight.

"How are you?" I asked.

"I'm in love," replied Jemima.

"Great!" I said. "Are you going to tell me about it?"

"Oh yes, if you don't mind." Over the last month or so, Jemima and I had established quite a pleasant rapport despite my earlier misgivings. We enjoyed occasional Sunday walks and popped down the pub every now and again. As I had very little in the way of other social life, I was very grateful to her.

We had even been to the cinema. Jemina had taken me to see *Waterworld* because she had a thing for Kevin Costner (and was sure, webbed feet or no, she would enjoy his screen presence). And, of course, I was planning to take her to see *GoldenEye*, the new James Bond film just as soon as it was out. Brosnan looked good in the trailer – and I was looking forward to a fine compromise between cruel Connery and comic Moore, with none of the earnestness of Dalton.

I made myself a strong normal tea, and rummaged around for some chocolate biscuits. Handing her the camomile and placing the biscuits between us, I sat on the floor next to the bed.

"Speak!" I said. "Spill the beans!"

"Well," she began sheepishly, "there's this man – he's been in and out of the department. He's ever so nice."

"What does he look like?" I asked.

"Oh," she exclaimed, "he's so handsome. He's so polite. He's *very* clever."

"Well, we always tend to think of men we fancy as perfect when we first meet them," I said, pragmatically. "What's wrong with him?"

"Oh, nothing," said Jemima with a sigh.

"Has he asked you out?" I asked.

"Well, sort of," said Jemima, smiling coyly. "He said that I could come to one of his seminars."

For some reason, 'a man who'd been in and out of the department' had conjured up one of two images, a vigorous antipodean postgrad., or a maintenance man. I was thrown.

"So what does he do for a living then?"

"He's a doctor," she said.

"A researcher?" I asked.

"Yes. That's what he told me."

"What's the seminar on? He sounds a brainy fellow."

"I can't remember what the seminar is on actually," said Jemima.

"You mean you weren't really interested in the seminar," I said, smiling. Jemima giggled.

"Do you think I should go?"

"Well, I don't see why not. But you're sure you didn't misunderstand him? I mean, going to a seminar is hardly a date, is it?"

"Well, not really, but he said they often go for a drink afterwards."

"Well, doesn't seem any harm in it," I said. We took gulps of our respective drinks. My head began to clear.

"Are you in love with anyone?" asked Jemima. "You don't have to say."

"Well, no – I don't seem to have much success in that sphere, but I do have theories on the subject if you're ever interested. They are based on maths and biology O level. Both are good for getting such things in perspective."

8

HAVING ABSTRACT THOUGHTS

Grace's thoughts were not work-related as she arrived at the office the next morning. She had hoped that a cold shower and a good sleep would make a sensible decision obvious, but they did not. It was too late. She recognised the symptoms and felt helpless. She had the irrepressible smile that comes from a good evening out with an eligible member of the opposite sex. She knew she shouldn't build a mythical man on limited data, but it did not stop her. Her mind couldn't help reminiscing. She broke down the conversations and actions, categorising and labelling them with the efficiency, but not the objectivity, of an anthropologist. Jack was waiting for her when she arrived. He greeted her with a few platitudes concerning the conference abstracts.

"I see you've had the last few faxes in."

"Yes, I expect we'll see a few more though, don't you think? People are so last minute."

"And what is the quality like?" By the forced nature of these opening words, Jack betrayed the fact that he would rather be talking about something else.

"Oh, variable," Grace replied, conscious that he was not really listening to what she was saying. "Jack, you're looking edgy."

"Oh, it's er nothing, er, by the way," he said, clearing his throat, and attempting a levity he obviously did not feel, "how did you get on with our friend Mr Tramane last night? Is he still a chauvinist pig?"

"I'm not entirely sure. He was better behaved on that front. He's not quite so bad when you get to know him."

"You got to know him, then, did you?" said Jack, with a curious mixture of satisfaction and sadness.

"A bit," continued Grace. "In the end we had quite a nice evening. We talked about political correctness, politics, world views."

"I wanted useful information, Grace; I'm not interested in the way the man votes. Did he say anything about his work?"

"Not a great deal, no. Look, what's the problem?" asked Grace, crossly. "What's the big mystery? You told me to take him out – you didn't equip me with thumbscrews. It wasn't an interrogation you know."

"Look, I'm sorry. It's nothing." He left the room. 'Yeah, right,' thought Grace, and sat down at her desk, her good mood deflated.

During the morning, Grace placed all the abstracts she had received into three piles. The first, she thought they should accept; the second, she wanted to discuss with

Jack; the third, she wanted to reject. Jack also would have undertaken a similar procedure with his copies. They had put aside the afternoon to discuss them. Theoretically, he would be using the same criteria as Grace, as they were both guided by Amity Action's protocol, but as with any of these things, there was room for subjective judgement.

Jack stayed in his office all morning, to Grace's relief, but by two o'clock, her anger had surrendered to concern, heightened by Jack's tardy arrival for their meeting. It was apparent from his face that his mood had not changed.

"Look, Grace, I'm sorry about this morning. As you can tell, I'm not one hundred percent at the moment – got a few things on my mind."

"Is there anything I can help you with, Jack? Is it work-related?"

"Well, yes and no, but let's not worry about that now. Abstracts!" he said, clapping his hands with false enthusiasm and sitting down next to Grace.

They were aiming to have ninety papers in all. In this initial appraisal, they wanted to keep about a hundred and twenty. These, including any the two of them could not agree on, would move onto the second stage of the assessment procedure – peer review. They ended up discussing the content of several abstracts at length, arguing one way or the other that the paper was good or bad. Jack wanted to keep about seven abstracts Grace had objected to outright, including the contribution from Hardnox.

"I thought that one of the criteria was that the research should have yielded results – and here that would mean at least the survey instrument. To me, it's entirely unclear where they're at – they imply they have something, but the abstract is terribly vague. What's more, it's full of annoying and unnecessary jargon," said Grace. Jack looked uncomfortable.

"Yes, I know what you are saying, but it is accepted that this group has a good reputation."

"Well, you know my opinion of that, Jack."

"It would look very bad if we didn't keep this project, Grace. You know it is important to include studies that we have funded."

"But don't you think it's a little premature? I guess if you insist, I don't mind including it one of these days, but can't it wait until they've got some clear results?"

"It may well be that they have something already."

"Look, you know as well as I do that that is highly unlikely; we only gave them the grant a few months ago."

"But they could have undertaken quite a bit of work in that time."

"I'm doubtful about that," said Grace.

"I'm sorry, but we have to include it."

"Why? Look, we always used to agree about these things. I'm beginning to lose confidence in myself. It seems so obvious to me that the work does not meet our criteria. It's the same with these other papers – some of the projects may have potential, but they are not ready for presentation at our conference yet," she indicated the other six abstracts which were spread in front of them.

"We'll let the reviewers make the final decision, eh? How about that?"

This always seemed to be his backstop: the 'reviewers'. It was yet another thing that had been bugging Grace.

Quite a few of the grants she had recommended for rejection of late had come back with glowing reviews. She could not understand it, and every time it happened, it undermined her judgement and depressed her. She could only hope that for these abstracts at least, the reviewers would agree with her.

Grace stayed late to finish off preparing the packages for the reviewers. Comments would be sent directly to Jack and when he had a complete set, he would have another discussion with her.

It was quite dark when Grace left her office and she could see that Jack was still in. It had been a strange, hasslesome day, and she thought she should see how he was and say 'goodbye'. As Grace arrived at the door she could hear the rumbling of his voice on the telephone. She paused, wondering whether or not to peer round the door and wave.

"Look, it'll be OK," she heard him say, "they've got through the first round. Yes, I know it's important, but it's under control. No, I've got that sorted. It'll be fine. It'll be OK. Yes, I know. You know I will. I need it." She heard the click of the receiver being replaced, waited a few seconds and then knocked. She heard Jack moving in the room, and knocked again.

"Jack?" she said, and popped her head around the door. He had his back to her, and turned abruptly.

"I, oh, Grace, it's you," he said. "Hi."

"Is everything OK?" She was shocked by his countenance. He was pale and tense, and although the building was cool, he was sweating.

"Oh, yes, yes, fine!" he said emphatically.

"Look, would you like a drink? You've seemed so uptight of late, I think you need an hour or two off," said Grace.

"I, um, look, give me a minute. Yes, that's a great idea." She had occasionally had a drink with Jack after work before. She cared about him and his recent behaviour deserved her concern. It was affecting their working relationship. She did not want things to change. Perhaps if she got him into a more relaxed environment, he might tell her what was on his mind. When Jack emerged from his room, he seemed a lot calmer. They agreed to go to the bar Grace and Tramane had been to the day before.

"Seems a while since we've done this," Jack said, once they were out of the building, "an after-work drink."

"That's because it is a while," said Grace, smiling. "And in any case, I'm a bit worried about you."

"That's very kind of you," Jack smiled back, "but there's no need."

"You haven't been yourself for, ooh, I would say six or seven months. And we always seem to be disagreeing about something. We used to agree all the time."

"Well, I've had a lot on my mind."

"So you keep saying. Do you want to tell me about it?"

"Well, I'm not sure it's appropriate," said Jack, stalling her, "and how have you been? It seems ages since we had a good chat about you." They had reached the bar, ordered a beer each, and took a couple of the stools by the window.

"Well, there's not a lot to say really," said Grace, continuing the conversation. "I was rather hoping I might be able to help you out. Look, I don't want to pry at all, but if you can think of anything I can do ... Well, what I'm trying to say is that if you ever want to talk, well I'm here, that's all."

Jack didn't answer immediately but stared into his beer.

"That's good of you, Grace, but it's, well it's a personal matter. I'm sorry if it has affected our working relationship. I do try and keep up a professional front, but, well, we all lapse from time to time." Another pause.

"Are you doing anything interesting at the weekend?" he asked, rather lamely.

"I thought I might go over to the Island; it's a while since I've been. I'm beginning to get 'the call of the wild'." Jack spilt some beer.

"Don't worry," said Grace, smiling, "it's only lager." She picked up a napkin from the table, and leant over to dab his tie.

"Grace, I ..." started Jack.

"Yes?" she said.

"Oh, never mind," he responded. "Look, I don't want you lacking confidence in what you do. You know I trust your judgement. I'm talking about this afternoon – the abstracts. It's just that in this field there are certain political pressures. I'm sure you understand."

"Look, I understand and I'm pleased to hear you say that I'm doing OK. I can't pretend that I haven't been getting a slight complex."

"I'm sorry," he said. "What you do is fine. It's great, in fact."

"Thanks." Another pause. "What about this thing with Alec Tramane. Why are you so jittery about him?"

"Oh, I'm not, I mean, I know it may seem that way but he was a little out of the blue, that's all. He's a new donor. I usually know a bit more about the organisations which offer us money. It's nothing really." Yet another pause: a little uneasy. Jack was looking at her.

"Grace, I ..."

"Yes?" she said, with encouragement.

"You know that I ... I would like to confide in you ... I have great respect for you, but I ..." Grace put her hand on his.

"Jack – tell me when you feel you can – and only if you want to."

"Thanks," he said, and, after yet another silence, during which he seemed to physically adjust himself, "now I ought to be getting home."

"I'm sure it'll work out OK in the end," said Grace, as they parted. She wondered what Jack's life was really like. Despite his great success at Amity Action, he seemed so very vulnerable. She thought how peculiar it was that jocular exchanges in the workplace were so unrevealing; that the characters one saw day after day were strangely lacking in dimension. She sincerely hoped he was sharing his secret with someone sympathetic. There was too much there for him to cope with alone.

The next morning, Friday, Grace received a call from Alec Tramane. He gave her the name of his hotel in Tofino, and she told him she would catch the ferry out from Horseshoe Bay the next morning. The conversation was brief and to the point. She felt good about this one. Ironically, Jack's anxiety had fuelled her curiosity about the man. She would have to be cautious, but even as she thought this, she acknowledged the futility of the observation: when it came to men, caution was not her forte.

9

ARSES AND ELBOWS

I arrived at work one morning, shortly after the steering committee meeting, to find Terry Spigot hovering outside my office. He was blowing his nose on a paisley handkerchief, and the corridor was filled with his aroma. After a cursory inquiry as to my health and well-being he requested a copy of the meeting's minutes which I printed out for him. This need sated, I expected him to scoot off to an urgent appointment as usual, but instead he loitered in the doorway, appraising me with a hint of paternal disapproval.

"Bond fan, eh?" he said after a minute, during which I had begun to feel very guilty for no obvious reason. "I see you've got the fellow on the wall."

"Er, yes," I replied.

"And the music in your car this morning? Couldn't help hearing it." I was still awaiting my resident's permit at home and had come to a grudging truce with Mr Boffin, who had reluctantly given me a month of parking without penalty.

"*The Best of James Bond*," I said, feeling not only that my privacy had been violated, but that I had been caught doing something very naughty indeed. It was my fault, of course, for playing it loudly.

"Can't say I like the stuff myself. Hardly PC, is it?" He wrinkled his nose with jovial disapprobation.

"Well, I, er, it's pure fantasy – that's what I like about it."

"But it's so sexist!" I thought of that bit in *Goldfinger* where Bond wants a chat on his own with Felix Leiter and dismisses a lithe young masseuse with an outrageous name with a slap upon her bottom.

"Well, yes it is," I said defensively, "but it was written a few decades ago now. I view it as pure escapism." I was reluctant to discuss the matter further. I had not spent many hours pondering why Bond was so appealing to me. Whilst it might be considered sad by some, it was by no means an uncommon trait. I was sure that there were many learned texts on the matter to explain my weakness. There was no point fighting it.

"I'm afraid I have no time for it," said Spigot dismissively. "I think you'll find such things encourage prejudice, rather than equality between the sexes. Still, to each her own, eh?"

"Well, at least it makes people talk," I said, as he turned down the corridor. And besides there were sometimes a few spunky women: usually baddies, naturally. I was quite looking forward to Xenia Onatopp.

It was the day of Rosy's seminar. She was flitting round the room like an agitated bluebottle, fiddling with some overheads.

"It'll be fine," I said, "you'll be fine."

"Oh, gosh, I don't know," said Rosy. "I mean, these are supposed to be the main results to go into my thesis. What if someone completely blasts me?"

"They've no grounds for that. Your methodology is sound – you've done a fab job." I had had several conversations with Rosy over the last few weeks and she obviously knew what she was doing. "This kind of study is really difficult, but you've approached it appropriately. And in any case," I continued, "if you don't believe me, you must surely believe Dr Sweeble." Rosy smiled.

"You're right, of course; he's been an excellent supervisor."

"He'll be there, won't he?" I asked.

"Yes," she replied.

"Well, he'll squash any irritating, egocentric time wasters then."

"I hope so," said Rosy. I escorted her down to the seminar room, which had been valiantly re-arranged with the table at one end, and the plastic chairs in rows. She looked a little pale, and sneezed as the musty air hit her nostrils.

A few people had assembled. Irene was there, having a tête à tête with Terry. Professor Tweezer was in the back row, on his own, eating a banana, his satchel placed territorially next to him, in case Sally should appear. Christian was sitting in the front row, looking roguish.

Mike Sweeble greeted Rosy with a comforting smile, and I took a seat in the second row. There was a gentle trickle of noise that died down as Sweeble moved towards the centre of the room.

"Well, it's eleven o'clock," he said, "and I think we'd better get going. Now, I'm sure you all know the speaker for today, Rosy Cloudberry, who is in the final year of her PhD here at the DoA. Rosy has been studying a new staff development scheme set up by Hardnox Council. As you may know, her work takes an anthropological perspective to identify key factors that help and hinder the acceptance and implementation of workforce innovations. Rosy." He waved his hand in Rosy's direction, at which point Christian opened a bag of crisps and Rosy sneezed again.

"Er, thank you Bike," she began a little blearily, dabbing her nose with a tissue in an attempt to clear her nasal passages, and only slightly distracted by Christian's voracious crunching. "Yes, as er, Bike has just said, I have been looking at a new initiative at the council. For those of you who are unfamiliar with the scheme, I thought I ought to go through the system ..." I was just getting into her talk when there was an interruption.

"You say you are adopting an anthropological view," said Professor Terry Spigot, "but don't you think an action research model would have been more appropriate?" Rosy was momentarily thrown, but regained her composure.

"Well, no," she said, confidently, and went on to say why.

"We adopted an action research model to evaluate an appraisal system at the Cheery Chummy Bank in London," said Spigot when Rosy had nearly finished, "you might be interested to read it, it's in *Society in Flux*, volume 3, number 4, published this year, Spigot et al.."

"Er, thanks," said Rosy, and continued with her talk. Christian started polishing an apple on his fleece. After about ten minutes, Terry interrupted again.

"That's very interesting, Rosy," he said, with generous condescension, "but don't you think that training the personnel team in the 'Spigot Sympathetic Interrogation Technique' (which was first published in 1991, to much acclaim I might add, in the *Quarterly Qualitative Methodological Review)* would have helped in the way they negotiated the scheme with staff members?" Rosy hesitated for a second, sneezed, then went on to explain, with a mucosity worthy of the interruption, that it was not her place to intervene, merely to observe in the process. Spigot carried on regardless.

"But don't you think SpIT would have increased the scheme's chances of success? We have found that by using SpIT, people feel much more a part of the process; less threatened by the perceived imposition of new cultural frameworks. You'll find the details in Spigot and Spatchcock in the *Annals of Social Dynamics*, volume 861, pages 714 to 758." Rosy looked confused and Dr Sweeble stepped in to her aid.

"Interesting comments, Terry, but Rosy's work is an observational study. She did not participate in the intervention herself. That was not the point of the project." Spigot nodded sceptically, and, as Rosy began again, Christian sank his teeth hungrily and obtrusively into his apple.

At the end, Rosy sank relieved onto her seat, blowing her nose with finality. Dr Sweeble asked if anyone had any questions. Terry said authoritatively,

"Innocenti encapsulates the philosophy of the Spigot method, the changing of dream to reality. I do feel it would have been a great framework for succeeding in this context. It's easy for those in institutions to feel at sea when people threaten change. It's a stage of life where players lose their way. It's a transitory state. It's fragile, and can end in a slip down the metaphorical snake as in a game of snakes and ladders. I've written a chapter on that, Spigot, 1995 'Innocenti's Dream' in a book edited by Dr Spatchcock published by the University Press. You've probably heard of it: *Facilitating Happiness in the Workplace*."

Rosy looked blank. Dr Sweeble said,

"Thank you for that, Terry. Any other questions?" Not allowing much time for someone to speak up, he closed the seminar. "As we're running a little short of time, I'm sure we would all like to thank Rosy, in the usual fashion, for a very interesting talk." There followed a scattering of claps before the chair scraping and shuffling took over. Christian threw his apple core at the bin, and missed.

I went up to Rosy, who was a little flushed. She had gone and worn a slightly low cut top, against my advice, and I noticed that her collar-bone was dappled like a cloudy sunset.

"That was really good, Rosy," I said. "I was very impressed. It must have taken ages to transcribe all those meetings."

"Well, it was a very painstaking process. But what should I do? Terry Spigot thinks it's a load of rubbish – and he's the head of department."

"Oh, I wouldn't worry about that, Rosy," interrupted Dr Sweeble, returning from raising the projector screen. "Terry is surprisingly – well – focussed shall we say. He's very wedded to his own methods. He really knows very little about the type of qualitative analysis you've been doing."

"So Terry doesn't know much about qualitative analysis?" I asked, taken aback.

"Well, not the sort that Rosy is using," said Mike. "I've seen a few summaries of focus groups that he and Irene have touted at various meetings, but they don't pay any attention to the detail, and that's where all the interesting stuff is. Terry's approach to using SpIT seems to involve quantity rather than quality, although there is no reason why one couldn't use it for a more in-depth approach."

"How long would you give someone to transcribe and analyse data from thirty focus groups?" I asked.

"Well, that would be almost the size of the qualitative component of Rosy's work. So I guess at least six months, probably more."

"I've been given eight weeks." Mike Sweeble looked a bit surprised, and then a bit embarrassed. I think he thought I'd been asking a hypothetical question.

"What should I do?" I asked, plaintively. "I want to get to the detail, but I simply can't with the time-scale that I'm working under." Having trodden on forbidden territory, I could see Mike was happy to charge in with abandon.

"Do you want my personal or my professional opinion?" he asked.

"Well, how about both," I replied, smiling.

"Hmm," said Sweeble, stroking his beard, "my professional opinion is that Spigot, Spatchcock and Snoode don't know their arses from their elbows when it comes to the kind of analysis you're talking about, so you should do what you think is best."

"Oh," I said, a little deflated, "and your personal opinion?"

"That Spigot, Spatchcock and Snoode don't know their arses from their elbows when it comes to the kind of analysis you're talking about, so you should do what you think is best! But then, it's not really my place to comment without knowing the specifics. Who am I to pass judgement?" he asked rhetorically, and turned to Rosy for some words of congratulation on her presentation.

I left the seminar with an uneasy mixture of relief and distress. Relief that, at last, I had some proof that I was not a complete idiot, and distress because I could not see a solution to my predicament. I disappeared to the Ladies' to calm down. Is it the lock on the door, or the coolness of a lavatory cubicle that provides spiritual balm? It gives you time out – relief in more ways than one. After about twenty minutes of solitary contemplation, I walked over to the Students' Union canteen and bought myself a sausage and tomato sauce sandwich. Not very sophisticated, I know, but homely.

It was a pleasantly bright October day, and I could see right out of the campus into the countryside. There was only a wire fence between freedom and me. I was unable to repress the theme tune from *The Great Escape*. If only I had a motorbike. There was a helicopter sweeping across some farmland a few miles away. A chopper would be just fine.

What an inconvenience it is that we are paid a wage for taking on responsibility. What a ridiculous feeling of obligation this inspires. How frightened we are of being seen as failures in the things we undertake. How large and out of proportion they become in our small lives. A doughnut. Maybe I needed a doughnut to hide behind.

I decided that I should have a chat to Dr Max Snoode. He had equal power amongst the triumvirate, and perhaps he could be lured into a treacherous alliance with me. Unlikely, I knew, given my lack of general attractions, but it was worth a try. I rang his extension, but his secretary said he wouldn't be back until about six. I spent the afternoon writing up my concerns in detail with very specific examples. By six o'clock I felt I had quite an eloquent document, full of flawless logic.

I walked with great determination across the campus and into the Sociology building. Max's office was apparently room 1.01, most inauspicious. The first floor corridor was dim, and there was a light only in one room, from which emanated the throb of a machine. This noise, and the auditory anonymity supplied by the carpeted floor, meant that I could approach without detection. Peering through the door's window, I could see several dormant photocopiers in an L-shaped room. Clearly the one being operated was round the corner. I went in and walked to where the machine was running. To my complete amazement I saw a man's hairy buttocks pumping rhythmically on top of the machine. I beat a hasty retreat.

"Oh, Max!" came the voice of the excited female beneath. "Oh Max! Get me another grant, you beast!" It appeared that I had located Dr Snoode, and that Dr Snoode, at least, did know his arse from his elbow. I didn't know what to do with myself. I was fuelled by an unwavering resolution to sort out my work, and I was not going to leave, yet it was preposterous, if not voyeuristic, to stay. I went back out into the corridor,

116

and waited in the shadows. After about five minutes, the photocopier went off, and I slipped into an office to wait for Max to appear. I don't know why it came as such a surprise when Irene Spatchcock emerged glowing and dishevelled into the corridor, but it did. On reflection, the connection was obvious. She disappeared down the stairs quietly, readjusting her clothing.

Again I questioned the wisdom of tackling Max at this post-coital moment, but I was a driven woman. I gave him time to get his trousers in place, and went back into the room.

"Oh, Dr Snoode," I said, beaming. "I'm so pleased to have found you. I've had a really good look at the focus group material, and I just wondered if you could spare a few minutes to help clarify some points." He was shocked at my appearance, but was no doubt comforted by my light and innocent expression[19]. He was rummaging through a pile of paper, which was lying by the photocopier.

"Oh, I, er, Ellinora, this isn't really a good time," he said. I was delighted to see his usually creepy composure destroyed.

"I've spent all afternoon doing this, please Dr Snoode."

"Well, I, er, Ellinora, can you give me a minute, I, er, for a course, on er, interpersonal communication skills, I er, just need to get a few handouts sorted."

"Oh, alright then," I said brightly, "shall I wait in the corridor?"

"Er, yes, if you could," he said. I turned and went out of the room, but as I did so, I caught a glimpse of his

---

[19] Never underestimate the power of an innocent look.

hand holding what appeared to be a ream of double-sided backsides.

I did not have high expectations of the few minutes that Max could give me. I felt that given the circumstances, his judgement was bound to be a little out of kilter, but I was surprised at the instant and rapid progress we made. He readily agreed that I should concentrate on the data from the twenty more consistent focus groups that Irene had facilitated. He said that he would have a look at the ten odd groups and analyse them himself. We could then compare the findings. He was keen for me to hand over the relevant tapes and any transcripts I had completed. Astoundingly, he also agreed that I should have longer to work on the data and suggested a deadline of late March for a draft set of themes to inform the questionnaire. Bingo! I hoped this was not simply an attempt to fob me off. He was certainly in a hurry when he left. He said it was his wedding anniversary.

The next day Irene came in to see me. I half expected a reversal of all things promised to me the day before, and was contemplating blackmail.

"Now, Ellinora," she said, decisively, "you may recall when you first started I thought how wonderful it would be if you had a little SpIT training. Well, Terry is in full agreement and we think you should come along to the course we are running in January. It is only right that you get a proper initiation into the system. We've all benefited from it so much ourselves, it would be quite neglectful for us to withhold such a privilege from you. You are the only member of the team, you see, who hasn't done it. It will do wonders for your personal development."

"OK," I replied, simply.

"To be honest, I think Terry is a bit worried about your taste in music," she said. "Of course, I don't exactly approve of all that Bond frippery myself, but we all have our little vices. SpIT has holistic repercussions. I rather think he hopes you'll be listening to Mozart by the end of the course."

"I already listen to Mozart," I said defensively.

"Oh," she said. "Oh well, that's just fabulous. Now Max says that you and he have sorted out something for the analysis … very sensible of you to give the more tricky transcripts to someone more experienced."

"Huh?" I said, my concentration momentarily directed towards a vision of Irene dressed as the Queen of the Night.

"You and Max," she repeated. "Tremendously generous of him to help you out; he is such a wonderful person."

"Absolutely," I nodded with agreement.

10

NOT LITTLE NELLIE

It is somewhere in England. The land is flat; field upon field squared and regular like infinite Battenberg cake. I am in a hangar, dressed in khaki. I am feeling determined and a great spirit of togetherness prevails. I have an objective. We share an objective.

Outside it is sticky. The sky is purple to the east, brooding, lugubrious. There is no rain yet, but I can see flashes of light in the sky. I am a pilot, and beside me is my machine. It is menacing, yet comforting. I touch my cheek against the cold steel of the helicopter. This is mine, and I can do what I like with it.

I am brought to attention by a woman dressed like myself. I think it is Jennifer. I have never met her before, but Rosy has told me about her. We are kindred spirits.

"Will you come into my office, please," she says. I think she is in charge. "We have a mission," Jennifer points with a wooden stick to a chart on the wall, "and it's just you and me, Lieutenant Flop, but the others are backing us all the way. If we succeed, it could mean an extra scale point, but it won't be easy. This is the target." She points to a building in what appears to be a campus. "You can't hit any of these other buildings," she says, "civilians, and we're talking about a full-blown gunship here, not Little Nellie."

"Yes, Sah," I say, "understood, Sah."

"Our mission is to deliver a consignment of logistics to the building. Do you understand?"

"Yes, Sah!" I notice how anxious she looks. She has deep circles round her eyes, and despite the confidence and directness with which she speaks, she looks as if she has been crying. There is no doubt that she has been Spatchcocked.

"The enemy are cleverer than you think. They are protected by a fiendish mouse, stationed here." She draws a cross on the map with a thick red felt tip. "It won't be easy to overcome," she says, "you will need a barrel of Horologist's Hokum, and a mean line in computer jokes."

"Permission to speak, Sah."

"Permission granted, Flop."

"Computer jokes, Sah. Do we have any leads?"

"You'll find a catalogue in the cockpit, Flop, version 3.1."

"Thank you, Sah!"

"This is it, Flop." Jenny embraces me. "Remember, we're in this together." A manly tear comes to my eye; I pat her firmly on the back. We come out of the office and back into the hangar. The place is full of people; they are professors and lecturers and researchers. They look at us wide-eyed. One of them comes up to me, he is bent and thin; he has Research Grade 1B written on his forehead.

"I'm only sorry I can't be with you, Flop, but I've got grants to get, papers to publish. But someone's got to do it, and you're the one for the job." I shake him by the hand and walk to my helicopter. It is an evil brute. I get in and put on my headset. A few of the academics push me out of the hangar and into the wide, open airfield.

"Flop, do you read me?" It is Jenny.

"Yes, I read you loud and clear," I reply.

"Ready for take-off. Stick to me like glue; you're new at this game," she says.

"Sah." I switch on the blades. They begin to thud, thud, thud above me, and suddenly the ground isn't there any more: I am swooping over the countryside below.

"Follow me," crackles Jenny over the radio. She is heading towards the storm. The lightning is flashing ahead of us, but I keep a steady course. I feel the wind buffeting the machine.

"Steady," says Jenny, over the radio. We hurtle across the sky, over churches and rivers and towns, deeper and deeper into the storm. The sunlight that had fallen on the ground beneath has disappeared and everything becomes grey and dark.

"Mouse at two o'clock!" exclaims Jenny. "Do you see it, Flop?"

Up ahead I see a large, smooth, rounded rectangle soar into the sky. Cold fear surges into my bloodstream.

"I see it, Sah! Should I fire the Horologist's Hokum, Sah?"

"No, Flop. Soften it up with a computer joke first. Then finish it with the ale. Try number 11." I open the book of computer jokes, but number 11 is obscured by a big, iridescent beetle, who wiggles its wing-casings at me, singing in a tinny voice,

"Nah nah ni nah-nah!"

"Sah!" I shout in a panic. "There's a bug in computer joke 11, Sah!"

"Damnation!" replies Jenny. "I knew we should have stockpiled version 3.1.1! Try number 12!"

But it is too late; the object rears up, then stays at a constant distance from Jenny's helicopter. It is like nothing in this world, something extra-terrestrial; something with a deep rumbling power. A great bolt of light comes out from the front of it, and rams into Jenny's machine.

"I'm hit!" she cries, "you must read ... you must ... aaarrrghh!" A great tortured cry rings out of the receiver, and the helicopter explodes: the embodiment of Lichtenstein. A great shockwave pushes against my craft.

"Jenny!" I cry, feeling suddenly bereft and alone, "you never even came to pick up your cardboard box!" But the airwaves are silent. Jenny is gone, and in front of me the strange, sinister craft hangs in the air. I lose my nerve.

"Help me!" I cry, "help me!" I suddenly remember that I don't know how to fly a helicopter and everything seems foreign to me. Up ahead I can see the object powering towards me. I am going to die! And then I recognise the pilot. It is Christian, sitting astride his mouse, pumping down the button, making it fire at me; he is laughing.

"Back end of a bus! Back end of a bus!" But his taunts pull me to my senses.

"I'll get you, you bastard," I say, and launch my barrel of Horologist's Hokum.

Christian's smile vanishes. He stops pumping.

"If you think I'm going to blow up a barrel of real ale, you've got another think coming." He manoeuvres his mouse out of the way and pursues the beer.

I have got through the defences! The air all around me is electric. I am knocked by the turbulence, but keep in control of the machine. Beneath me, in the gloom, I see my target. I know it is the Department of Administrative Studies.

"Time for a bit of music," I shout, and the *Bond* theme rings out over the skies, drowning out the thunder and the rain, the drops of which are smashing against the cockpit. I fly low over the building and flick the switch marked 'cargo'. I unleash my load. There are thousands of logistics: friendly, blobby, purposeful logistics, winking at each other as they fall.

"Wheeeeeeee!" goes a particularly cute one.

Professor Spigot is below. He is amazed at the deluge of happy spheres. He looks at them quizzically as he scoops them up. The logistics bounce gaily into his clothing. In the department, Irene and Max embrace. Terry waves his handkerchief, leaping up and down. I wave back. A tidal wave of relief comes over my body. A great weight lifts from my shoulders. I can hear people cheering and laughing; the world is liberated, and I have done this. Everything is going to be fine.

And then I fell out of bed.

11

WAY ABOVE THE TREE LINE

Grace Lefavarie caught the 9.30 car ferry from Horseshoe Bay. In an hour and a half she was in Nanaimo, and driving her hire car on Highway 4 to Tofino. It had been a while since she was last on the Island, and it was refreshing to get away from the city, much as she loved it. Vancouver Island was part of the tourist circuit. She would direct her friends from Ontario here after they had been to the Rockies. It was a mysterious place, full of dark, moist temperate rainforest: immense trees and cavernous groves. To the south of the Island was Victoria, the capital of British Columbia, a sliver of England, full of tea shops and rose beds.

Grace insisted to herself that she had not made up her mind about what should happen this weekend. Although she had a few taxonomic problems with Alec Tramane, she was keen to overlook them. A few things passed through her mind. Was he purely interested in her for a fling, or was he considering her in the longer term? More to the point, what did she want from him? Grace was intrigued by his controversial conversation. When he patronised, he seemed to relish the rebellion it inspired, but in the ensuing talk he showed no sign of bigotry, and every willingness to discuss his point of view, to the extent of admitting that he might be wrong.

The Orca Hotel in Tofino was a modern brick building with an attractive wooden balcony at first floor level. Grace checked in. Alec Tramane had assumed nothing. A room was booked in her name. She asked the woman at reception to give Tramane a ring, to tell him that she had arrived, and made her way up to the room. The hotel was simply but tastefully decorated in light colours, with a series of pictures on the walls, depicting the Pacific in several of its many moods. Grace was just brushing her hair when Tramane knocked at the door.

"Come in, it's unlocked," she said, turning round. "Alec, how are you?"

"I'm fine, I hope your journey was pleasant."

"No problems at all. The weather is so good at the moment, the crossing was really smooth." She went to the window and opened it. It looked out over part of the inlet that made up Clayoquot Sound, and out towards Meares Island. She could just make out a little cluster of wooden houses with their satellite dishes; a juxtaposition of tradition and technology. Tramane sat down in one of the armchairs.

"I hope you like the room. I'm in number seventeen, down the corridor on the left. I must admit, this part of the world is growing on me. It's quite unusual to get this feeling of wilderness only a stone's throw from a city."

"It's great, isn't it," agreed Grace. "Have you seen much of the national park?"

"I've driven through it. I took a ride down the coast to Ucluelet yesterday. I thought perhaps we could go for a walk in it this afternoon."

"Oh, yes, you have to see the rainforest at close quarters. They have some superb boardwalks. It controls where you go rather, but takes you through the heart of it all. I'll be your tour guide." Grace had come prepared for the trip, wearing jeans and a pullover, and she had her walking boots and mackintosh to hand. When she had unpacked a little, the two of them went down to the hotel bar for some lunch. Although the whale-watching season was not yet over, the hotel felt tranquilly under-utilised.

"I can't get over how quiet it is here," said Tramane, "it makes me feel very conspicuous."

"Ah, you are a man who likes anonymity then," replied Grace. "Empty hotels always make me feel special – as if all these facilities are laid on just for me."

"A deprived childhood perhaps?" queried Alec.

"Not at all – a flat and humid one perhaps, but plenty of toys. What about yours then, with your desire to remain incognito?"

"Institutional. I'm a product of the great British public school. Maybe that does explain it: a childhood full of little boys just like me."

"I've no doubt you took every opportunity to assert your individuality. I don't see you toeing the line."

"Well perhaps not, but I was always very stealthy when I broke the rules. On the surface, I was an exemplary student."

After two unnecessarily large club sandwiches, they set off in Tramane's hire car, an outrageously comfortable Buick, with large, soft leather seats. It was like flying on a cloud. They drove for about twenty minutes, after which Grace suggested they stop. Tramane pulled into a lay-by and they got out of the car.

"Now follow me," said Grace, in her best formal 'tour guide' voice, "lesson number one. You see these trees here," she pointed, "these are Sitka Spruce. They can tolerate the salt water that blows off the Pacific. They're quite old, I think." They entered a grove and suddenly the light level dropped. They were surrounded by prolific vegetation. The trees were dripping swathes of moss and the ground below the boards, upon which they walked, was covered in ferns. A deep, peaty, pungent smell arose from between the planks.

"When one of these big trees dies, you'll often see young spruce colonising the trunk. Nothing's wasted – it's a continuous process."

"They seem to manage things well out here. I mean, the fact that this forest is allowed to remain."

"Well," said Grace dubiously, "the national park might be well managed, but there's been a massive amount of controversy about timber. A couple of years ago there were thousands of protesters here. Did you notice all the woodland on your way to Tofino? That used to be temperate rainforest. You destroy a whole ecosystem when you tear it down. It might take a thousand years to restore it. I couldn't bear them to fell

Clayoquot Sound. There's been some progress but not enough yet."

"I didn't realise you were an eco-fascist," said Tramane, laughing at her earnest expression.

"I suppose you support the timber companies – after all, I expect you get business out of them," responded Grace, annoyed at his flippancy.

"Well yes, I suppose we do – but hey, I'm not here to be labelled a capitalist pig as well as a sexist one. I do see your point of view, honestly." He spread his hands out defensively, but stopped suddenly. "Good gracious, what's that?"

"That," said Grace, laughing, pleased that he was not going to make her dislike him again, "is lesson number two – one of our famous banana slugs." Beneath them oozed a pale yellow slug, about twenty centimetres long. "They're great, aren't they?" Tramane looked doubtful. "Don't worry, they don't bite." They continued a little further along the path. It was getting quite dark now, simply because the undergrowth was so thick. Every now and then a glitter of sun would catch on a damp leaf, or silhouette the great furred branches above them. The walk was a circuit and they found themselves back at the lay-by before too long.

"It's amazing how small this national park is really," said Grace. "I think they should extend it to include the sound. There's another boardwalk on the other side of the road. Come on." They crossed, and dived once again into the gloomy verdure.

"It is peculiar," commented Grace, as they stomped along the springy boards, "this all seems so out of context. I mean, here I am, tromping along in the wilderness with a client from work. It feels very strange."

"I rather hoped you'd stopped thinking of me as a client," said Tramane.

"Maybe. Maybe not – I haven't decided yet," lied Grace playfully. "Oh look, here's the road again. How disappointing. I wish these walks went on for a bit longer."

"Where do we go now?" asked Alec.

"Well, I think we should pay our respects to Long Beach. There's some more slimy wildlife I'd like to show you."

They drove a little further down the road and stopped. From the car park they emerged out of the trees into a wide open empty beach, littered with great skeletal tree trunks, their roots helplessly stranded in the air, weathered to snake-like appendages.

"They have incredible winter storms here," said Grace. "These trees get ripped from the coast and dumped on the beach. It's very desolate, isn't it? They look so pathetic; so undignified." They were walking along the beach now, sand underfoot. To the south a small headland poked tentatively out to sea. Behind it a few lines of thin grey cloud broke up the otherwise blue sky; they occasionally obscured the sun, creating a strange enclosed glow. Every so often, the two of them perturbed a flock of littoral birds which rippled in front of them before resettling a few metres ahead.

"Here we are," said Grace, clambering up some rocks on the shore, "let's see what we've got in here. There," she said, pointing into a rock pool. Alec came up to join her.

"Good grief," he said, "they're quite impressive." The pool was filled with large anemones stuck to the rock like giant green dandelions.

"I think we should have a bit of a sit down here," said Grace. "Lesson number three is all about absorbing the atmosphere. You just have to be part of this place for a while." Perched on top of the rocks, they looked out to sea, sitting close together in silence. It seemed only natural that she should lean gently against him. Grace had not been sure how Tramane would react to this part of the world. The very fact that he had suggested coming out here made her feel that he was drawn towards these types of places. That put him in her good books. She might be a city person herself, but wilderness was important to her. It was a world where schedules and deadlines were meaningless; a world that brought home to her the small role she played in the big picture. In a hundred years' time she would be gone, but Long Beach would live on: waves bombarding the shore; anemones pullulating in their pools. She had feared that Tramane was totally urban – he emanated that type of sophistication. Now, feeling him next to her, seeing him in casual clothes, he seemed like a different man.

"What's that bird?" said Tramane, interrupting her musings, and pointing upwards. "It's been going back and forth along the shore ever since we've been here. It's massive." Grace looked up.

"It's an osprey," she said, looking at its long thin wings. "It's hunting, I expect." On cue, the bird swooped down into the sea, wings held jagged and aerodynamic, only 20 metres from where they sat. The osprey grabbed at a fish with its talons and, after a brief, one-sided struggle, the bird lifted it above the waves, still thrashing, and moved over to the trees and out of sight.

"Gosh," said Tramane, "that was a bit of natural drama: 'Nature, red in tooth and claw'. You expect to see that sort of thing in nature programmes, not in front of you with the wind in your face."

"That's what I like about this place. I always think it's strange that we feel so attached to Nature. That sitting here, you do feel part of something greater, and yet it doesn't care about you, does it? I mean, if there were a storm, this place wouldn't think twice about chucking one of those great logs at us or drowning us."

"I didn't have you labelled as a country person, you know, Grace. You look so comfortable in the city, so suave, and here you are waxing lyrical about the wind and the rain. Is there anywhere you don't feel comfortable?"

"Actually, I'm not very comfortable on this rock. It would be better like this," she said, placing his arm around her. "At least I won't fall off now." She smiled, and caught his eye. He leant forward and kissed her.

"There's no-one here," said Alec gently, "and I'm rather looking forward to lesson number four."

"So am I," said Grace, exploring his hand with the tips of her fingers. She kissed it, then looked up into his face. He was looking quite radiant: his cheekbones sculpted, smooth and strong, his grey-green eyes vivid against the tanned skin. They kissed, and she felt his hand move quietly over her body: caressing, discovering. She did not object, and felt for the warmth of his skin beneath his pullover. Touching him sent a delicious sensation through her body, lapping around her like the waves in the Pacific only metres away. He pushed her back softly and moved his lips to her neck. She felt his breath hot and passionate as his fingers slipped under her clothing. She would not resist him this time: it was too exotic, too dreamlike, too elemental; too ridiculously romantic to be resisted.

They held hands as they made their way back to the car. The grey clouds had grown into streaks of orange, running at angles to each other in the sky, and the wind had begun to antagonise the water, creating little angry turrets of white, and a haze along the shore. The warmth of their encounter was dissipating to the chilliness of the evening, and they were both pleased to get back to the car. They drove along the darkening road to the hotel, and went straight to the bar, which was more populous now with the return of weather-beaten tourists swapping grey whale stories.

"Are you warm enough yet?" asked Alec.

"Yes, I'm fine now thanks, and you?"

"I think I shall be feeling very pleasantly warm for a while yet."

Grace smiled. "I've had a wonderful day," she said.

"So have I," replied Tramane, "and I'm pleased that it's not over yet. Shall we eat here?"

"I would like that," said Grace. After about half an hour they moved into the dining room. Alec ordered a bottle of wine, and they ate local fish, talking with easy intimacy, legitimised by their new relationship. Afterwards, they made their way up to their rooms.

"I suppose if I offered you a nightcap, you would take it as an 'obvious cue'," said Grace.

"Yes, I would take it as an obvious cue," confirmed Tramane.

"Good," she said. "Would you like a nightcap?"

When Grace awoke, it was dark, and she was conscious that she was alone. She glanced over to the bedside table. The red glow of the digital clock told her that it was half past two. Why had she awoken? Could she hear something? She strained her ears, but could hear nothing, apart from the gentle swish of the sea outside. Where was Alec? Perhaps he had just nipped to the bathroom. But moving her hand out into the bed, she could detect no warmth. Alec had been gone for some time. She sat up, and switched on the light, shading her eyes at first from the brightness. She looked around the room. His clothes were gone; there was no hint that he had been there. For a moment she thought that perhaps she had been dreaming, but she saw the sand on her boots by the wall, and the afternoon came back to her with all the force of the emotions she had felt. She began to worry. Why would he have gone? She got out of bed, wrapping a shirt around her, and moved towards the window. Suddenly a hand clamped over her mouth and pulled her back. She tasted salt on fingers and she tried to struggle free, her heart surging with adrenalin.

"It's OK!" said Alec Tramane. "It's only me; it's OK."

She tore herself away from him.

"Then why did you have to do that!" She put her hand to her mouth. He had been a bit rough and her upper lip felt sore.

"I'm sorry. I didn't want you to scream."

"For fuck's sake Alec," she said, calming down a bit, "I thought my time was up. Where have you been anyway?" She sat on the bed, gradually feeling her pulse return to normal. He moved over to the chair, and unstrapped a leather holster from under his arm. Grace gradually began to take in what she was seeing. Alec Tramane had been out. He was dressed in black and had sand on his trousers. The holster contained a gun.

"What on earth is going on?" she asked, standing up again and instinctively moving backwards to the door.

"I shouldn't have come back here," he said. "I thought you would be asleep."

"I was asleep until you woke me up," she said indignantly. "Now I want you to tell me what the hell is going on?"

"Look," he said. "I don't think that's wise. It could be dangerous for you. The less you know the better." He was irritated.

"Don't treat me like an idiot!" said Grace. "Whatever you were trying to conceal, you've blown it now!" She could feel herself losing control. As it became clear that he meant her no harm, her initial fear had turned to anger.

"Look, Grace, calm down, sit down, and for heaven's sake keep your voice down!"

"Not until you tell me what's going on!" she exclaimed. He came over and guided her reluctantly back to the bed. He sat down on a chair facing her.

"Look, I didn't mean for this to happen," he said. "I'm sorry." He was speaking more gently now, and he held her hands. "I didn't mean to scare you. Listen, you need an explanation, I know, but can't it wait until morning?"

"No, it can't," said Grace. She took her hands away from him and stood up again. "I can't believe this is happening."

"It's a long story," he said, "please sit down."

"Tell me now," said Grace, regaining her composure. "I want to know now."

"OK," said Alec. "OK. Look, sit down." She sat down once more, but some distance away from him.

"I'm not what I appear to be," said Tramane. "I work for the British Secret Service."

"You what!" exclaimed Grace.

"I work for the Secret Service, and I'm here on an investigation."

"Oh, come on," said Grace.

"It's true."

"And what exactly are you supposed to be investigating then?" she asked, incredulously.

"Amity Action," he replied. Grace's mouth opened, but she didn't say anything for a few moments. When she managed to get words out of her mouth, they were dismissive.

"Oh, don't be so daft!" She almost laughed, waiting for him to tell her it was all a joke, but he remained resolutely solemn.

"Look, Grace, I'm sorry, but it's true, and now I've told you, you must keep quiet. You could put yourself in danger."

"What on earth do you mean?" she said. "Look, if what you are saying is true, then I want to know everything."

"I really don't think that's a good idea," said Tramane, "and anyway, I'm not sure about anything myself at this stage. I'm still doing some groundwork."

"So where were you tonight then?" asked Grace. "There's nothing out here remotely to do with Amity Action."

"Well, that's where you're wrong," said Tramane. "You mentioned a couple of days ago some courses Jack D'Oretz is setting up out here. Well, he plans to use a building near Chesterman Beach. I've been there."

"Well, that doesn't mean anything," said Grace. "That would be expected."

"It's who owns the building that's the problem."

"Who, then?"

"Praefortica," said Tramane, "and the man behind Praefortica is Zuserain Nexus. He is under investigation. We have reason to believe he may be plotting something. And the link with Amity Action is not coincidental."

"It could be," said Grace, feeling suddenly very protective of Jack. "I know Jack. He's a sound man. There can't be anything wrong." She felt the taste of untruth in her mouth as she said these words, recalling her recent conversation with Jack and her latter disagreements with him. Annoyingly, Tramane seemed to pick up on her lack of certainty.

"Is there something wrong, Grace? You said that you and Jack had had your differences?"

"No, I ... he has personal difficulties at the moment, that's all. It's nothing to do with work."

"That's your opinion, Grace."

"And what have you been doing this evening?" she said, responding to his scepticism with a counter-attack. "Snooping round other people's private property?"

"Yes."

"And did you find anything?" she asked.

"It's too early to say."

Grace stood up again and walked round the room slowly.

"And where do I feature in all this?" she asked. "I suppose I'm just a useful contact, an information source."

"I'd be lying if I said there wasn't an element of that at first," said Tramane, coldly, "but you know as well as I do, there's more to it than that now."

"Do I?" said Grace. "What am I supposed to think? Someone like you, some calculating Bond-like robot, would care about me?" Tramane made no attempt to calm her down, his habitual equanimity tempered only slightly with an impatience which Grace felt was directed at her.

"I think you'd better leave," she said, turning away from him.

"Grace, you mustn't say anything about this. You could put yourself in danger."

"As if that would cause you an ethical problem," she said, bitterly. Tramane picked up his gun and walked towards the door.

"I'll be in touch," he said, and left.

Grace sat heavily on the bed and put her head in her hands. She felt confused and humiliated. She was even peeved at the professional distance at which Tramane had placed her. How could she have misjudged this man so completely? The thought of what had passed between them that day revolted her. She had gone and done it again! She had leapt into a relationship with a man she hardly knew and was paying the price for it. But it was so much worse than just that. Tramane had taken a swipe at the other half of her life – Amity Action. Jack was under suspicion. What could this mean? What should she do? Jack's behaviour of late now raised some questions in her mind. What if he was involved with something? Who could she turn to? Tramane had been so bloody unspecific. What if there were others in Amity Action involved? Suddenly everything about her life was uncertain. Her cosy ecological niche was under siege.

Grace lay back on the bed. It was three fifteen. She had to leave. She couldn't stay in this place a minute longer. Gathering her belongings, she went down into the foyer and pressed the night bell. A bleary-eyed young man with tousled hair materialised from a dark back-room, trying to suppress a yawn.

"I want to pay the bill for room fifteen," she said.

"Is everything OK?" asked the young man, gradually registering her distressed expression through his drowsiness.

"It's fine," she said, "but I've had an urgent message. I have to go."

She handed over some cash. She would owe Alec Tramane nothing.

12

THE ICE QUEEN INVESTIGATES

The first ferry was due to leave Nanaimo just after six, so Grace dozed off in the car at the ferry terminal. She was reluctant to contemplate recent events. Each time she did so, a wave of anxiety flooded her mind. She found herself in a cycle of weariness leading to forgetfulness leading to dreaming leading to waking and shocking reminder. On the one hand she was horrified at the doubts Tramane had raised within her. On the other, she felt that somehow she had betrayed Jack by letting Tramane use her. She dismantled every conversation she had had with him, checking for morsels of unwitting incrimination. She was so angry with herself for not pressing him for more detail.

Grace arrived back in Vancouver before eight o'clock. She collapsed exhausted on her bed, but her mind was far too active for sleep. Instead she unpacked, had a shower, drank some coffee and began to feel better. It was clouding over outside and she guessed that the good weather that they had enjoyed was on the way out. Soon it would be raining, and the cold, wet nights would start.

What is the purpose of anxiety? At one level it seems such a negative emotion, and left to run riot it undoubtedly is. But sometimes that initial rush of predicted disaster prompts a counter-attack of logic, and a rational plan of campaign. Grace had options. (1) She could put the last two days aside and carry on with her job as if nothing had happened. She need not say anything to anybody. Let Tramane get on with whatever he was doing. It might all come to nothing anyway. (2) She could tell Jack everything. His suspicions of Tramane were plainly well-founded. But she had reservations. Why had Jack been so nervous? Did he have something to hide? What about their own work disagreements of late? Could there be a connection? They might be small grounds for distrust, but they were sufficient. (3) Grace could do a bit of detective work herself. She had a name – Zuserain Nexus; and a company – Praefortica.

Grace slept better on Sunday night, but annoyingly, she had dreamt about Tramane. Having made a decision about how she would deal with him professionally, she now had to reconcile how she felt about him personally. It was probably best to forget him entirely. He had been another mistake. Given that there was a good chance he felt nothing for her, she would have to take the blow with fortitude. It was humiliating, but manageable.

Her resolution was challenged immediately on arrival at work. Amid the small sheaf of faxes was an envelope which had been delivered by hand. It was from Him – his business card: 'Alec Tramane, Amatheia Exports, Canary Wharf, London, UK'. There was a telephone and fax number. On the back, he had written 'I have told you the truth. Take care of yourself. Don't hesitate to call, any time.' It was simple and unsentimental, but affected her nonetheless. She put the card in her wallet, stuffed underneath her bankers' cards: out of sight; out of mind.

The following week, an opportunity arose for Grace to do some investigating. Aware that the conference was under control, Jack was keen to involve her in the residential courses he was planning with Praefortica. She could not believe her good luck. She could now legitimately probe the company. Jack brought a pile of paperwork with him, and suggested she talk to Sevi Janus in Accounts about the finances. The documents proved disappointing, however, consisting mainly of glossy annual reports. Praefortica appeared to have a good ethical record and exemplary employment practices. Amity's dealings with them had been long-standing and regular. There was no reference to Dr Zuserain Nexus, though. If he was behind the company, she would expect him to be referred to in the literature.

Grace did not like Sevi Janus. She could not pinpoint the exact reason. He was tall and muscle-bound – too thick and burly and physically overbearing. The latter was not his fault exactly but he carried his gym-honed body with a confident swagger, which bordered on arrogance. He was loud, blonde, icy-eyed, and expected women to find him attractive. Needless to say, Grace had caught his attention, and although he was always overtly professional, he harboured an unspoken undercurrent of desire which would occasionally surface – a detectable ripple in their otherwise formal conversations.

Grace went up to Janus's office late one afternoon. They had just sat down at his computer to look at the files when he was called out of the office to deal with a telephone call in an adjoining room. He apologised to Grace, saying that the call would be a long one, and shut the door. She looked at the computer. His screen saver was on – Arnold Schwarzenegger as a T-800 Terminator – a role model perhaps? Did he see himself as the bad one or the good one, she wondered. Looking guiltily at the door, Grace jogged the mouse. The screen saver disappeared – Janus was logged on.

Whilst Grace could access certain summary files using her networked terminal, Janus stored all the main company finances on his stand-alone. Now she had access to them all. A list of files came up – one of them was marked 'Praefortica'. This in itself was not surprising. She clicked on the file and waited for it to load, the disk whirring with conspiratorial compliance. Up it came. She opened a few files but they were the expected spreadsheets. She leaned back in the chair and swung it from side to side meditatively. She was not making much progress.

It was as she was rotating that she spotted a locked plastic box on a filing cabinet next to the desk. It rattled when she picked it up. She found the key in the top drawer of the desk. Inside was a floppy disk. On closer scrutiny, the disk was labelled 'ZN'. That was too much of a coincidence to be ignored. She popped it into the disk drive and one file came up labelled 'Personal'. She clicked on it, and a request for a password appeared.

This would take too long to pursue now. She could hear by the tone of Janus's voice that he was trying to draw the call to a close. She needed more time. She would have to get into Janus's office after hours, but given the financial data he was responsible for, it was likely that he kept it locked. This would be tricky.

She removed the disk, put it back in the box and locked it, replacing the key in the drawer. The desktop was back where it had started. After an agonising few seconds, the screen saver reappeared, and Grace relaxed. Janus re-emerged almost immediately afterwards, saying how sorry he was for the delay. He then spent twenty minutes showing Grace the budget details for the courses. Grace nodded politely, hardly listening. She was plotting her next move.

When Janus had finished she said,

"I'm so grateful to you for going through all this. It's given me a good feel for what we can and can't do." Turning the chair in his direction, she smiled, "You really work out, don't you?" She consciously looked him in the eye with a calculated hint of admiration.

"I go to the gym every day." Janus was visibly flattered and adjusted his posture, pulling his shoulders back. "So, the Ice Queen has finally noticed the fine specimen on her doorstep then?"

"The 'Ice Queen'?" Grace pulled a face.

"I'm afraid that's the nickname you have around here. You appear impervious to the charms of the Accounts Department and it's getting them down. I shouldn't tell you, but there's a bet on – a crate of microbrewery beer to whoever gets you out on a date first."

"I see," said Grace, concealing her distaste. She may not like it, but she would have to finish what she had started. "I guess that's not the worst I've been called; it has a certain poise and dignity to it – and being super cool – well that can't be bad either."

"You're taking it very well!" said Janus. "I'm not saying I approve of it, of course."

"Well that puts you in my good books," replied Grace. "Tell me about the gym you go to," she continued, "I'm looking to join one."

"It's the one on Beach Avenue," he said. "I've a visitor's pass if you're interested. Perhaps you'd like to try it out sometime? How about tomorrow? I'm meeting some friends afterwards – perhaps you'd like to join us?"

"That would be perfect," she said. "That's really kind of you. Why don't I come and find you at five. Would that be OK?"

"Great – it's a date then," said Janus. Grace smiled. 'Not if I can help it,' she thought.

"I hope you're not in it just for the beer," she said playfully.

"It hadn't crossed my mind," replied Janus, laughing, his straight white teeth catching the light, "but now you mention it …" Grace smiled,

"I'll see you tomorrow."

The next day, a little before five, Grace was up at Janus's office, kit-bag in hand. He invited her in and she went over to the window, popping the bag on the floor. She was not looking forward to this. It reminded her of the night she met Tramane at the Fraser River Hotel. The red silky dress; the hypocrisy. Again she convinced herself that the end justified the means. But there would be fall-out from this one, no doubt.

"Great view," said Grace. "being on the top floor makes a big difference. I'm sorry I'm a little early by the way."

"Not at all," replied Janus. "I'm nearly done here …" He picked up a sheaf of papers and put them clumsily into a filing cabinet, keen to get the evening started. "That'll do – I can sort them out another day." They left the office together, Janus locking the door behind them. They were half-way down the stairs when he said,

"My kit's in the car in the basement. I hope you don't mind coming down an extra flight of stairs."

"Oh gosh! My kit!" exclaimed Grace, innocently, "I'm so sorry! I left it in your office. Look, don't let me delay you. Give me the key and I'll just nip back upstairs to get it. I'll meet you in the foyer." Janus laughed,

"I always suspected that underneath that efficient veneer was a ditsy blonde – there usually is. Here you are," he said, tossing her a bunch of keys, "I'm sure you will recognise the right one. I'll see you in a couple of minutes." He disappeared through a double door, shaking his head in amusement. Grace went back to Janus's office, unlocked the door and quickly found the floppy disk. Popping it into her handbag and picking up her kit, she left, leaving the door unlocked.

The gym was quite luxurious and Grace enjoyed trying out all the machines. Janus had a serious regime, and he took every opportunity to flex his muscles in front of her. She would have found it amusing on another occasion, but subterfuge and spying did not come easily to her and as the session drew to a close, she felt the butterflies rising in her stomach.

When they had showered and changed, they met in the hallway. Janus was in good spirits. He was sure he'd

146

made a good impression and conceit osmosed through every pore of his body.

"Right – my friends should be along soon. Let's go to the bar." He placed his hand firmly on her lower back and started to guide her.

"Look, I'm really sorry," said Grace, disengaging herself, "I should have mentioned it earlier, but it turns out I have to be somewhere else at seven."

"Oh," Janus was visibly put out, and Grace could see his jaw tense up, "so you just wanted to try out the gym, eh?"

"No Sevi, honestly – it was a last minute thing – it only came up late last night." Janus paused, checked himself, and reconfigured his face quickly.

"I'm sorry," he said,. "I'm just disappointed. "You've time for a drink though?"

"OK," said Grace, mustering a smile, "that should be fine." Janus became more cheerful with a beer in front of him and proceeded to bore her with fitness stories, but at least it meant she did not have to say anything. She left at ten to seven, apologising again, just as Janus's friends arrived. She heard a few jeers as she exited the building; the crate of microbrewery beer was still up for grabs.

Grace went back to the Amity Action building. It was virtually empty. She had an hour before the security guard would come round. She took the disk to her office and popped it into her computer. Up came the 'Personal' file, along with the password request. Grace thought for a moment. She knew the Amity guidance on passwords – up to a twelve digit alphanumeric. Janus was clearly a fan of *Terminator* – in fact, a comparison between the former and the cyborg felt quite apposite.

She typed 'n0fate': nothing. 'Far too profound for Sevi Janus,' she thought to herself. She tried 'hastalav1sta,' and miraculously, she was in.

Grace's excitement at having hacked into Janus's 'Personal' file was quickly replaced by confusion at what she found. It was clear that some payments were being made regularly into Amity Action from an unnamed source, and that further payments were being made to several people. In fact, both Sevi Janus and Jack D'Oretz were on this list. The payments amounted to thousands of dollars each quarter. The whole thing was obviously done separately from the main payroll, so any external auditor would not notice it. Grace scanned down the list of recipients. There was no-one else from Amity Action, but for some reason, one or two names were familiar. Where were these payments coming from? She was not even sure that it was through a Canadian bank. It was all obviously designed to disguise the donor. She printed out the list.

It was a quarter to eight and she could hear the security guard further down the corridor. She peered out of the room and went quickly back up to Janus's office, slipping the disk into its box and locking it. She left quickly and quietly. As she reached the top of the stairs, she glanced back at the office and saw the security guard locking it. She hoped he wouldn't mention to Janus that he had found the door unlocked. But, hey, it would probably be all right. She had already established her credentials as an airhead. What more could Janus expect?

13

A DATE AT THE PIG AND TROUGH

I arrived one morning to find a devastatingly attractive man in the academic staff tea room. He was tall, with grey-green eyes and a subtle tan. He wore a neatly tailored suit which fitted his broad shoulders perfectly[20] – all in all an intimidating presence. He wasn't my type, exactly, but one can't help admiring from a distance. Needless to say, he made me very self-conscious. My jacket was worn at the cuffs, there was a hole under my left armpit, and I found myself cursing the haze of dark hair that adorned my upper lip. I would have to invest in some strip wax[21].

---

[20] Frumpp's Fashion Tip Number 13: don't always believe he's a hunk. They use a lot of padding in men's jackets these days.

[21] Frumpp's Fashion Tip Number 14: all depilatory methods are appalling, but strip wax is nothing compared to the epilator, which takes the biscuit.

"Er ... are you waiting to see anyone?" I enquired as I put the kettle on.

"Dr Irene Spatchcock," he said in a cultured English voice. "I was told to wait for her here. I have an appointment."

"Fine. Er ... do you want a coffee? Instant only I'm afraid." I had this feeling he would be the proud owner of a Deluxe Espresso Plus and would only accept the finest beans, newly roasted and ground on site. "Or tea?" I asked. "Er, bog standard, regrettably." I had another feeling that any tea in a bag would be out, and that he would only accept loose leaf delicately scented with bergamot, crumbled lovingly into a teapot by a hauntingly attractive geisha.

"I'll have some coffee, thank you," he said. "Let me give you a tip – don't go into sales." I smiled, and adjusted my glasses with my sleeve.

"Milk?" I said, reaching over to the fridge.

"No thank you," he replied, as I dropped the lid of the milk onto the floor, sticky side down. I rinsed it under the tap. He smiled in a gentlemanly, tolerant way.

"Do you happen to know when Dr Spatchcock is likely to appear? I've already been waiting for half an hour."

"Have you spoken to Sally Whimbrel, the secretary?" I asked.

"She sent me here."

"Hang on a sec. and I'll try and find out for you." I went down to Sally's office. She was trembling, as usual, behind a pile of paperwork.

"Sally, there's this man in the tea room waiting for Irene. Is she around?"

"Oh Dr Frumpp!" exclaimed Sally, in despair. "She's not in, and she's not answering her phone at home. He's in her diary. She must have forgotten. You couldn't see to him?"

"Well, what's he here about?"

"The project. I'm sure you could talk him through it."

"What if Irene comes along?"

"Well, she should be grateful to you," said Sally. Her telephone rang: it was Tweezer. I left. Returning to the tea room, I explained that Irene had been delayed, and that I was quite familiar with the study if he would like to chat to me about it. He seemed slightly put out but was happy to follow me down the stairs with his cup of coffee. I pulled Rosy's chair over so he could sit next to me, although he was forced to twist slightly after his legs clashed with the cardboard box under the desk.

Dr James Ross from the Docklands Institute for Work and Social Life Research, in London, had been commissioned to do a piece of research for an import-export company who wished to evaluate workplace satisfaction. He had a large sum of money from them, and was interested in the questionnaire we were developing. About an hour into our discussion, we wandered back to the tea room to get further refreshment. I popped out to see if Irene had arrived and found her in Sally's office.

"Irene, I hope you don't mind, but Sally suggested that I explained the project to Dr Ross as you weren't around."

"Good, Ellinora," said Irene, smiling sweetly. "I think this will be very good experience for you."

"He's got some money to look at workplace satisfaction. I think he's looking for a collaborator."

"Is that so?" said Irene, thoughtfully. "Where is he now?"

"In the upstairs tea room," I replied.

"I'll be along in a minute," said Irene definitively.

I found Dr Ross thumbing through an ancient copy of *The Daily Telegraph*.

"Dr Spatchcock is here now," I said, "I think she's on the way."

"Oh," said Dr Ross. "I must say I'm very grateful for your time. Maybe we should finish our meeting anyway." Irene waltzed in; her eager expression changed immediately to one of pleasant surprise. I suspected a recognition of mutual good grooming.

"Dr Ross," she said charmingly, "I'm so glad that Ellinora has been entertaining you. I was, er, unavoidably detained."

"Dr Frumpp has done a good job," said Ross, nodding towards me.

"Do call me Ellie," I said.

"She's been taught well," said Irene, with a strange combination of girlish giggle and patronage.

"I was wondering whether Ellie and I ought to finish our discussion, rather than bother you, if you are too busy," he continued.

"But why talk with the monkey when you can have the organ-grinder," laughed Irene lightly.

"I'll leave you to it then," I said.

"Er ... thank you, Ellie," said Ross as Irene escorted him down the grey corridor.

I was just finishing my lunch, a floppy sandwich from the canteen, when Dr Ross reappeared. He produced a banana from his pocket and put it on my desk.

"Something for the monkey," he said with a grin.

"How very generous of you," I said, surprised. "Did you have a good chat with Irene?"

"Yes, in fact, I think I'll be attending Spigot's famous Sympathetic Interrogation course."

"If you're coming in January I'll be a fellow student," I said. "Professor Spigot felt I was in need of a bit of personal development. I shouldn't tell you why of course, but it was to do with my taste in music."

"Music?" said Ross, raising his manly eyebrows.

"I rather like Bond music."

"Ah, yes, I noted the man himself on your wall."

"Well, Professor Spigot doesn't really approve. Personally, I like the fantasy element. I mean, you're never going to come across a secret agent, let alone be seduced by one, not if you look like me."

Ross looked at me curiously. 'Uh-oh', I thought. Prattling again: the sure way not to impress a man. Not that I wanted to impress him, you understand.

"I wondered if we might go over the study again. Dr Spatchcock seemed a little hazy on the detail."

"Take a seat. I'm so sorry about the box," I added as his knees collided with cardboard for the second time that day. "Now, what do you want to know?"

"Well, we discussed the Spigot approach earlier, but I wondered if I might have a look at some of the source material for the questionnaire. Is it good, reliable stuff?"

"Well, er, yes – on the whole. We had a few, er, consistency problems to begin with, but that's been sorted out now, from my point of view at least."

"What do you mean by 'consistency problems'?" He was looking at me intently, as if he were making a decision about me. "Look," he said, smiling, before I could reply, "we seem to have a lot to talk about.

Perhaps I could take you out to dinner tonight, and we can discuss this further. Unfortunately I have something to attend to right now." A moment of panic. Goodness knows why, but something in his manner suggested more than a business dinner. The whole idea was completely ludicrous, of course. The man was a stunner, and to be frank, although people give you all that gobbledygook about a person's character rather than appearance being important, let's face it, it's a lie propagated by people like myself. There was no way he would fancy me.

"Er, a er, *business* dinner," I said, stressing the word, just to set the record straight.

"Yes, if you like."

(Phew) "Maybe I should see if the others are free? Irene or Professor Spigot?"

"Oh no, I, er, I'm sure that that won't be necessary. They are obviously very busy people. And in any case," deep breath, "I quite enjoy your company."

Oh no, no, no, pull the other one! This is not real. Behave yourself!

"Oh, I er, thank you. I, er," I could almost see my glasses steaming up before my eyes.

"Shall I pick you up, or meet you somewhere?"

"Um, how about The Pig and Trough, in Bloort Street." Stupid idea. Studenty pub.

"Sounds great. About seven thirty then." He rose with natural grace, and walked to the door with perfect posture: noble, but nonchalant. "I'll look forward to it," he said, giving me that strange look again.

It is obvious that I was quite taken aback by this conversation. Now, I'm not saying that I can read a man's mind, but after a few years of blind stumbling and misinterpretation, you learn a little of the language of, well, the language of love; and a man like that simply does not pay attention to a woman like me. Not unless they're a member of the aristocracy with a large dowry, and I'm strictly middle, middle class. I assured myself that I must be mistaken, and by the time I left the office I was laughing at myself.

I bumped into Jemima in the hallway of our shared residence. She was looking very smart, and I thought I detected a sheen of iridescence on her lips.

"Jemima!" I exclaimed. "You look lovely!"

"*Do* I?" she said sweetly. "Thank you so much. I'm going to that seminar. Remember, that doctor I told you about. It's tonight."

"Whereabouts?"

"Oh, it's at the university. I feel so nervous!"

"Why do you feel nervous?" I asked.

"Oh, I don't know. I, I just have a feeling about this man. I, er I really like him. I think he likes me ..."

"Well, if he does, Jemima, you'll impress him even more tonight," I said, "but don't get too excited, in case it turns out to be only a bit of academic chit-chat."

"Well, you never know. Why don't we go for a drink tomorrow so I can tell you all about it?"

"Great idea. Actually, I've got a date tonight too," I said smiling.

"*Really,*" she said.

"No, not really," I said, "it's to do with work." I laughed. She left in a floral haze. I trudged up the stairs and into my bedsit and whacked on *Reality Crescent.* Marjorie had just slept with her sister's second husband's Brazilian stepson, and her own husband, Derek, had rescued a small puppy, accidentally trapped in a black bin bag he was about to throw in the dustcart (he was in waste management).

My room was a mess. For some reason I felt I ought to clear it up. When I realised why that had crossed my mind, I was angry with myself. As if I would ever dream of bringing a man back with me! What would I do with him? It's all very well what we see in the movies, but it is so deceptive. We are given a diet of romantic encounters culminating in unbridled passion. And yet, do you ever see a heroine ponder upon the wisdom of her actions? Or pause to take precautions? Does she ever cheerily produce a three-pack? Still, what would I know, struggling as I was to graduate from the 'Jane and Peter and Pat the dog' primer of sex education?

I was ashamed of myself. The prospects of this particular encounter were zero. The man was just being polite. For once, I did not pander to fantasy, and did not tidy up my room. The same pangs of shame crept over me as I considered what I should wear. IT DOES NOT MATTER! I repeatedly told myself. And yet ... There was no point pretending. I would definitely not wear women's clothes. Besides, I was never the proud owner of a scarlet eurobabe number. Heaven forbid! I would look like a postbox! I decided to go for smart casual and went for a pair of printed trousers and a jacket. At least it was *me*.

I arrived at The Pig and Trough, briefcase borne defensively like a shield. James Ross sat at a small table in the saloon bar. He waved at me and stood up.

"Can I get you a drink?"

"Er, yes, thank you. I, er ... half of bitter?" I said. He went to the bar. I was comforted by the fact he had a pint, although aware that he was probably used to women ordering spritzers and cocktails. We sat on maroon chairs with bulbous and ornate legs, rather vulgar, now I considered it.

"I brought my work files," I said hastily, as he returned, hoping to stave off any words which I could misinterpret. He patted the attaché case at his feet.

"I brought my homework too," he smiled. And it was a very nice smile. His teeth were white, enhanced I think by his tan. Bloody hell. I opened my briefcase, immediately conscious of its somewhat tatty appearance.

"Er, it's an old and faithful briefcase[22]," I said, blushing slightly, "um."

"It's got character," he said, sympathetically. "Now, you said you had some odd data?"

"I, er, well I shouldn't really dwell on them now I don't have to deal with them. I expect you are more interested in where the questionnaire is heading in terms of content."

"Actually, I am interested in the data. My background is in this type of research. Maybe a second opinion would be useful."

"I, er, well OK then. I had copies of Max's tapes and the transcripts I had made of them, and produced an example of the latter from my bag. "Max Snoode – the facilitator here – was supposed to be eliciting experiences from a group. If you look through the manuscript it really is a focus group of two halves. The first half is what I'd expect – people getting round to sharing their experiences in the usual, polite, roundabout

---

[22] Frumpp's Fashion Tip Number 15: 'old and faithful' clothing and accessories should not be worn/ used for important occasions.

way; but in the second half they are so direct – this is a typical example:

'MS: How would you describe the administrative support in your organisation?

Respondent 5: Yes, well, we have a lovely admin. team really. They are rather hard-pressed though – you know – so much to do – so – well I suppose what I'm saying is that they could be better, but it's not their fault, if you know what I mean.'

Now in the second half:

'MS: So do you enjoy working here?

Respondent 5: No, not at all – it's the bane of my life. I'd rather be writing my novel.

MS: How would you describe your attitude to work?

Respondent 5: Well, if I'm honest, I'm a lazy sod.'

Obviously one can argue that as the focus group progresses, people may become more relaxed, but you don't usually see such a radical change. It happens to everyone in the group – it's as if they've all been given a licence to be bolshy – or maybe it's a licence to tell it how it really is. Difficult to say."

"Are all the groups like that?"

"No – only ten out of the thirty are internally inconsistent."

"Did anything go on between the first and second halves?"

"No, I don't think so. There was a break for tea and biscuits I think, but that was no different to all the groups and the rest are OK. Anyway, Max is going to analyse the weird ones himself, then we'll compare the themes coming out of his to those emerging from the others. If they don't fit, I'd be inclined to exclude them."

It was pleasant talking to someone who seemed to know a bit about qualitative analysis. We discussed some of the practical issues for fifteen minutes or so, and I was beginning to feel quite relaxed when Ross looked at his watch.

"I've booked a table at *Le Joli Chou-fleur*," he said. For a moment I thought this was a cue for me to leave him to get on with his evening before remembering that I was supposed to be dining with him. I blushed.

"*Le Joli Chou-fleur!* That's rather posh!" It was a spontaneous response – I'm not proud of it.

"Don't worry – it's on me and besides, I'm sure you're worthy of it." Oh gosh, that look again! He stood up and insisted on helping me into my coat (the lining was ripped). He lingered with his hands on my shoulders, and gently turned me round. My composure was ruined, and I blushed yet again. Ross was just looking at me meaningfully when I heard a bawdy laugh from the bar.

"Hey, Frumpp, how much are you paying him?" It was Christian who was drinking with a group of rather unattractive nerds. He was pointing at me. This was a nightmare.

"Come on, let's go," I said quickly. "It's just someone from work." I led the way, ignoring Christian, but feeling awful. I was very annoyed with myself because I could feel the tears welling up in my eyes. If I went first they might just be reabsorbed before we got outside. It was all so embarrassing. This man, whoever he was, leading me to think the most ridiculous thoughts; Christian punishing me for them.

I was relieved to get out into the fresh air, and managed to take a few calming breaths before Ross caught up with me.

"I'm, er, I'm sorry about Christian – he doesn't realise this is a working thing. I er, I mean, if it wasn't, I think he would be right. I would have to pay you." I tried to make a joke of it, but James Ross looked serious. He stopped and gently caught my arm.

"You don't have a very high opinion of yourself, do you?"

I walked on. He was making me feel uncomfortable.

"So, do you think you might use our questionnaire in your evaluation?" He was polite enough not to pursue his question.

"It's certainly a possibility. Perhaps you can give me an idea of what it might look like over dinner."

We talked business for the rest of the evening. I think he knew that he had made me uneasy. It was very nice of him.

14

REVELRY AND REVELATION

There were potentially legitimate explanations for what Grace had seen in Sevi Janus's 'Personal' file, but the concealment of it away from the mainstream Amity accounts and the 'ZN' on the disk prevented her from dismissing it all as inconsequential. Jack had only once mentioned Alec Tramane since Grace's Vancouver Island trip and that was to say he had received a letter to thank him for their hospitality and that a donation was still on the cards. Grace had just nodded an acknowledgement. It was a difficult time. She felt a certain duplicity every time she spoke to Jack. He was, after all, a friend as well as her manager.

It was a dark, wet afternoon in December – the type of day that obliges artificial light to make a tasteless, brazen substitute for the inadequacy of Nature. It had been raining for over a week and the damp was penetrating, rusting the Christmas spirit. Grace had been running a few possible speakers past Jack for the Praefortica course and he was now staring out of his office window at the blank bay.

"It's all a bit dreary, isn't it?" he said.

"I guess it's to be expected," replied Grace, conscious that this was about the level of their conversation nowadays.

"How about a company do?" he asked.

"Pardon?" said Grace.

"Everyone seems a little down at the moment. I was thinking perhaps we should have a party this Christmas, here at the office. Perhaps before Christmas lunch in the café?" Grace was not a great fan of enforced jollity and Jack detected her lack of relish.

"Come on, Grace! Let's see some enthusiasm!" he laughed. "It's Christmas! We'll do it!"

The next week, Grace dutifully made her way down to the conference rooms. Today, the false wall separating the neighbouring spaces was concertinaed back, making a capacious meeting-place. The usually sober decoration was supplemented by assorted paper chains and sparkly orbs which hung incongruously above crudely concealed business paraphernalia. Jack was tinkling his glass as Grace came in.

"Friends," he exclaimed, "Merry Christmas!" A slightly subdued reaction – the wine had not been flowing long enough. "I thought I would take this opportunity to thank you all for working so hard over the last year. As you know, business is booming. We've had a record income, which has meant that more projects than ever before have been funded. I don't have to say that none of this would have been possible without all your hard work. Here's to you!" There was a smattering of clinks as glasses were raised and conjoined. Grace helped herself to some wine, and retreated to a seat in the corner. She did not feel like socialising.

After about half an hour there was a general migration to the staff café. The earlier self-conscious murmurings had become more strident and oblivious. People were finally acknowledging that they were allowed to relax. Jack collared Grace as she stood up.

"Is everything OK?" he asked. "You've been looking so grim here, sitting in the corner."

"No, everything's fine. I'm just a bit tired," she said, limply.

"I'm sorry," he said. "You've been very quiet lately. Perhaps it's time for me to lend you an ear or a shoulder for a change."

"That's very sweet of you, Jack, but honestly, there's no problem. I just need a holiday."

"Well, you mustn't worry about anything over the break. Everything's going to plan. I got the last peer review back on the abstracts today."

"You did?" said Grace, at once interested. "I wouldn't mind a quick peek at them all."

"Then follow me, you workaholic!" said Jack with a flourish, and led her back up to his office. There was a large folder on the desk.

"Here," he handed it to her. "Have a quick look. I've got to get downstairs. They won't start without me. A *quick* look remember – and don't dwell on them. I'll come and drag you away if you're more than five minutes."

At the top of the pile, Jack had typed out a summary page, listing the projects, the reviewer's name and the suggested course of action. The first project to catch her eye was Spatchcock et al.; and next to it, the word 'accept'.

"No!" she said to herself with incredulity. It was happening again. As she worked her way down the list, she found that the seven studies she and Jack had argued about were all accepted. The results of the reviews sapped Grace's spirits further. It was all bad. She had either lost her capacity to judge what made a good conference paper, or something suspicious was going on. She made her way reluctantly down to the staff café, feeling detached from the good humour all around her. She would have to leave as soon as possible. She could not cope with this.

Arriving late, she realised that the only seat left was next to Sevi Janus. He had been a little off-hand with her since she had left him prematurely at the gym and he had not attempted a second date. Now he was ruddy-faced and verging on rowdy, laughing with a group she had labelled the 'gym squad'. The latter raised a cheer as she took her seat next to him and he shrugged and laughed, playing to the crowd. Clearly they were aware of what (little) had passed between them and they persisted with various schoolboy pranks to make Grace smile. She finally subdued them all with a look she had spent her life refining: one of anger, aggression and contempt all rolled into one, along with the words,

"I am *not* in the mood!"

Janus's pent-up humiliation and anger boiled over at last.

"Wrong time of the month for Jack's 'bit of skirt' is it?" he whispered nastily. "We all know why you got the job, Grace." He waited expectantly for her to react, a sneer on his face. They were interrupted by the arrival of the starter – avocado and prawn cocktail. Momentarily frozen by the insult, Grace found herself staring at a prawn poised with balletic artistry on the top of her food. In full crustaceal glory, its beady black eyes met hers, cross and accusatory. It was hardly an invitation to eat, but this aside, her thoughts were suddenly elsewhere. She had remembered something. Without acknowledging the feigned disappointment of her other dining companions, Grace got up and left the room.

The quiet should have been a relief, but Grace's mind was focussed elsewhere, her thoughts generating anything other than calm. She went straight up to her office, unlocked a drawer in her desk, and reached for a piece of paper. With this in hand, she headed to Jack's office, and the package on his desk. Every one of the seven projects she had recommended for outright rejection had been reviewed by people on the list she had obtained from Sevi Janus's 'ZN' disk.

Grace carefully copied the summary sheet from Jack's package and, feeling sick, left the Amity Action building. Oblivious to the rain, she walked briskly to her apartment, slammed the door behind her and leaned back against it, taking a few minutes to recover her breath. She would be missed in the afternoon, but staying at Amity was simply not an option.

Along with the summary, Grace had brought her copies of the conference abstracts and Janus's list. She laid everything out on the floor in front of her, determined to detect that hint of contradiction that would permit her to laugh at the frenzy she was in. But it was not there. Although the names on the list occasionally appeared on projects she had thought were worthy of inclusion, the poor projects were consistently reviewed by the same names – all on the list. As far as Grace could see, the only common factor was their failure to meet Amity Action's protocol for acceptance. They were either low quality or at too early a stage for presentation. They came from organisations in several different countries. The whole thing was absurd! It was only an academic conference. Why should an accepted paper be so important? It could not conceivably justify corruption. And yet, people cheat at board games. Maybe nothing was too trivial?

The question was: what should she do? Should she contact Alec Tramane? An unappealing option. How could she find out more? Maybe she should pay Praefortica a visit to look for a connection. It would be a perfectly normal thing to do – pretty much expected. They were running the last of their in-house courses in the New Year. It would make sense for her to observe it – it would help her finalise the draft course she was planning. A strategy in place, Grace felt a little more relaxed. It would all have to wait until after Christmas. She was due back in Ontario in three days' time.

15

MAXIMILIAN

When I came into the department the next morning, there was a note stuck clumsily onto my door with a piece of sticky tape. It read 'Dr E. Frumpp, still *Virgo Intacta*?' It was surrounded by hearts and flowers in red biro. The handwriting was unmistakably Christian's. I was less upset by the public acknowledgement of my (at least recent) virginal state, than I was perplexed at how Christian could possibly have known of it. There is no shame, after all, in 'virtue'. Knights in shining armour will only undertake brave and reckless deeds if they are promised a maiden (although whether they would slay a dragon for a maiden-*aunt*, on whose territory I was encroaching, is another question). I supposed that he had made an educated guess; either that, or my sexual status was a readable physiognomic characteristic. I tore down the note with a sigh.

Later that morning, I was having a chat to Sally Whimbrel in the postgrad. and admin. tea room, when Christian came in. He was smirking. I blushed slightly.

"Did you like my artwork?" he said, smugly, "you know it's a well-known fact that you should never share a secret with Spatchcock." It took me a moment to realise what he meant, but before I could react he said, "well, did you do the deed? And how much *did* you pay him?" These were, of course, outrageous remarks, but I was learning that Christian was a man for whom boundaries were non-existent in an environment bizarrely tolerant of his deficiency. Rather than explode I answered softly,

"No – none of your business – nothing."

"A likely story," he jibed, "he was all over you."

"What's all this?" Irene wafted in with a pile of papers, which she handed to Sally with no comment.

"Ellinora's got a boyfriend," said Christian.

"Oh really?" said Irene. She sounded surprised. I suppose it was a little unlikely. "And who might that be?"

"Oh, Ellie, the photocopying cards have arrived. Perhaps you'd like to come to my office to pick one up." The angel, Sally Whimbrel, rose to her feet and motioned to the door with her eyes. We left together, leaving Irene's question neglected in the air.

"Thank you, thank you!" I said with relief, when we were in Sally's office.

"Christian can be such a mischief," said Sally, a little too charitably. "You looked rather uncomfortable."

"I was; very uncomfortable. He's making it all up, you understand. Dr Ross just wanted some more information on the study. He thought it would be good to do it in style."

"The Pig and Trough, Bloort Street?" queried Sally, sceptically. Christian had been gossiping.

"Well, actually he took me to *Le Joli Chou-fleur.*"

"Did he now!" Sally raised her eyebrows.

"Oh not you too!" I exclaimed. Sally laughed.

"Here's your card. Just punch in the number and it'll be charged to the project account."

"Thanks," I said.

Later that afternoon, I received a summons from Irene. I suspected bad news because Christian delivered it with such relish. Irene was busy at her desk when I knocked on the door.

"Oh Ellinora, it's you," she said, with a hint of disappointment in her voice. "Have a seat. Christian tells me you were in a pub with Dr Ross yesterday."

"Yes, that's true," I said, matter-of-factly.

"But what were you doing with him?" she enquired. It was the kind of question that could have provoked a sarcastic or jovial remark under lighter circumstances.

"Dr Ross was particularly interested in the focus group analysis. He didn't have time to talk through all the issues with me at the department, so he suggested getting together later to go through a few things. It was a business meeting."

"Well I know *that*, Ellinora," said Irene, rolling her eyes. "I couldn't have believed that it was anything else. But if it was a business meeting, don't you think it would have been appropriate for you to involve Terry and myself? It is our study, after all." Her expression changed: carefully calculated confusion and hurt scampered across her eyebrows.

"Dr Ross didn't want to bother you. I did suggest it myself."

"Well, that may be the case, Ellinora, but this was wrong of you. Dr Ross is a potential collaborator. He could be valuable to the future of the department. You don't have the experience to deal with someone at his level."

"I'm sorry," I said, "but he wasn't interested in talking about funding. He wanted to know more about the data."

"Well exactly, Ellinora. If it had been Terry or myself, funding would have been at the top of the agenda, and now you may have spoilt our chances."

"He still seemed very interested in the study, and the possibility of using the questionnaire."

"But Ellinora – The Pig and Trough in Bloort Street!" She looked at me with despair. I thought better of mentioning the restaurant.

"He's coming to the course," I continued defensively.

"Well, that is most fortuitous. At least we may be able to pick up the pieces. I can't say I'm not disappointed, Ellinora. As you know, we put a great deal of trust in you. I just hope that it is not misplaced." I said that I was sorry again, and as Irene simply shook her head sadly and shrugged, I assumed that I was dismissed. As I got up to leave she said, "I know he's a very attractive man. Believe me, I do understand, but he's really out of your league. Besides, one should never mix work and pleasure. It's most unprofessional."

I had arranged to go to the pub with Jemima that evening and I was looking forward to an unstressful pint or two at The Jaunty Scholar. She popped in as the credits for *Reality Crescent* were rolling. Derek had just discovered about Marjorie's affair and in a fit of pique had poisoned Twinkletoes, not realising that the bird was about to predict the numbers for the ten milllion pound national lottery roll-over.

"Are we still on for tonight?" she asked, as my heart went out to the small green and blue bird with the amiable nostrils.

"Er, yes, if you're still game," I replied, pulling myself together. She hovered by the door. "Is something up?"

"I, er," she smiled coyly. "He's coming!"

"Who?" I said.

"The doctor I told you about. He's coming to the pub."

"Tonight! Oh Jemima. Look, you'll not be wanting me there then, will you?"

"Yes I will! Look, he thinks it's just an informal drink with friends. He's not expecting me on my own."

"Are you sure you want me there?" I asked again dubiously.

"Quite sure," she said with certainty. "We'll go at about half seven. OK?"

"Fine," I said. She left and I put the kettle on. The evening had taken on less satisfactory proportions. I would now have to be polite and interested to a stranger. Oh well.

Jemima and I wandered towards The Jaunty Scholar at just past seven thirty. Her friend had not yet arrived, so we bought a couple of drinks and squelched down in our favourite sofa. Jemima was a little uptight and kept looking at the door, but I was feeling all right. The alcohol had just reached my legs when in walked Dr Max Snoode. As a reflex, I slunk lower in my seat, and simultaneously said,

"Damn." I was just about to explain my discomfort to Jemima when she sprang up and cooed,

"Over here, Dr Snoode, Maximilian!"

Snoode came striding over with a look of cool manliness. 'Oh no,' I thought, 'this can't be true!' When Max saw me slumped with my pint next to Jemima, he checked his pace, his compact bravado off-balance.

"Hello Maximilian," said Jemima with shining eyes, "can I get you a drink?" Like myself, Max was temporarily dumbfounded. "Maximilian?" she persisted.

"I, er, I'll have a gin and tonic, Jem, thank you."

"This is my friend Ellie," said Jemima gaily. "Ellie, this is my friend, Maximilian."

"Er, actually we know each other," I said.

"*Really*?" said Jemima.

"Yes, really," I said.

"How exciting! Well, you have a chat while I get Maximilian his drink." Max sat on a stool opposite me. I was not quite sure what to say. Jemima was under some illusion. She was definitely not the sort to go round with a married man, so deception or misconception had occurred. I was not sure what my role should be – I hardly felt in a position to lecture Max on his wedding vows.

"Well, er, hello, Maximilian," I said, smiling slightly.

"Ellinora, what a surprise. I, er, Jem and I. Er, we're just friends. I'm doing some, er collaborative work at her department. Asked me if I fancied a drink. Seemed harmless enough." Now it could be, of course, that Jemima had deluded herself into thinking that Max liked her, so it might not be his fault. I was a bit concerned at the way in which he had approached her, though. There was the definite swagger seen only in men bent on making an impression.[23] I was convinced that, if I hadn't been there, there might have been a kiss.

"Oh, er, so, you're just friends, then," I said, for want of something better to say.

"Oh, yes, definitely just friends," confirmed Max, a slight irritation rippling his forehead. I was not convinced, but this was neither the time nor the place to get to the bottom of this.

"And what has a sociologist got to do with the Department of Biochemistry?" I asked, curiously. Unfortunately (or perhaps fortunately), Jemima arrived before Max could answer, with a fancy glass which she set lovingly in front of him.

"So, tell me how you know each other?" she said. We explained, and there followed an uncomfortable hour in which Max repeatedly looked at his watch, and Jemima earnestly looked into his eyes. I slowly sipped my pint, and made frequent visits to the Ladies' to relax.

When we got back to the bedsit, I felt that there was a thing or two which Jemima should know, so I invited her in for camomile.

"What do you think then?" she said, as I handed her a mug.

"Look, Jemima, are you sure he, well, are you sure he regards you as a potential, well, date?"

"Yes, he really likes me. He told me after the seminar yesterday. I wanted to get your opinion first, but we're going on a proper date tomorrow. You know, that really nice restaurant – um, The Riverweed, out of town. He's a lovely man, Ellie, and he goes to church." I couldn't

---

[23] Frumpp's Fashion Tip Number 16: deportment speaks louder than words.

believe what I was hearing. There was something going on and I didn't know how to tell Jemima. It was going to hurt her.

"Jemima, I work with Max."

"Maximilian," corrected Jemima, giggling, "it sounds more mature."

"I work with him and, well there's something you should know." Jemima looked excitedly at me.

"Please don't look like that," I said, "this isn't good news at all." Jemima's smile lessened a little. "Look Jemima, from what I know, he's married." For some reason this did not have the impact I was expecting.

"Separated," said Jemima firmly, "he's separated from his wife. They have been for two years."

"Are you sure?"

"Absolutely. He hasn't seen her for six months." I thought back to that awful evening in the Department of Sociology. He had told me then that he was going home to celebrate his anniversary.

"I'm not entirely sure that's true."

"Oh, it is. Maximilian told me."

"Look Jemima, men sometimes say things that aren't true."

"Not Maximilian."

"Jemima," I said.

"What?" she said impatiently. I was deliberating over how much I should tell her. There was no way I could be mistaken about Max and Irene, even if I was mistaken about Max and his wife.

"I'm not sure that he's the right bloke for you. Look, I think he may already be having an affair with someone." Jemima stood up.

"Ellie, what is wrong with you!" This was uncustomary. Jemima was angry. "There's nothing wrong with him. He's great. I love him. It feels right."

"OK, I'm sorry Jemima. Look, sit down, please. I was only telling you what I thought was the truth."

"Well, it's not true, Ellie." She walked to the door. "I'm going to bed."

"Look, I really am sorry," I said. But she had gone.

16

MINUTES, MEETING, DEPARTMENT OF ADMINISTRATIVE STUDIES, UNIVERSITY OF HARDNOX, DECEMBER 5TH, 1995

Present: Professor Terrence Spigot (chair), Emeritus Professor Ronald Tweezer, Dr Mike Sweeble, Dr Irene Spatchcock, Ms Rosy Cloudberry, Dr Ellinora Frumpp, Miss Sally Whimbrel (minutes), Mr Christian Wynde-Ryder

Apologies: Dr Hermann Peewit

1. Notes from previous minutes

Professor Spigot congratulated Miss Whimbrel on her excellent minutes of the last meeting, but pointed out that 'mugwort' (*Artemisia vulgaris*) was spelt with an 'o', not an 'e'.

2. Matters arising

(a) Colourful perennials

Miss Whimbrel reported that as yet she had only heard from Professor Spigot with regard to colourful perennials. His suggestions were as follows: lupins, bear's breeches. Miss Whimbrel is inclined towards a mallow. Professor Spigot suggested that these ideas be discussed with Mr Ramsbottom.

Action: SW to convey list of perennials to WR.

(b) Car parking

Professor Spigot reported that the Vice Chancellor is currently on sabbatical in the Okefenokee Swamp in the US, but that the issue of bollarded car parking would be raised with him on his return.

Action: TS to speak to VC on return from sabbatical.

(c) Stationery

Miss Whimbrel made another request that staff fill in the book attached to the stationery cupboard, as it was still important to log items. Recently her last treasury tags disappeared without being recorded. Whilst she has had a new batch on order for eight weeks, it will be at least another four before they arrive.

Action: All to fill in book on string attached to stationery cupboard.

(d) Update on LOOFAH licence

Miss Whimbrel reported that UCLOG were still negotiating the site licence for LOOFAH.

3. Formal welcome to Dr Ellinora Frumpp

Professor Spigot formally welcomed Dr Frumpp to the department. Dr Frumpp has recently gained her doctorate from the University of Swinbrooke, and will be working with Professor Spigot, Dr Spatchcock, and Dr Snoode from Sociology.

4. Newsround

(a) Update on Ms Biffing's job

Dr Spatchcock reported that Ms Biffing's job had been advertised during the summer in the university pink pages, but no-one had come forward. It was recently advertised in *The Guardian* but as there are only two years' worth of grant left, she expressed some scepticism over the possibility of filling the vacancy. Professor Spigot felt that a two-year position was something of a luxury in the 'cut and thrust' of today's academia, and, with the university's reputation, he was sure that the post would be over-subscribed.

(b) International Workplace and Productivity Meeting, 1996

Professor Spigot reported that the abstract for next year's IWaPM had been submitted successfully. He reported that Dr Max Snoode, who has the ear of Amity Action, had assured him that acceptance was likely. Professor Spigot thought that as this was the case, it was important to consider possible travel plans. Because of his chronic back problem, it would regretfully be necessary for him to fly business class, which would mean that the travel budget would be diminished. As with last year, however, he promised to share his in-flight champagne and salmon and asparagus roulade.

(c) Publications

Professor Spigot was pleased to announce the following publications:

Spigot T., Spatchcock, I. (1995) From clock-makers to fish breeders: the universality of the Spigot Sympathetic Interrogation Technique (SpIT) through time and specialty. *Archives of Administration*, 5(1): 61-93.

Spigot, T. (1995) Carry on sympathising: what we can learn from theatrical relationships. *Curtains*, 64(3): 1112-1120.

Spatchcock, I., Snoode, M., Spigot, T. (1995) SpIT meets ET: sending the right signals. *Manx Journal of Communication Sciences*, 10(4): 21-24.

Spigot, T. (1995) It's all about me: using SpIT in phenomenology. *Ego*, 77(4): 57-107.

(d) Dr Hermann Peewit

Professor Tweezer asked if anyone knew where Dr Peewit was, as he had not attended a departmental meeting for a while. No-one had seen or heard anything of Dr Peewit for the past three months. Dr Sweeble said the Annex was not tremendously accessible. He also suggested that Dr Peewit might be working in another dimension.

5. Library

Miss Whimbrel reported that the keeper of the Hardnox University Library had requested her to inform staff of the following addendum to the current rules and regulations concerning use of the library. The library will now be open on Saturday mornings from 8.30 until 12.00, but not the third Saturday of each month, as the library needs the latter for staff training. Other exemptions include: Saturdays which form part of bank holiday weekends, the weekend of the Chancellor's annual garden party, and the Saturday of the annual inter-departmental hurling competition (where the library parking area is required for Red Cross volunteers). Usual rules apply for non-card-holders, who may not use the library unless accompanied by a registered user. A card-holder may provide access to the library to no more than three non-card-holders during the period of one academic year, and only one non-card-holder at a time. Exceptions to this rule are non-card-holders who graduated from Hardnox after May 1st 1954, and any non-card-holder sharing the birthday of Brunhilde Waterwell, the Founder's wife (29th February).

6. Christmas party

Miss Whimbrel reminded staff that it was the departmental Christmas party Wednesday fortnight. She had agreed to provide a variety of salads but would be grateful if other members of staff could also contribute. Dr Spatchcock wondered if the party was really necessary. Professor Spigot suggested that everyone should bring a bottle of wine, beer or soft drink as his entertainments budget was at an all-time low. Professor Tweezer volunteered to provide alcohol. Dr Sweeble said he would be happy to provide sausages on sticks. Miss Cloudberry said she would bring in some Christmas pudding. Dr Frumpp said she would provide cheese and pineapple, crisps and dips. Miss Whimbrel suggested that Dr Spatchcock might be able to bring in Christmas cake and Mr Wynde-Ryder could provide some crackers. Dr Sweeble suggested a departmental comedy review, but Professor Spigot felt this was unwise. He said he had not been amused by Dr Sweeble's impersonations last year.

7. AOB

Next meeting: First Tuesday in June.

17

DR NEXUS

Christmas week passed in slow motion. Although present in body, it was obvious that Grace's mind was in Vancouver. In the small moments when the warmth and comfort of the familial home penetrated the haze of her preoccupation, Grace felt tempted to stay. It would be easy. Her mind-reading mother attempted several sorties into her daughter's reverie, but this was something Grace could not share, even though she desperately wanted to. This lack of communication made her stay in Ontario a tense affair, and her departure on January 2nd, a painful relief.

Vancouver was cold, dull and unfriendly on her return. Even Grace's flat seemed to lack colour and amiability. On her first day back at work, she went to see Jack D'Oretz and after a few minutes of tiring platitudes, Grace informed him of her plans to visit Praefortica in

Banff. Her explanation to him was straightforward: she had the conference under control and was beginning to turn her attention to the courses. A trip up to Banff would enable her to consult with the company, observe their last in-house training and enjoy a spot of skiing at the same time.

Midweek, Grace took a flight to Calgary. She had lined up at Vancouver Airport laden with skis and boots she had no intention of using. At least it made her feel one of the crowd. After the short flight, she caught the shuttle bus to Banff and was sitting in her hotel by late afternoon.

Grace mindlessly sipped her coffee, vaguely conscious of the heat of the large log fire nearby. The Rockies were *her* kind of landscape and yet she felt unmoved. She had been to Banff several times before – either skiing, or hiking in the summer – and had always been astounded. Manufactured in the Earth's forge and coerced by tectonic upheaval into chains of stark, angular forms, the Rockies, like the great beaches of the West Coast, were another reminder of the insignificance of *Homo sapiens*. She would usually find herself gasping in amazement at it all: the glaciers, rippled and torn with centuries of grinding progress, trammels of dirt clustering in moraines littering the snow; the encrusted Columbia Icefield, presiding over vast U-shaped valleys and dramatic waterfalls; coyotes trotting by the roadside and bears peering shyly from grassy ditches and woodland. But not today. As she stared out of the window, which perfectly framed the awe-inspiring mountain scenery, she was furious at her lack of response. She went to bed early, feeling flat, weary and sad.

Praefortica was based just where the town gave way to wilderness. On first appraisal, this mountain community seemed a strange location for a company; but city living had left young, sporty employees jaded, and the quality of life was good here. When Grace arrived, she was struck by the thought that had gone into the building. Its stylish modernity fitted surprisingly into its surroundings. It had mirrored windows which acted as a kind of camouflage: doubling, not blighting, the snowy beauty all around. Elk steamed and snorted nearby, staring at their reflections with faint ennui.

A woman in her early thirties came to meet Grace just as she was disentangling herself from various layers of outdoor clothing and handing them to a friendly receptionist. She introduced herself with directness and confidence, as Sorrel Surrido from Human Resources. She was smartly dressed and very good-looking, with short, fashionable, dark hair. Her face was engaging, not least due to her amber eyes, which were verging on the uncanny. She explained that the course began that afternoon, and took Grace on a tour of the building. The interior fulfilled the promise of the external design. It was spacious and decorated with taste. They ended up in a bright, airy staff dining room, its large windows looking out onto some tall, thin conifers. Whilst eating, and discussing the logistics of Grace's stay, Sorrel said casually,

"And, of course, this evening we've organised a small dinner for you up at The Banff Palais Hotel. Dr Nexus is very keen to meet you." Grace was momentarily speechless.

"Dr ... Dr Nexus?" she finally stuttered.

"Yes, he's our biggest investor. He has a particular interest in the personnel programme – for obvious reasons!" Sorrel paused. "Are you OK, you look a little pale?"

"Oh yes, fine, sorry," said Grace, regaining a more suitable demeanour. "I'm just a little tired after my trip. So, er, Dr Nexus. He's Praefortica's main investor. What is his background?"

"Well he's a very serious businessman. He has interests in a number of companies – lots of links in the Pacific, Hong Kong, you know. He started investing in us seriously about four years ago. The general feeling is that he saved the company."

"It's funny, I mean, obviously I've done a bit of background reading on Praefortica, but I don't recall any reference to Dr Nexus in the reports. Don't investors usually like to advertise their involvement?"

"Not always," replied Sorrel. "Dr Nexus likes to stay in the background." Grace was beginning to feel she was being a little too overt in her enquiries and changed the subject, asking Sorrel what it was like living in the Rockies. She was very positive, and within seconds the conversation came back round to Nexus of its own accord. It transpired that he had funded the company's relocation. She said that Nexus had liked the idea of having his company near a national park. That inevitably limited the workforce to certain types, but Nexus wanted young, healthy employees with plenty of fresh, creative ideas.

"Does Dr Nexus have a big say in how things are run here?" asked Grace, taking advantage of the turn in the conversation.

"He does really. Officially he leaves everything up to the Board, but they all defer to him."

"He's beginning to fascinate me," said Grace, smiling.

"He is a fascinating character, believe me," said Sorrel. "I think he'll like you."

The seminar room where the course was being run was plush with pale wood flooring and modern furniture. A circular table filled the centre of the room, surrounded by green padded chairs. Like the rest of the building, the windows were large and with the snow, a strange brightness filled the room. Sorrel closed some of the blinds. A projector and screen were set up, along with a laptop computer. Grace took a seat and watched the proceedings. As she was an observer, the group had no expectations of her and she was surprised at how relaxed she began to feel.

The afternoon went quickly. The course attendees consisted of a small group of employees. Sorrel led the sessions on problem solving and team working with admirable eloquence and efficiency. At about five o'clock, Grace trudged back to her hotel. The course had provided a pleasant distraction, but now her mind was freed up, she was beginning to feel nervous about what the evening might bring. It was discomforting to have some vague negative knowledge about a person. Fear based on hearsay. Prejudice based on someone else's bad opinion. Alec Tramane had implied that Dr Nexus was a villain: villain or not, she was going to meet him; she had no choice in the matter.

At seven o'clock, Sorrel picked Grace up in a black four-wheel drive.

"Do you know The Banff Palais?" she asked, as Grace got in.

"Is it that very grand affair up the road?"

"Yes."

"I think I've walked around it in the past, but I've never been in."

"Nexus has a suite of their rooms. The food's very good. It should be an enjoyable evening." They drew into a car park next to the hotel, which looked like a Bavarian castle. It was lit from the ground, giving the dramatic building a gothic grandiloquence. Vast shadows were cast up towards the turrets like blackened flames. Grace moved to open the door, but Sorrel stopped her by touching her arm.

"Nexus is a powerful man," said Sorrel, "and powerful men do act strangely sometimes. He is known to be a little eccentric, but please, don't be put off by him. He likes to play games with people, and that can seem odd. Just play along with him." Grace was not sure how to respond, and simply nodded. She was feeling even more nervous now and climbed out of the car reluctantly. With a deep breath, she began to walk towards the hotel entrance, her boots crunching on the icy surface. After a few metres, she paused, conscious that Sorrel had not joined her. In the next second, she heard a car start, and before she had a chance to turn round, Sorrel was next to her, still driving, with her window wound down.

"You're on your own, I'm afraid. Dr Nexus prefers to meet new people one-on-one. You'll find him an interesting man. I'm sure you will enjoy the evening." She drew away, the rear lights of the car disappearing round the corner.

Grace stood transfixed for a while. She had certainly not been expecting this! Everything that Sorrel had said had led her to believe that this was more of a 'works' event and now she was to be the centre of attention. There was to be no hiding in a crowd. What if Alec Tramane was right about the man? What if Nexus knew of her association with him? What if this was some fiendish plan to kidnap her? But what a chance this was! Curiosity got the better of her. She went up the steps to the main entrance of the hotel, took off her coat and changed into her shoes in the cloakroom. She looked at herself in the mirror. Was she dressed appropriately? She was wearing her suit, which was good. This was already beginning to feel like a blind date. She didn't want to encourage that feeling. She opened her handbag and touched up her make-up nonetheless – she had to feel confident – and went out to main reception.

"I'm here to see Dr Nexus," she said to the man behind the counter.

"Ah, yes. You must be Miss Lefavarie. He's expecting you." The man smiled knowingly, or was Grace being paranoid? "I'll ring his suite." A moment's pause. "Good evening, Dr Nexus, I have Miss Lefavarie in reception … Of course, Dr Nexus." He replaced the receiver. "I'll get one of the porters to escort you up," he said, and caught the attention of a young man in a green uniform with gold trim. "A young lady for Dr Nexus," he said. The porter nodded. 'A young lady for Dr Nexus,' sounded a bit dodgy to Grace – it smacked of a call girl paying a visit. She could feel her palms sweating slightly, and she was hot in her jacket, although she had only just got in from the cold. The porter gestured to her.

"This way, please." Grace followed him across the hallway and into the elevator lobby. The carpet was soft and quiet underfoot, and Grace was aware of some background music: Mozart's *Magic Flute*. The elevator arrived with a 'ting,' and the porter swept her in with a gracious wave of his arm. Ordinarily Grace was sure she would have made small talk, but she felt too tense. What had she got herself into here? Simply a business dinner with a client – an attempt at self-comfort. The elevator jolted gently to a halt: the twelfth floor; and the porter directed her into a corridor.

"Dr Nexus will greet you in a minute," he said, retreating back into the elevator like a hermit crab. The doors slid shut, and Grace felt suddenly alone and vulnerable. There did not seem to be many ordinary hotel rooms along this corridor. In front of the elevator was a notice indicating 'The Sunshine Suite,' off to the left. Perhaps they were in one of the turrets. A smoke alarm blinked silently above her head. She waited. About five minutes passed, and she began to wonder whether Nexus was going to appear. She took a seat in an armchair to the right of the elevator. Still no sign of life. Maybe she should leave now. What did she have to lose? The contract, maybe? That would be bad for Amity Action. If Nexus had as much power as Sorrel had implied, he could easily decide to give the work to someone else. She waited another five minutes.

"Miss Lefavarie?" The voice came as a shock. Grace stood up.

"Oh, er, Dr Nexus?" she enquired, looking from left to right. There was no sign of anyone.

"Yes," replied the voice. A small loud-speaker was positioned on the wall above the chair. "Follow the signs to the Sunshine Suite." She did as she was bidden. The corridor went round to the left and led directly to a large wooden double door. She paused for a moment, and then knocked.

189

"Come," said the voice. Grace turned the handle and went into a large, richly decorated room, full of dark, antique wooden furniture. The walls were painted a pale green, and adorned with still life oil paintings. In front of a many-paned window, which looked out over the lights of the town below, sat a man behind a heavy desk. Zuserain Nexus stood up as she entered.

"I make no apology for keeping you waiting, Miss Lefavarie. I like to study human nature. I believe one can learn a great deal about a person from observing at a distance as they anticipate something unknown." His voice was rich and steady, with an unnatural precision of speaking which hinted of a foreign origin.

"I see," said Grace, "so you were observing."

"Yes, I was observing," Nexus moved round to the front of the desk, took her hand, and gave a nodding bow, "and I liked what I was observing."

"Dr Zuserain Nexus," he said.

"Grace Lefavarie," she replied. Nexus was dressed in a dinner jacket. He was a middle-aged man, well built; a subtle thickening of the waist perhaps, but an aura of fitness and strength. His hair was greying at the temples and he had a finely barbered moustache and goatee. His cheekbones were well defined but not bony, and his eyes were light hazel with a distant, dreamy, detached expression. Grace immediately felt under-dressed.

As if reading her mind, he said, "You look business-like, Miss Lefavarie. Perhaps you would feel more at ease without your jacket?."

"I, er, yes, thank you." She handed it to him. He looked at it for an instant, and then lifted it to his nose.

"A very respectable perfume, Miss Lefavarie."

"Thank you," she said, unnerved by the personal nature of his remark.

"Please, Miss Lefavarie, make yourself at home," said Nexus, hanging up her jacket on a stand near the door. "Can I offer you a glass of champagne – I have quite a selection, all chosen by myself."

"I, er, that would be perfect," said Grace. She would have to get into her stride; take command of this situation.

"Do take a seat," said Nexus walking to a large ornate dresser behind the sofa onto which he had motioned her. Grace heard the professional thud of a bottle opening, before being presented with a chilled glass of champagne, the confusion of bubbles vying eagerly for her attention.

"I am so glad we have this opportunity to meet, Miss Lefavarie. I have every faith that you will sort out our courses excellently. Tell me, how are your plans progressing?" Nexus had taken a seat in a large, leather armchair. A peculiar juxtaposition, thought Grace, sitting in a large, grandiose hotel room, talking about an educational course. There should have been the sophisticated rhubarbing of rich men and women, the click of a roulette ball, a shuffle of a game of *Chemin de fer*, the aroma of tobacco, and cocktails, jewels. Or he should be trying to seduce her ...

"Very well, Dr Nexus, and I'm busy getting some hints from Sorrel Surrido."

"Another very competent young woman," said Nexus.

"Indeed," replied Grace. Nexus paused and took a sip from his glass. "Perfect," he said, with satisfaction, "I am, however, equally partial to our New World wines. I hope you will appreciate the selection I have made to complement our dinner together." As if on cue, there was a knock at the door, and a waiter came in with a silver trolley. Nexus directed him with his eyes to a table in the corner of the room, which the waiter proceeded to set with great deftness.

"I have heard a great deal about you, Miss Lefavarie, or may I call you Grace?"

"Do, please," she said, attempting a smile to hide her concern at the notion that he might have heard a lot about her. "Who has been telling you?"

"Oh, Jack D'Oretz speaks very highly of you. We have met on several occasions. Personally, I think he is a little in love with you. I've observed him, you see; the way he talks about you." The waiter looked up momentarily from his duties, but returned instantly, professionalism getting the better of his natural human curiosity.

"You are very blunt," said Grace, "but I think you are mistaken." She could not help remembering Janus's cruel comment at the Christmas dinner. Perhaps Jack did rather like her?

"I am never wrong, Grace, when it comes to such matters. I think you will find his affection for you will make itself known in due course."

"He's a happily married man," protested Grace, beginning to laugh. "I am sure his feelings are entirely honourable."

"And Jack is an honourable man," said Nexus, cryptically. "One couldn't blame him, naturally, for admiring a woman of your evident beauty and intelligence." He smiled, and Grace felt herself blush: a most unusual response. The waiter had finished. He bowed and left the room, unacknowledged. "Please,

Grace," Nexus had stood up and was holding a chair out for her to sit on. She obliged him.

"Scottish smoked salmon to begin," he said, raising the silver dome from one of the plates, and taking his seat opposite her, "and a fine white from one of the more exclusive Californian vineyards." He removed a bottle from its nest of ice, and poured.

"Well, Dr Nexus," said Grace, as she tasted the salmon. "I confess this meeting is leaving me disorientated. I am unsure whether I should be talking with you about business, or whether I am allowed to discuss other things more appropriate to this ambiance."

"Please, let us talk of anything you wish," said Nexus grandly." He smiled but Grace could detect none of the usual signs of a man who was interested in her. There was no appraisal of her body, no glance up and down, taking in her shape; no attempt to catch her eye. His body language remained remote, polite, neutral.

"May I ask about your background?" enquired Grace. "I am always curious about successful people." She felt a rush of confidence. It could just be the champagne, but this was an ideal opportunity to get some information, and she would take advantage of it.

"My background is fairly uninteresting," he replied simply. "I am merely a hard-working man. If I desire something, I strive to obtain it. I know how people function; I make it my business to know their business. I can usually get them to do as I wish."

"You mean you manipulate people?" asked Grace.

"Manipulate is too strong a word," replied Nexus, unmoved. "You have heard of horse whisperers? They learn the body language and behaviour of those animals. By so doing, they can control. I have merely learned to understand how human beings behave. I can see what is in their minds by reading their bodies. But I also make it my business to know the strengths and weaknesses of those around me. Knowing the truth of their character, Grace, gives me a certain power over them. Thus I can control their destiny – and that of the companies I work with. But I never force anyone to do anything they do not wish to do." It was there, now, he had caught her eye; he was giving her that appraising look. He reached across the table and touched her hand. She did not withdraw it, but was fascinated.

"You see, Grace, this is what you expect of me. I have given you the messages that you usually see. I can turn them on and off as I wish." He withdrew his hand, and his eyes again took on a far-away look.

"You are very skilled," she said. "Can you make anybody do anything?"

"I think that would be a dream, rather than my reality."

"Don't you think it would be boring being able to control everyone?"

"On the contrary, it would give me a sense of complete security."

"But if you could make people do what you wanted, there would be no one to challenge you. You must have a lot of faith in your own judgement."

"I do."

"But what if your judgement is wrong?"

"That is unlikely."

Grace smiled slightly. The conversation was becoming entertaining.

"Your power would be absolute – and you know what they say about absolute power."

"I would be a benign dictator," he said.

"I suspect that is what every dictator in history has considered themselves to be."

"Possibly. But I am an honest, strong man. I detest hypocrisy and corruption. I would rout it out. The control I would exert would be for the benefit of all. I would create a true community, free of the darker side of mankind."

"I'm sure you would think that to be the case," concluded Grace, "but what you perceive to be good and bad for the population may not be everyone's view. I think I would prefer a world where we all have a say. You have to take the rough with the smooth. It's part of living in a human society."

"You are a lively conversationalist, my dear Grace," said Nexus, a glimmer of amusement flickering in the lines around his mouth. "But let us move on to a more trivial subject, namely the second course: poached breast of squab in a mustard and tarragon sauce, and a selection of fresh Californian vegetables."

"You seem to like California. Wine and now vegetables," Grace picked up his cue for a change in topic.

"I more than like it, I am one of its citizens. Do not be deceived by my accent. I was born an American. I own a small vineyard in the Napa Valley and spend much of my leisure time there. California is a state offering most of what people think will make them happy: sun, sea, money, beautiful scenery. Would that make you happy, Grace?"

"Well, the sun is heartening; the sea makes me contemplative; money is always useful. I'm usually on holiday when I'm surrounded by beautiful scenery, and that makes me happy."

"A very full answer." Nexus took a sip of wine. "You have been interrogating me, Grace. It is my turn to interrogate you. Do you like the squab?" The conversation drifted into platitudes as Nexus asked Grace about how she enjoyed Vancouver. The waiter returned with some fresh fruit and liqueurs, which he served with discreet gentility. It was a quarter to eleven when Nexus looked at his watch and said, "The evening has gone so quickly, my dear Grace, but now I must draw it to a close. I rise early. I look forward to seeing you again."

There was no hint of that desire in his eyes. He handed over her jacket, and saw her formally to the door. Before she had really registered that the dinner was over, Grace was out in the thickly carpeted corridor. She walked round to the elevator, conscious that Nexus was probably spying on her. She cast her eyes around the lobby for a camera, but could not see anything – just the loud-speaker.

"Goodnight, Dr Nexus," she said.

"Goodnight, Grace Lefavarie," came Nexus's voice.

It was a relief to be out in the cold night air and Grace decided to walk the short distance back to her hotel. She came down the imposing driveway into the lively streets of après-ski Banff. Grounded again in reality she felt herself unwind. What a strange man Zuserain Nexus was. She smiled to herself as she recalled their conversation. It seemed so ridiculous. Maybe he was just having fun, with his sonorous voice and serious look. She couldn't help thinking that it was all a bit of a joke. And yet there was something quite eerie about his obsession with control and his ability to turn his humanity on and off.

Grace reached her hotel at just past eleven. At least she felt she had learnt a little about Nexus's character, and yet part of her was disappointed not to have unearthed some great conspiracy. From the way Alec Tramane had spoken about the man, she had almost expected a gangster, spats and all. Instead she had found a mildly odd businessman with an unhealthy interest in controlling people. But many rich men were odd, she reflected. She couldn't help wondering what Tramane would say now if she told him that she had just dined with the infamous Zuserain Nexus. The thought made her reach in her bag for her wallet where she kept Alec's number. Her hand searched for a second or two before she realised she no longer had it. She was struck by a moment of alarm, but told herself to be rational. She must have dropped it on the way back from Nexus's hotel. That was hardly any distance. She sat on her bed, reluctant to step outside again into the freezing cold night. She was just bracing herself for a midnight jaunt when the hotel telephone rang to say that there was a message for her at reception. She took her coat, anticipating a stroll. To her great relief, her wallet was there.

"A Dr Nexus had it sent over," said the lady at the desk. "Apparently you left it at the Banff Palais." She gave Grace a snooty look as if to say, 'so we're not good enough for you, eh?'

"Oh, thank you so much," said Grace, ignoring the glance. "I was just about to go out and look for it!"

Back in her room, Grace considered what it was she was trying to achieve. Fine, she had met Nexus, but she hadn't really found out anything substantial. How could she spend her remaining day to maximum effect? She would have to attend the workshop again for at least part of the day, but could not see herself sneaking into offices and rummaging at random. She needed a bit of guidance so she could direct her energy.

Grace thought again of Alec Tramane. Should she give him a ring? It was an awful thing, pride. If he had truly been a friend or business colleague and nothing else, she felt that she would get in touch. But more had passed between them than that, and it had created a great hurdle for her to leap over psychologically.

She looked around the room. It was nicely appointed. She had a king size bed, and all the gadgets one could wish for: a mini-bar, a coffee machine, a hair dryer. She walked to the mini-bar. If she was going to contact Alec Tramane she would need another drink. She would see how she felt after a bit more Dutch courage. She looked at the array of mini bottles, and at the back found one containing 'Californian champagne'. She smiled; why not – it seemed to encapsulate the evening's themes. She opened it and poured herself a glass. As she drank, she went over her conversation with Nexus. He had let nothing slip, nothing incriminating. Perhaps she had asked the wrong questions. It was harder than she thought, this espionage malarkey. Her 'investigations' had been confined by etiquette – or was it simply that she had not been brave enough to pursue the odd promising line of enquiry? Grace felt the wine do its job – that wave of 'what the hell'. It was now or never.

She rolled over to the telephone and cast her eye over the instructions. They seemed straightforward enough. She got up and had a quick rummage in her bag, found her wallet, and flicked through her cards. She pulled one out: 'Alec Tramane, Amatheia Exports, Canary Wharf, London, UK'. She turned it over in her hand for a while before picking up the telephone. It would be quite early in the morning in England now, but he had said she could call any time. She looked at the brief, handwritten message and started to dial. She heard the strange English dialling tone, and waited for two or three rings. Someone picked up,

"Good morning, Amatheia Exports. Can I help you?"

"Oh, hello," said Grace. "I wonder if it would be possible to speak to Alec Tramane." There was a pause, during which Grace could feel her heart beating.

"Mr Tramane is out on business at the moment. May I take a message?"

"I, er," Grace had not really been prepared for this. "Do you have a mobile phone number for him?"

"I'm afraid I'm not at liberty to give you that number. If you would like to leave your name and number, I can contact him, and ask him to call you."

"I, er. OK then." Grace read out the hotel number, "but I need to speak to him urgently. I'll only be here tonight and tomorrow."

"And your name?"

"Grace. Just tell him Grace," she said. When she put down the telephone, she wished she'd left her full name. It occurred to her that he might know half a dozen Graces; a Grace in every port, perhaps. The tenderness that had begun to creep back was ejected unceremoniously, as she remembered their last encounter. All the humiliation of that moment came back in a flood. "Damn you," she said, under her breath. It had been a stupid idea to contact him. This whole thing was stupid! She should forget it all and just get on with her job.

Grace poured herself another glass of wine, which now seemed ludicrously inappropriate to the way she was feeling. She drank it down quickly, as if to insult it, and slammed the glass down on the bedside table. She lay for a few minutes, staring at the ceiling before going to bed.

Grace couldn't sleep. She kept expecting the telephone to ring. Things always get out of proportion when we are alone in bed. Grace could not rid herself of a sense of anger and betrayal, and yet, deep inside, she knew Tramane had only been doing what he was paid to do. Perhaps he had been telling the truth when he said he had felt something for her. Their last conversation came back to her time and time again, and she flipped from anger to love and concern to anger again within minutes. Finally, at about two thirty she went to the bathroom, splashed her face with water and returned to bed. Enough of this! Tramane was probably eating his breakfast, with his mobile phone switched off. No doubt he had company.

18

PERSONAL DEVELOPMENT AND SANDWICHES

Dr James Ross appeared in my office on a cold, bright January morning, the day of the SpIT course. He was gorgeously smart, and had that white-toothed, chiselled, healthy look. In short, he could have just strolled out of a commercial for shaving foam. As I was to grow personally and sympathetically that day, I had taken extra care over my appearance, but this effort was instantly dulled by comparison to him. I had forgotten that Dr Ross was to be there, and his presence was a pleasant surprise.

"Hi, Ellie," he said very casually, "how are you?"

"Fine, thank you. It's good to see you. Are you ready for a bit of personal development?"

"Sadly, I'm beyond that," he remarked, "beyond the pale. In any case, I'm here to observe. I'll enjoy watching you getting sympathetic, however." He smiled. "I believe we're in the seminar room."

"Yes, if you hold on a minute, you can follow me." I gathered up a pad of paper and a pen, surely the prerequisites for any workshop, and we walked down to the seminar room.

"How are you getting on with your research?" I asked.

"Well, we've done quite a bit of groundwork for the company we're working for – looking at structures and so forth. We still hope to use your questionnaire, but that depends on coming to a suitable agreement with Irene and Terry. They seem keen to collaborate."

The seminar room looked much as usual: stale, small, dark. Being in a basement, the only natural light came from a single, narrow, oblong window on one side of the room. Peering up through it one could see the grille that covered the path outside; it really was a prison.

A lack of windows is disappointing. After all, one cannot be expected to be interested in every talk, and it is nice to be able to look out at the world instead of at a blank, grey wall. In fact, it is definitely healthier to have something half decent to catch one's eye on such occasions: a flitting bird, a creeping cat, a tree or a flower wiggling in the breeze. Unless I am thus diverted, my mind unaccountably turns to sex, a most frustrating subject for me.

This time, the plastic chairs had been laid out around tables placed in a giant U-shape. On one side stood the OHP, and in a corner, three blank flip charts, an intimidating presence indicating impending obligatory participation. When Dr Ross and I reached the room, there were already a number of others accumulating there: a gaggle of floral skirts and dogtooth check, grown-out perms and rather unimaginative ties. I felt rather important, swanning in with such a stylish person.

We took seats next to one another and awaited the grand entrance of Spigot and Spatchcock. Max Snoode, brooding sultrily on the far side of the room, nodded as I came in. He, like James, was intending to 'observe'. I had heard through Sally Whimbrel that these courses were a major source of income for the department. It seemed the world was very unsympathetic.

Irene came in after about five minutes, beaming at the collection before her. She introduced herself, and said that Professor Spigot would be along later to help. She began with the inevitable 'going round the room introducing yourself' routine, and the 'what I hope to get out of the course' bit. I never like this very much. I find it more stressful to make a brief, unrehearsed statement, than to stand up and give a formal talk. A lady on Irene's right spoke first, some health authority manager with a very long and intricate job title.

"My name is Mrs Geena Froggit, I'm from Waterhampton Shires Community Services NHS Trust, and I'm the Deputy Manager of Clinical Research, Audit and Personnel Development. I hope to learn better communication skills for staff interviews and appraisals."

James whispered, "I reckon they keep appending the latest fad onto the end of her job title." I smiled, and whispered back,

"I bet they have a good acronym for it." James chuckled quietly. Irene had turned her gaze expectantly to the next person in line, who happened to be a man looking very uncomfortable in a brown 'off-the-shelf' suit. His broad kipper tie was twisted exposing a label reading 'dry clean only'.

"I'm, er, Colin Clatter," he said, obviously suffering slightly from my problem. "I er work in er the Statistics Department at Trethreen Borough Council. I'm er supposed to be improving our survey methods, finding out er people's opinions er that sort of thing, you know." He was a diffident chap, and despite (or perhaps because of) his brown attire and the aforementioned neckware, I felt he was someone to whom I could relate.

The next lady was formidable. She looked Irene straight in the eye and said, "Britt Boulder-Smyth, Inspiracol Technology, Director of Human Resources. I'm here to learn about the Spigot Sympathetic Interrogation Technique." Irene flinched slightly. I suspected the two would not get on. I think Ms Boulder-Smyth was another 'man's woman'. Her *haute couture* suit[24] was from a world Irene would like to feel she was part of but was not. This was a fish from a bigger pond where everyone wore suits.

It was James's turn next.

"Dr James Ross, Docklands Institute for Work and Social Life Research, London. I'm here as an observer, to learn more about the Spigot method." Irene looked pleased, and turned to me.

"Er, Ellie Frumpp, researcher here at the DoA. I'm here to, er," I was tempted to say 'to help improve my musical taste' but Irene was giving me one of her 'acute' looks. "To, er ..." Actually I didn't really know why I was there. "To, er, to experience SpIT," I said lamely,

---

[24] Frumpp's Fashion Tip Number 17: beware two women in the same room with suits. There will be sparks.

conscious that 'experiencing spit' sounded rather disgusting. The baton passed to my neighbour, I slumped back in my seat, relieved.

"I thought you were here to improve your musical taste," said James, his eyes glinting.

"Actually I'm rather proud of my musical taste, Mr Bond," I replied. James laughed again. Irene noticed, but turned her attention politely to the next person in line saying,

"I must say, it's so nice to have such a mix of clients on this week's course." All in all the process took about twenty minutes. There were fifteen of us and once the introductions were done, Irene began by taking everyone through the SpIT methodology. There was nothing new here for me. In fact, I knew it backwards, so I didn't really listen that carefully. Towards the end of the lecture, Irene explained the relevance of SpIT to personal development, and how being aware of non-verbal signals during conversations could enhance more than just one's professional life. I thought that whilst this was possibly true, most of us had been reading visual cues since birth, and frequently opted to ignore them, or to use them to manipulate rather than communicate. Still, no harm in a bit of revision. James looked sceptical.

Terry Spigot came in at the coffee break, his suit crumpled fashionably. He brought with him a waft of his strong perfume, and a raisin bagel from the canteen. Irene introduced him and then talked a bit about the workshop. We were to do a bit of 'role play' to begin with, to demonstrate the importance of body language in social interactions. Irene had devised a series of scenarios that required us to relate to each other or not, as the case dictated and to note our reactions. The groups were pre-ordained and James Ross was sent to a different group to mine.

It was quite an interesting experience. There were five of us in my group including the power-dressed technology lady and the nervous council officer. Needless to say, Britt (we were all on first name terms) dominated the proceedings whatever role she took. I tried to cheer on Colin, who was supposed to be 'bossy, oblivious company director' in one scenario, but he was obviously too much in awe of Britt ('put upon secretary'). You could see his sense of inadequacy rising within him like a blush, until he completely withdrew and took on a tortured expression. He was not heading for the Board Room.

Terry and Irene chatted idly at the main table where the initial lecture had been presented. Occasionally, the two of them made brief inspections of the groups to keep an eye on progress. By now Britt had procured the flip chart to summarise our group's experiences as instructed. As the incisive comments were few and far between, she made a list herself. About half way through, her mobile phone rang and she had to leave the room. At this juncture, I thought I'd better try and egg the others on. We managed to add a couple of things to the list after a brief conversation, during which Geena Froggit went off on a tangent about her holiday in Ibiza. I attempted to bring the conversation round again, but was silenced by the return of Britt, who, unsmiling, took the magic marker between her finely manicured fingers and began once again to scribe. I noticed that Max was watching our group intently, and after a while he came and sat nearby.

"How are you getting on?" he asked Britt, taking in her precise and orderly form.

"Fine," said Britt. "I think we've picked out the important themes illustrated by the role play."

"Yes, you've quite a list there, Britt," he said. "Incidentally, I'd like to talk to you later. I have a feeling that Inspiracol may be just the company I need for a study I'm planning, and you look just the sort of person I should be consulting about it." Max looked at her meaningfully, propelling a barely disguised vibe of animal magnetism in her direction. Britt smiled archly in response, her frosty expression on hold for the brief second that their eyes met.

"Speak to you later then," she said, a slight huskiness in her voice. She turned back to the flip chart and added 'importance of eye contact' to the list.

I glanced over to James's group and he winked at me before rolling his eyes to the ceiling. I could hear that an argument had broken out between two of his group-mates. A woman and a man were squabbling over who should be writing things up on the flip chart. Eventually Irene moved in to try and clear up the spat, and she seemed to bring things to order for the next ten minutes or so, after which voices were raised once again. The third group appeared to be working very diligently.

Lunch arrived towards the end of the workshop with a crocodile of middle-aged ladies in stained white clothing. It was provided courtesy of the Students' Union canteen, which was somewhat daring, and consisted of a range of tatty, damp, white sandwiches, filled with a variety of yellow to fawn lumpy fillings which were hard to discriminate. A vegetarian participant had great difficulty discerning animal from vegetable and consequently stuck only to the less than fresh fruit that accompanied the sandwiches. Cartons of orange juice were placed unceremoniously on one of the tables. Various attempts were made to open them, culminating in a fountain of sticky liquid down Colin's trousers, bringing the man to within a micrometre of a nervous breakdown. An urn of coffee set next to the juice bubbled and belched digestively at impolitely frequent intervals.

James Ross found me contemplating a soggy sandwich next to the urn.

"You're not going to eat that, are you?" he enquired with apprehension.

"Do I have any other option?" I asked. "I'm sure it's good for my personal development."

"That may be," he replied, "but I doubt that your intestinal tract would appreciate it."

"Have you eaten anything?" I asked.

"No. Actually I was wondering if we were allowed to escape for lunch."

"I suspect that they will put a black mark by your name if you do," I replied.

"Do you fancy a sandwich from Doralie's Deli? I discovered it when I was here last." Doralie's had a great reputation for the yummiest sandwiches in Hardnox.

"Will we be able to get back by two?" I asked, dubiously.

"Look, I'll drive – you can hop out. We'll be back in fifteen minutes." I paused indecisively.

"Come on then," I said, "but let's be unobtrusive about it."

We left the room inconspicuously. People were milling about making small talk. The two protagonists from Ross's group were still arguing. Max and Britt were engaged in an intense dialogue.

James's car was parked outside, courtesy of a visitor's parking permit – a rare privilege. It was what I expected: flashy, sporty and expensive. He had one of those little handsets which bleeped and with a magic 'grunch' opened all the doors at once. Needless to say, I had never owned a car with a magic 'grunch'. Inside, there were all sorts of buttons and gadgets, even a very superior mobile phone in a hinged compartment. We sped off campus. This was a new experience for me. I was not accustomed to having friends with fast cars (I did not count my trip with Irene; she was no friend), and I must confess, it gave me a certain buzz. Why James Ross was showing me such attention was incomprehensible, but at least he was no longer giving me those funny looks. He was natural, relaxed, and surprisingly interested in what I said. Five minutes from the university and James paused ostentatiously on a double yellow line, while I leapt into Doralie's and had two excessive baguettes made up. The lady behind the counter was friendly as always, and peered curiously out of the window at James's panting car.

Back inside we went round the one-way system twice for fun and arrived back at the space in the university car park.

"To be honest, I'd rather stay here and eat," said James.

"If we're spotted, I'm going to get an earful," I said, "but it is sunny, and the seminar room is an inappropriate venue for such good food." We clambered out of the car, or at least I did. James rose gracefully from his seat. My leg got stuck in the safety belt, and I almost tripped out onto the gravel. But it didn't seem to matter. Somehow there was no need to impress. We sat on the scrap of beetle-eaten lawn in the winter sun, and made a mess. Well, I made a mess. For, despite the depth of filling in his lunch, James remained in complete control. I, on the other hand, managed to slop egg mayonnaise on the lapel of my jacket, and kept allowing chunks of tomato to regularly flop out onto my chin.

"What do you think of it so far?" I asked.

"Well," said James, "I can see what they are trying to do, but in my group the take-home message so far is that if you are pig-headed or immature, it is impossible to work with anyone. You may have noticed that there are two people in our group who don't seem to see eye to eye."

"What exactly were they arguing about?

"I think Deborah works for a local council. Martin works for some construction firm. There may be something ideological going on there, but my suspicion is of a more personal affair. There was definitely an immediate prejudice on both sides." I looked at my watch.

"Oh, goodness, is that the time. Quick!" It was five to two. If we left it any later, we would lose the chance of creeping back unnoticed. We trotted to the seminar room where the darkness almost blinded me for several seconds. The air was even staler, and now it had a distinct savoury tinge. My absence had been noted, I was sure, for Irene looked at me with a smidge of hurt when she caught my eye.

Terry was to take the afternoon session. He began by saying how well he thought we had done in the morning. The first part of the afternoon involved feeding back what we had learnt from the morning session. Once this was done, we had a lecture on, among other things, the importance of looking at people when you speak to them.

As Terry droned on, I couldn't stop my mind wandering to James Ross. I must admit that in workshops and conferences my first priority is usually to find a soul mate: someone to drink with, someone to have amusing conversations with. I suspect this explains my lack of success in academe – nattering, not networking. James was fitting the bill today. Physically, I find it hard to attract people's attention – let's face it, it helps if you are good-looking. That is why James was such a mystery to me – he was a man giving 'li'l ole me' the time of day. During the evening we had spent together, he had even emanated flirtation. Perhaps, in retrospect, that was just the way he dealt with women. He was a natural charmer, but I was flattered that now we seemed to be beyond that. Goodness! I'd be flattered if he looked at my shoes!

Terry had quoted himself at least ten times during his presentation, which touched on subjects such as the importance of trust and letting people have their say, before the statutory urns of tea were wheeled in. I found myself chatting to a nice lady from some council in Scotland. She had been in the group which had got on, and was clearly having an enjoyable day. As I took a slurp of my tea, I noticed Irene making a bee-line for James. I could tell she was in a gushing frame of mind, and she started chatting with her earnest, intelligent look. James was responding, and I could hear the odd word. I think they were talking about Amity Action. Irene kept glancing over to Max who was once again deep in conversation with Britt. All this merely confirmed my prejudices. The best looking man and the best looking woman on the course were getting the most attention. Yes, I could tell that James and Irene were flirting now. I restrained a pang of jealousy. I had no right to feel it.

The object of the rest of the afternoon was to think constructively through some possible work-related issues that required diplomatic handling. Irene had some hypothetical examples for us to work with. By the end of the afternoon we were to have a list of 'sympathetic actions' we could use to facilitate the interactions without causing upset. Tomorrow we would have to use our list to formulate and then apply a 'sympathetic strategy' in an interview or focus group context of our choice. Britt dominated the session yet again, and was basically encouraged by Max, who, for some strange reason had decided to join our group. He agreed constantly with Britt, who was busy scribbling on the flip chart again. Irene had joined James's group, and seemed to be keeping the peace.

At the end of day one, I was feeling quite exhausted. I had to admit, the experience had been an interesting one. The fact that the groups had functioned so differently showed how important individuals were in determining the success or failure of the task in hand.

There was a general drift towards the Union bar, and I felt obliged to go along. Irene had again engaged James in conversation, and seemed set upon ignoring me. In a way I was pleased because I was sure that our lunchtime excursion had been duly noted. I couldn't help watching the two of them, though. He was doing it again, and I didn't like it. I sat next to Deborah. She had taken the day's events very seriously, and was busily filling in an evaluation form. I asked her whether she had had an interesting day.

"Very, very interesting," she said, brow furrowed, "although I think there should be some vetting of who attends these courses. After all, we have a right to expect some degree of basic reasonableness in a person. Unreasonable people have no place in team work." She turned again to her sheet. I noticed Martin, the construction man, poring over a pint of subsidised beer. He wasn't talking to anyone. In fact he looked quite ostracised, so I went to say hello. I was intercepted by Geena, who touched my arm and nodded towards him.

"Do you know what he said to Deborah?" she asked, in that confiding way women discuss things together. "That man is so rude. Deborah said that she's come across him before through work. Did you know he's been in trouble with the police?" Geena tut-tutted and moved on, no doubt to spread this juicy piece of scandal.

Martin was not in the mood for talking. Before I could sit down, he got up and walked out of the room. It was clear that he was emerging as the course's black sheep, whether this judgement was fair or not. I stood alone for a while, nursing my half pint of bitter. I was beginning to feel that awful 'alone in a crowd' sensation, and had started looking purposefully at the grubby notices that adorned the walls, when James tapped me on the elbow.

"Hi," he said, lightly.

"Oh, hello," I replied, with just a little bit of distance. "I was beginning to feel rather lonely."

"Look, I've been invited out to dinner this evening with Irene. It seems a little rude to say no. Apparently a message has been left for me at her office – I've been away from my mobile and I expect work is trying to get hold of me. We're going to pick it up first, and then go into town to discuss the details of our collaboration – you know, 'dot the i's, cross the t's'."

"Yes, sure. I understand," I said nobly, with just a hint of disappointment in my voice. "I'm sure I can find another drinking partner."

James smiled. "I may see you later," he said. 'But probably not', I thought, as he and Irene left the room. I glanced at Max, who looked put out, but he turned purposefully back to Britt and offered to buy her another drink. I didn't really fancy staying, but there wasn't much to look forward to that evening. I suspected that Jemima would still be avoiding me.

As I walked up the stairs to my bedsit, the air became infused with a wholly noxious odour. The U-bend had been neglected again, but today the pong of human excrement had an additional dash of industrial waste which made a change. At least *Reality Crescent* was on. Twinkletoes had received a reprieve because Marjorie, suspicious of Derek's intentions, had swapped the poison he was going to use with sugar. The high produced by this sudden intake of sweetness, however, meant that the poor budgie only correctly identified three of the lottery numbers. Derek had overcome his hatred for Paolo, his estranged cousin, and now, finding him attractive, was having doubts about his sexuality. Marjorie, in the meantime, was having problems house-training the puppy that Derek had saved from the dustcart. A full and life-affirming evening beckoned.

19

THE INDUSTRIAL SPY?

The next morning, Sorrel Surrido picked Grace up and they drove over to the Praefortica building. Grace was conscious that Sorrel seemed a little distant, preoccupied perhaps with the course.

"I had a good evening with Dr Nexus," Grace said. "He's an interesting fellow, I'll say that of him. Does he only ever dine with one person at a time?"

"Not necessarily," replied Sorrel succinctly.

"Did you have to go through that particular rite of passage?"

"Yes, I did."

"What did you make of it all?" asked Grace.

"He was very courteous."

"He seems to pride himself on being able to manipulate people."

"I think manipulate is too strong a word," replied Sorrel, echoing Nexus himself, and for the first time that morning becoming animated, defensive even. "In the business world you have to know how people work. If you look at any great entrepreneur you'll find they know how to get people to do things for them. Dr Nexus is a formidable man, but he is a good man."

"I confess I was sure he was reading all my thoughts. He made me feel quite transparent." Sorrel said nothing, and as she seemed disinclined to continue the conversation, Grace remained quiet for the rest of the short drive. She was a little bleary after her bad night anyway.

They entered the Praefortica building and headed back to the main seminar room on the top floor where they had been the day before. Sorrel remained taciturn as they took the elevator and walked along the corridors. Grace tried to make eye contact with her, but she looked straight ahead. Grace wondered what was up. It was almost as if Sorrel was cross with her.

"I'll er, I'll leave you to it then," said Grace, accepting that she would get little out of her for the time being and taking a seat with the other attendees.

The workshop progressed smoothly, as it had the day before. Grace was greatly impressed with the way the group interacted. She had never witnessed people working so well in teams. Despite the varying degrees of seniority represented in the groups, there was an equality and maturity in the conversation that she had not seen anywhere else. The morning session ended with lunch in the staff dining room, but pains had been taken to make the participants feel they were doing something special. Part of the room had been cordoned off for them, and they were served at their tables by a waiter. The food was of a high quality. Not surprising, perhaps, given Nexus's gourmet tastes. Maybe he thought the real secret of success lay in keeping his employees well fed. Sorrel had left the group briefly, but she returned towards the end of the meal and said to Grace,

"I've just been speaking to Dr Nexus. He's coming over this afternoon. He wondered if you wanted to see the production side of things." Grace was enthusiastic, and shortly after lunch, Nexus met her in the foyer.

"Good afternoon, Grace," he said, warmly. "I know that Sorrel has shown you round the administrative part of the building, but it occurred to me that you may wish to see our production facility."

"That's most thoughtful of you," she replied, noting Nexus's suit, which fitted him perfectly, emphasising his athletic shape and complementing his regal face.

Grace followed him along the corridor that linked the administrative block to a large building which housed the production line. The comforts of the former gave way to a utilitarian, almost clinical, décor.

"I suspect that, with your usual diligence, you have read our brochures?"

"Yes, I have, and I'm impressed at how quickly Praefortica has established itself in what must be a very crowded market-place."

"Yes, indeed, we have made considerable progress. As you know we produce a range of products and supplements related to health and wellbeing. We are keen to promote healthy living and combine this with the philosophy that each one of us should always move forward in what we do, whether it is striving physically or mentally. This is what keeps us alive and interested."

"That sounds very sensible," said Grace, "there's nothing worse than stagnation."

"Indeed no, and my great desire is to see every human being reach their potential, and live their life out enjoying the satisfaction that this brings. We can't avoid the inevitable need to profit from our work, but most of this we re-invest in the company. We have no shareholders to please." He smiled a very natural smile, and proceeded to tell Grace simply about the usual processes involved in product development, starting with research, then design and manufacturing. By now they had reached a small ante-room.

"I'm afraid you'll have to wear these, Grace," Nexus handed her a white coat, hat, gloves and overshoes. "We have to keep this zone exceedingly clean – and I'm sure you do not want anything on that suit of yours either." He laughed slightly. Grace had not heard him laugh before. He opened the door to a large, brightly lit room, where a number of technicians, all with white over-clothes, were supervising an immense production line.

"Today we are making one of our latest health drinks," explained Nexus, as Grace looked in awe at the automated machines with glistening bottles being shunted gently from place to place, filled up, secured and labelled.

"This is fascinating," replied Grace, genuinely interested. Nexus introduced her to one or two technicians who gave resumés of what they were doing. They were visibly delighted by their work, and were easy and friendly with Nexus.

"Good R&D is at the heart of our success," said Nexus, as they strolled around the factory. "I have developed a practical system to ensure we have the finest academic minds working with us in food science, biochemistry and product design. Many are reluctant to work full-time for a commercial company. Obviously they like to develop their own ideas, to write and publish their own papers. I therefore offer a good secondment package to academics and their institutions. Scientists come and work for me for six months or a year at a time and I compensate them and their universities. I get to work with a wide variety of great minds for a short time, and then I return them to their natural habitat, having signed suitable confidentiality agreements, of course. Everyone wins. The individuals see a handsome boost to their otherwise minimal incomes, the institutions get much sought after funds, and I get brainpower. There are too many competitors out there to get complacent – and believe me, the competition is aggressive: they are happy to employ any means at their disposal to keep ahead of the game."

They finished their circuit of the factory and returned again to the ante-room where they removed their protective clothing. Nexus straightened his tie, and continued,

"Industrial espionage, even in our area, is surprisingly common. Health supplements may not sound particularly life-changing, Grace, but we have been investing a great deal of money in a particular product recently: very new and very powerful. I have great hopes for it and the impact it could have on people's lives. I fear word may have got out. As you know, our main R&D facility is on Vancouver Island. I wanted it right out of the way, but despite all our safeguards, we have reason to believe that we had a visit from an industrial spy."

"Really?" said Grace, nervously.

"There are a number of people, we know who – or at least we know who they are working for – with a particular interest in our new product. A few months ago, we were aware that our installation was broken into."

Grace looked up. "You were broken into?"

"Yes," said Nexus placidly, "classic industrial espionage. We didn't capture the person concerned, but it was obvious that he, or she, had looked through our development files."

"You said you knew who it was?"

"Personally, I think it was our old friends, 'Amatheia Exports'. It's a cover name for a number of agents who work contract by contract." Nexus smiled, and looked her in the eye. But behind the smile, he looked hurt. Perhaps it was even a vulnerable look. Grace was shocked. Was it possible that Tramane was an industrial spy? Had he fabricated some preposterous story to make himself seem like the good guy?

"There is no need to look so worried, Grace. The person failed to find any details concerning our current project. If he, or she, got away with anything, it was old and abandoned ideas." He smiled. "And now for some afternoon tea."

When Grace returned to her hotel, there was a message for her. Alec Tramane had called, and wanted her to ring back urgently, day or night. He had left his mobile number. She looked at the note briefly in the hall, ripped it up and threw it into an ashtray by the elevator.

20

LATE NIGHT COFFEE

I was not particularly looking forward to the next day of the course. It was likely that James, my main source of amusement, would be preoccupied with Irene and Terry, finalising their collaboration. Of course, I did not expect anything special from James. I may be a frump, but I'm no fool: I knew that romance was out of the question. But I felt that perhaps we were becoming friends. We were opposites, certainly to look at, and I suspected, from his steely eyes, that his core was hard. But we had our wit in common, and we had shared a number of naughty asides.

When I arrived in the office, I found a small pile of treasury tags on my desk. They were rather exquisite – a tangled mass of coloured cords in lime green, orange and luminescent pink. Just the ticket for holding together the transcripts I had been analysing. I made a mental note to thank Sally.

James was in the seminar room and I asked him how his evening had gone. He replied that it had been a mixed pleasure. He and Irene had worked out the arrangements for the work. She was to be a formal collaborator, and receive a proportion of the funding to organise and analyse the quantitative data. He looked slightly down. I asked if there was anything on his mind, and he said that he was expecting an important telephone call. Further conversation was curtailed by the sound of Terry Spigot clearing his throat.

Spigot's lecture, a pep talk on picking scenarios and formulating our strategies, was not greatly revealing. The latter resembled the type of pop psychology more common to women's magazines than anything especially academic and innovative. Uninspired, I took to observing those around me. I could not help but notice that a certain tension had developed between Max and Irene, who seemed to be ignoring each other. There was a general aura of upset about the room; an ominous disquiet, like distant police sirens on a balmy night. Even Britt was subdued. Every so often she would play with her wedding ring, taking it off, fiddling with it, and then putting it back on. The upside of this was that when it came to the role play, there was a lack of inhibition in our group, equivalent at least to a shot of good whisky. Colin, his confidence bolstered by a fresh pair of trousers, began to come out of his shell a little, gently coaxed by Geena and myself. There were still fireworks in James's group though. The evening before had obviously gone well for Deborah. She had managed to convince the majority of those attending that Martin was a complete cad with a criminal record. The women outnumbered the men three to two and the sisterhood was strong. The situation was quite dire because at regular intervals both the other groups would stop and listen to what was going on.

Deborah shouted,

"I really feel, Martin, that with your particular history you are in no position to be the 'manager leading the interview'. For this, one should be sensitive, diplomatic and have the respect of colleagues." There was a general murmur of agreement from the women in the group.

"For crying out loud, woman, I am a manager, it's what I do every day of my life!"

"I am merely pointing out that we need to be realistic if we are going to succeed in this task. We are supposed to be allocating roles which have responsibilities. Personally, I think you are completely irresponsible. In fact, I know you are completely irresponsible." The other women in the group began to look a little nervous. There was less support for that one. It was only a matter of time before she commented on the size of his genitalia. Irene and Terry had slipped out of the room temporarily and I began to feel a little responsible myself, as the only member of the DoA present. After a period of slightly lower voices, the 'discussion' escalated.

"You couldn't organise a piss-up in a brewery, Martin!" yelled Deborah.

"As if you know even the slightest thing about me, Deborah!"

"I know all about you, Martin. Every little sordid detail! Your brain is in your bloody boxer shorts!"

"You just can't take rejection can you, Deborah! And I might say that rejecting you was the best decision I

223

have ever made in my life!" James's suspicions were publicly confirmed.

"You bastard, Martin!" shrieked Deborah, and she stormed out of the room. I felt that I should follow and soothe her, but one of her stalwart women friends did the job. As they left the room Martin shouted,

"Stupid cow!" amid looks of disapproval and disbelief. James took him to the canteen, whilst I tried to bring a modicum of order to the groups. By the time Irene and Terry reappeared you would never have known that the fray had occurred.

I felt I should stay in this lunchtime, and mentally prepared myself for soggy sandwiches. James had not reappeared with Martin, although Deborah had returned, her tear-stained face stimulating a degree of sympathy amongst certain of her colleagues. There was a little back-patting and nodding. Irene looked vaguely curious, but made no immediate attempt to find out what the fuss was all about. James re-emerged in time for the urn, which arrived with its escort only a little late. Martin, apparently, had gone home. I felt I should mention that there had been a bit of a rumpus in Irene's absence, and my opportunity arose in the Ladies'. I explained what had happened.

"Oh yes," said Irene, "well, these things happen. Incidentally, Ellinora, don't think I didn't notice you sneaking off yesterday. However, I don't blame you. James *is* such a charming man, isn't he? We had such a good time yesterday evening."

The afternoon consisted more of a plenary session where Irene and Terry got us to do little presentations and fielded questions. It was quite enjoyable, and certainly less stressful than the role play.

The course was due to end at midday the next day, and tonight was the course dinner. Sally had booked a restaurant in town and we all met in the bar. This was evidently regarded as something of an occasion. Diurnal office-wear was replaced by smart jackets, and, I regret to say, the odd blazer[25]. The floral skirts had been accessorised with a variety of scarves and other garments (some with gold buttons)[26]. It was going to be a jolly evening.

Have you noticed how women who usually spend hectic evenings mashing potatoes and putting the washing on for their broods, let their hair down when freed from these housewifely responsibilities? Granted, there will be the odd telephone call, a sweet word to a small ear pressed against the receiver at the other end, but only after a large gin and tonic, and a few rude jokes.

Geena, who was a bit of a gossip, held the group entranced by her risqué stories, and even Britt, her leg gently resting against Max's thigh, looked as though she might thaw. Irene had positioned herself on James's left, but I had secured his right, hoping for a few witty observations.

Despite the day's drama, there were some surprisingly positive vibes about the course. It is a fact that a group of people with something in common, left in a room to talk, will enjoy themselves. The course dinner had been paid for in advance and the wine flowed freely. The jokes got ruder, and the more opinionated amongst the

---

[25] Frumpp's Fashion Tip Number 18: blazers should only be worn by those aged eighteen and under.

[26] Frumpp's Fashion Tip Number 19: gold buttons are often found on designer-wear. Do not be deceived, they do not enhance the item. Only the Queen is allowed to wear gold buttons in public.

group began to argue for the sake of it, but in a fairly good-humoured way. Deborah, who had played the injured party all afternoon (she had no shame – it was all Martin's fault, obviously), began to return to her normal self, talking earnestly to Colin, who nodded nervously in the corner.

Max and Britt moved closer together as the alcohol filtered through their capillaries. I could tell this without looking, because Irene moved closer and closer to James. Every so often he would chat to me, but Irene insisted on hogging him.

As is not uncommon on these occasions, the women with families got the bit between their teeth and suggested a night club. I wasn't ready for bed, so I tagged along. In fact, the only person to retire was Colin, who was all Deborahed out. We chose one of the student night spots, where, by luck, it turned out to be an '80s evening. I say, 'by luck', because it was the era of a good many on the course. Jackets and scarves were abandoned in a heap under the only chair which the party managed to procure, and the formerly sedate and relatively well-behaved freed themselves of all inhibitions, and took to the dance floor. I thoroughly approve of this. There are few occasions when we are truly allowed to let ourselves go, and a good elemental bop is one of them.

At about half past one, I was hot and sweaty, and desperate for a breath of fresh air, so I sneaked out. The little stamp the club had put on my hand now looked like an aged tattoo. In its molten, expanded state, I doubted its passport-worthiness, and accepted I would be stranded forever in the 1990s. Whilst I literally steamed in the cold night air, James Ross came out to join me to the strains of 'Everybody Wants to Rule the World' by Tears for Fears.

"It's a shame, isn't it," he said.

"What's a shame?" I replied.

"That everybody wants to rule the world," he said, smiling, "it causes no end of trouble, you know."

"It's Madness," I said, as 'One Step Beyond' started to play. Ross laughed.

"It certainly is," he said. "It's a while since I've been to a night club. I'm used to slightly more peaceful venues. You know, I'm really more of a casino man."

"Casinos!" I exclaimed. "How very sophisticated. Have you been to Las Vegas?"

"On several occasions," he replied, "but I'm not sure I would describe that as sophisticated. You see more purple rinses than dinner jackets. On reflection, a gentlemen's club is probably more my cup of tea."

"You're joking," I said.

"No, I'm not, I'm afraid."

"What else do you like for entertainment?" I asked. "Go on – tell me the three things you most like."

"What I'd most like just now is a coffee," he said. "We're not far from my digs," he said, "would you like to join me?"

"What about Irene?"

"What about her?"

"I just thought. Well, she seemed to require your attention."

"Didn't you notice? Britt has gone to bed. I think Irene and Max are making peace on the dance-floor."

"Well, I suppose that's less embarrassing than making love on the dance-floor. I must say, you are very observant."

"It helps in my job."

"Well, if Irene won't take it out on me tomorrow, I would like to join you." We wandered through the quiet, weekday Hardnox to one of the grander hotels. James checked with the night porter that he had no messages, seemed disappointed that he did not, and then we went upstairs together. I didn't feel the need to question the wisdom of this. I was anticipating nothing other than some refreshment and good conversation. The porter looked surprised though, and when I caught myself in one of the mirrors on the landing, I exclaimed out loud, "Oh no! Will you take a look at that! No wonder I was getting some odd looks."

It was quite awful. James and I stood side by side, and we looked a completely incongruous pair. There was he: tall, tanned, and despite the heat of the night club, only sexily dishevelled. And there was I: small, stumpy, the little make-up I had on cascading down my face in black loops, my wiry hair askew, my glasses steamed up.

"What a lovely couple," James remarked, laughing. I gave him a gentle push.

James's room was pleasant in a posh-hotel-institutional sort of way. The carpets were, as always, rather alarming, but their ferocity was dissipated by the sheer volume of the room. I sat in a very comfy wicker chair by a round, glass table, and he, flicking his shoes off, lay on the double bed. The coffee machine began to gurgle gently in the background.

"You haven't answered my question," I said. "Go on – your three favourite forms of entertainment."

"OK," he said, scratching his head. "I'm afraid I'm a bit of a gourmet. I like to eat good food, I've a weakness for very expensive wine and I like an adventure."

"Like a course in SpIT?" I asked, wryly.

"A true adventure into the depths of human dynamics," laughed James. "And what about your three favourite things?"

"Oh, I don't know; let me think: empty cinemas, very expensive beer and *Reality Crescent*."

"Empty cinemas?" enquired James.

"Yes. I dislike the intimacy of a crowded cinema. The fact you can smell and hear other people. The crunchy, salivary noise of the man behind your left ear eating popcorn; pungent training shoes, that sort of thing."

"I'm surprised you tolerated this evening."

"I prefer empty night clubs," I laughed. "I mean, let's face it, dancing is a way of letting go. When you are crammed together, how are you supposed to express yourself? If you are going to boogie – let it rip!"

"And I thought you were a person in control of herself."

"You mean I'm a bit anally retentive."

"I wouldn't say that. But you strike me as someone who likes things in reasonable order – the project, for example. You also seem rather self-conscious, which is no bad thing, but I suppose adds to the significance of your desire to 'let it rip' on occasion. You are also pretty hard on yourself," he added.

"And what do you mean by that?" I smiled uncertainly.

"You don't think highly of yourself." James got up and went to the coffee machine which had expired ungracefully with a chugging grunt. "Ellie, you have a great deal going for you: you are interesting, witty, reliable, trustworthy ..."

"Hang on a bit. You don't know me that well, surely. I could be grossly unreliable."

"No, I don't think so."

"Well, that's all very nice, James, but the fact is that I'm a bit of a frump: Frumpp by name, frump by nature, and despite all my other charms, I don't have a hope of attracting gorgeous-looking blokes like yourself."

"But that kind of attraction can be highly superficial, Ellie. At least it is in my trade."

"Work satisfaction in import–export?" I said doubtfully. James paused slightly on his way to the bin with the coffee grounds.

"What I mean is, when you are researching social relations, you come across people who do daft things for what they mistake for love."

"My, this sounds profound. If you don't watch out I'll give you Ellie Frumpp's Theory of Love and Sex."

"I'd be interested to hear it. Milk and sugar?"

"Yes please. Are you sure? It's a bit matter-of-fact."

"Then I thoroughly approve – go on!" He walked back to the bed, took a slurp of his coffee and settled down to listen.

"Well, it's all to do with Venn diagrams and biology – do you really want me to go on?" James was stifling a yawn but indicated his assent. "Well, I see all major characteristics like humour or kindness as 'sets' of characteristics and when we meet someone, different sets overlap to differing degrees. They can overlap a lot in people that we like, and hardly at all in people we dislike. So, take Irene for example, we really have very little in common apart from the project, so frankly, we don't really like each other at all. My friend Jem, well – we don't always overlap in the humour department, but she's a kind and moral creature and I respect her for that. Anyway, if someone is, or says or does something seriously outside of our own sets, well, any chance of friendship is gone."

"And where does love and sex fit in with all this?"

"Well, sexual attraction is just another 'set'," I replied, "but it is a bit different because it is so obviously driven by biology. It is delightful, but dangerous because it is quixotic and quite likely ephemeral. So where 'kindness' is a trait that you hope will last in someone you meet – sexual attractiveness may be quite transitory unless it is reinforced by the other sets in the Venn diagram. It takes time to get to know someone's full character, but the old sexual attraction is quite happy to drive us on regardless and we can end up in bed with a person we couldn't possibly love or even like. I guess that's fine if you are both aware of what's going on but horrible if there's a mismatch in interpreting the event. But love – now that is different, because it is really a feeling we get when lots of our sets overlap with someone else's; if sex is on board then – well – that's just great." I wondered for a moment about the state of Jemima and 'Maximilian's' Venn diagram. How could that possibly be viable?

"Makes sense to me." James looked a little ponderous.

"Are you married?" I asked. "I can't believe that you don't have someone."

"I'm afraid I'm a bit of a superficial bastard when it comes to relationships. I tend to act on my sexual urges and usually find it pleasurable. I like to think the other parties involved do too, but I've probably led a few women astray feelings-wise. It's not that I've never got more involved than a fling, but for one reason or another, it's best not to get too attached in my game," he frowned.

"There you go again. What is it about the study of people in customs and excise?"

James smiled. "How much do you overlap with me, d'you think?" he asked.

"Well I don't know you that well yet," I said, "and I have drunk rather a lot, but I feel very relaxed with you now. I must admit, though, that when we first met I found your manner very odd indeed. I thought for a moment or two that you were flirting with me, but that was so impossible – we are at opposite ends of the beauty spectrum. But I think we overlap here and there – humour at least."

"More than humour I think," said James, offering no explanation for his earlier behaviour. "I'm strangely comfortable with you too. You don't expect me to 'perform' in any particular way." James grimaced for a second and then burped out loud.

"I do beg your pardon!" he said. "Goodness. I think the last woman to witness something like that was my mother – about 30 years ago. I do apologise. I guess that shows how at ease I am just now. It's so nice to feel I can be a normal human being. Perhaps I should marry you and be done with philandering."

"My! I'll take the hypothetical proposal any day," I said, "but I'm not so sure about the comparison with your mother. I think on balance I'm flattered." We both laughed.

"Gosh, it's very late," I said, when we had recovered – my watch said three o'clock. "I'd better go. Irene will be very upset if you are not ready for a bit of SpIT later."

"Look, Ellie, I can't let you walk back on your own. I'll come with you." James rolled off the bed.

"You look too knackered for a night stroll. I'll get a cab," I said, standing up.

"You could stay here of course," he said. "I mean, you could have the bed – I'll sleep on the floor."

"Why are men always so chivalrous when it comes to me?" I said, smiling.

"I could sleep with you if you want," James replied, raising his eyebrows. "I've already warned you about my habits. I'm very good at sex, and I'm quite serious." I laughed nervously.

"I don't believe you," I said, but he spread out his hands as an extension of the offer. I looked at him quizzically. No one this handsome would *ever* make such a proposition to me again. What an initiation it would be into the wonderful world of sexual intercourse! I sighed.

"I think you would be shocked at my big pants and hairy legs, and I don't want to upset the happy Venn diagram we are in just now."

"I'll get you a cab," he said, giving me a kiss on the cheek, "just as soon as I've had a pee."

21

PERSISTENCE AND RESISTANCE

Flying back to Vancouver that weekend, Grace had time to contemplate the latest piece in her jigsaw. It could all fit! Tramane's interest in Amity Action, given that they had a long-standing link with Praefortica; Tramane's interest in her, as an employee likely to work with Praefortica; and Tramane's foray into the night on Vancouver Island. He really could be an industrial spy! And there she was about to help him! The only outstanding niggle was the business of the abstracts, and the payments, but perhaps there was a rational explanation for these. A coincidence? Or the acceptance of poor abstracts might be Jack's way of encouraging researchers who were not doing as well as they might. The payments could be completely unrelated to the reviewing exercise. A bit of consultancy work perhaps?

A horrible thought struck her – maybe they weren't poor abstracts at all? She cast her mind back again to the ghastly Christmas lunch and the awful Sevi Janus. Maybe she really wasn't any good at her job. Maybe she had been appointed for the wrong reasons? Damn! From the start, this whole business had been deeply undermining. Perhaps now was the time to have a chat to Jack about everything. He could probably reassure her. One thing was certain: she would leave Tramane to do his own dirty work.

That week, Grace's main task was to sort out the timetable and proceedings for the conference. She and Jack had finalised the list of abstracts following the reviewers' comments. She now had to classify and index them. She was just collating a draft programme when the telephone rang.

"Grace Lefavarie," she said, placing the receiver under her chin.

"Go to the telephone box outside the building," said a voice and hung up. Grace swore under her breath and as she put the receiver back, she knocked her neatly ordered document on the floor. It lay in chaos; its logic defeated – a visual manifestation of her discombobulation. She had recognised the voice immediately; and just as quickly the world she had comfortably reframed had broken in two. She swore again and grabbed her coat. He had not even given her time to tell him to get lost and now she felt she had no choice but to do as he said. She would end the conversation quickly.

The telephone in the booth outside the building was already ringing – nagging her – when she came out of the front door.

"Grace, it's me, Alec. Thank goodness you're all right!"

"Why shouldn't I be?" enquired Grace, sharply.

"You rang me. I didn't think it was likely that you would do that unless you were desperate."

"Well, I wasn't, and I don't really think we have much to discuss."

"Grace, you know how sorry I am about, about, you know ..."

"If you think I'm still bothered about that, you're mistaken," she said, curtly.

"Well, then, did you call for a reason?"

"Yes, but it transpired that the reason was mythical, so I didn't call you again. It was a mistake."

"Listen, we know where you called from. You were in Alberta – in Banff."

"What if I was?"

"We know Praefortica have an outfit there. Were you at Praefortica?"

"Look, Alec. If you must know, yes, I was in Banff; yes, I was at Praefortica; and yes, I even met your precious Dr Nexus. It's my job, OK? But if you think I've fallen for that secret agent nonsense, well, think again. I found him a perfectly charming person, his organisation is robust, and their working morale is enviable. I also learnt a thing or two about you. Believe me, your little 'breaking and entering' into Praefortica's property did not go unnoticed. Rather amateur, I would say, for a professional industrial spy!"

"You've completely lost me, Grace."

"I think I would like to keep it that way. Goodbye, Alec."

"Wait a minute, Grace, you're playing with fire ..." She put the receiver down and turned to leave the booth but the telephone rang again. Grace hesitated, sighed, and answered it, annoyed.

"Don't put the phone down," said Alec urgently. "I don't know what you've got into your head. All I can say is that I was telling you the truth, and if you have been in contact with Nexus, you may already be in danger."

"I'm not listening, Alec," said Grace flatly.

"I've been doing some research," continued Tramane quickly, trying to keep her on the telephone. "I've been to visit your friends Spatchcock and co.. I know what you think of them, Grace. You are, of course, right."

"You went to Hardnox because I didn't like the study? You must be mad!"

"No, I merely have a great deal of faith in your judgement, especially when it does not coincide with the judgement of Jack D'Oretz."

"What on earth do you mean?"

"There is definitely something going on. I've been making enquiries."

"And?" said Grace.

"Nexus has recruited several scientists from Hardnox over the last few years – most of them on secondment. He's also been funding other work – quite legitimately as it happens ..."

"So what then?" said Grace impatiently.

"It's a connection," said Tramane as if this piece of information was, in itself, earth-shattering.

"Why are you telling me this, Alec? It really doesn't interest me, and I'm not getting drawn into this conversation. I don't even know who you really are!"

"Grace," Tramane paused. "I can't tell you everything now, but you must believe me. We have intelligence that something big is afoot and the pieces are coming together. Ask yourself this, 'Why would an industrial spy go and spend an excruciating three days on Spigot's course in Hardnox?' Does that sound like fun to you? What has *that* to do with industrial espionage, for goodness sake?!"

"I don't know – but I hope the course did you some good. You certainly need a little relationship counselling."

"What did Nexus tell you, eh? If he's spinning you a tale about industrial espionage, it's because he's aware that you know something important. He's trying to put you off."

"And how might he know that?"

"Have you told D'Oretz anything?"

"No. He's only aware that we've had dealings professionally. He didn't even know about our meeting on Vancouver Island. To be honest, I think it's time I told Jack everything."

"Please, you really must *not* do that Grace. It's bad enough that Nexus may be on to you. He has ways and means of finding out anything." Grace did not answer. "I give up," said Tramane, after a pause. "Look, I know we've still got some work to do before you'll be convinced, but we are definitely on to something. If I don't speak to you before, I'll see you at the conference. I'm coming along."

"I don't think you are," said Grace. "Your name's not on the list – remember I'm in charge of the wretched thing."

"I'm coming to the conference," repeated Tramane. "For goodness sake, keep away from Nexus, please, and don't say anything to Jack D'Oretz." Grace did not respond.

"Please, Grace?"

"I can't promise anything," she said crossly, and put the receiver down. Back in her office, Grace looked at the mess on the floor. She had no inclination to pick it up and went to lunch instead.

In the afternoon, Grace went down to the Fraser River Hotel to check the booking and to go round their conference suite. She needed to assess their audio-visuals, and to have a word with the caterers. It was peculiar, wandering into that amazing foyer once more. She had not been back since her rather unpleasant conversation over coffee with Tramane. She looked up at the spiralling balcony winding round the sides of the hall. In many ways she had wanted to hear from Nexus that Tramane was the bad guy. It meant that the cosy world in which she had functioned for the last two years was secure. Although she was initially shocked by his comments about industrial spies, these had led to a sense that she was no longer responsible for finding out the truth; that somehow all the doubt and confusion had been swept away.

As she sat on a sofa waiting for the events manager to show her round, she found herself getting angry. Tramane had gone and spoilt it all over again! There he was, with his silly conspiracies and dramatic language about danger and playing with fire. Why had he gone to Hardnox? Surely not solely on the basis of her disdain for Spigot and co.? And how did that fit with Nexus's story? But why would Nexus invent such a thing? There was no reason for him to suspect any special relationship between them.

Grace opened her bag to take out the hotel brochure again, to refresh her memory. As she withdrew it, her wallet fell onto the floor. She looked at it for a second. Her wallet! Zuserain Nexus had had her wallet! He could have seen Alec's card and the note he had written!

"Ms Lefavarie?" A lanky man was standing next to her, jingling a bunch of keys. "Ms Lefavarie, I believe you wish to see the conference suite, is that right?" Grace jumped.

"Oh, yes, sorry. I was just admiring this amazing hall. It is really most intriguing." The platitude concealed her agitation, and as she followed the man, responding vaguely to his slick sales patter, she found her anger at Tramane being replaced by a cold apprehension.

22

TEARS AND TICKETS

I awoke at one o'clock. I knew it was one o'clock because I could hear the Hardnox bell, the local scourge of hungover students. At first I assumed it was the bell which had awoken me, but my bleary subconscious left me feeling uneasy and unsatisfied with this explanation. It would not let me fall back to sleep, my mind butting in with irritating thoughts. I was feeling a little peeved about work. Sally Whimbrel had congratulated me on having had the abstract for the Vancouver conference accepted. Apparently, Amity Action had written to Irene over a fortnight ago with the news. She had seen me at least twice in the last week without mentioning it. Her urgent requests for a project update now made sense, though.

This time I heard the noise properly: something like a cat yowling, but this was duller, more human. I uncovered my ear, which was habitually squashed beneath a curl of the pillow when I slept, and listened, a small infusion of adrenalin waking me still further. It sounded as if it came from within the house: it sounded as if it came from Jemima's room.

I had not had the opportunity to say much to Jemima over the last few weeks. I had tried to make conversation, but she would always brush me off, very sweetly and politely, but definitively. I guessed that 'Maximilian' was still proving a paragon of a potential life-partner, making my own criticisms of him appear implausible. I had missed her chit-chat and cups of tea.

The noise definitely came from her room. I sat up in bed. Actually, now my ears were feather-free, it sounded like crying. I waited for about five minutes but it didn't stop. I heard no other voice in Jemima's room, so I got out of bed cautiously. I had become a little wary of wandering around barefoot in the dark since I surprised a mouse in my Crunchy Wheaty Flakes one morning. Since then I had become more aware of the nocturnal scampering of my small, furry squatters. It was freezing, so I slung a jumper over my pyjamas, put on a pair of socks and poked my nose out of the room. The landing light was off. Looking at Jemima's door, I could detect no illumination. I put my door on the latch and listened at hers. She was still moaning softly. I knocked. The moaning stopped. I knocked again.

"Jemima?" I said quietly. I heard the floorboards creak and the door opened a couple of centimetres. She peered out, her eyes red and swollen. There was a strange look of hope or expectation in her eyes, which vanished as she recognised me. In fact, she looked very disappointed. "Jemima, are you all right?" She looked at me sheepishly.

"Of course I'm all right," she said, a little sharply.

"No you're not," I said.

"No, I'm not," she agreed. Her eyes welled up and she put her arms out like a child. I gave her a long and firm hug.

"Tell me what the matter is." She led me by the hand back into her room, and put on her bedside light. We both squinted. "Shall I put the kettle on?" I suggested. Jemima nodded. As I made some hot chocolate for us both, Jemima crawled back under her covers and stared at nothing. She sniffed at regular intervals, and with each sniff a fresh tear would roll down her cheeks.

"It's Maximilian," she said at last, after a draught of chocolate. "He dumped me. He dumped me today."

"I'm really sorry, Jem," I said.

"No you're not. You'll be saying 'told you so'."

"No, that's not what I'm saying. I *am* sorry."

"He said that we really weren't suited. He said he was going back to his wife."

"Two good reasons why this might be for the best," I said sympathetically.

"But you don't understand, Ellie," Jemima paused. "I, we ..." her voice trailed off, and she started to cry again. Great heaving sobs, that made the bed springs tinkle.

"Oh Jem," I said, "you poor, poor thing." I gave her another hug. "Ellie, I, I ... I was a virgin, Ellie ... I ... he said we would get married ... I never would have ... if I had known ... I never would have ..."

"I know. There, there," I said, trying to soothe her.

"I feel so used, Ellie. I was speechless when he said it was over. I couldn't say anything to him, but now I feel

243

so angry!" She emphasised the last word and threw her tissue on the floor. "I think he was just after my help ... I had to keep delivering things to him from one of the technicians, you know ... at the department ..."

"I'm sure that's not why he went out with you, Jem. I think he really liked you. I saw his face when he came into the pub."

"No, it was to get my help," persisted Jem, "because now it's finished, he's dumped me."

"What's finished?" My curiosity got the better of me.

"Oh, I don't know. Whatever he was doing," she said vaguely. "He never told me any details."

"Oh, Jemima. I do know how you feel, believe me."

"Do you?" asked Jemima. "Have you been dumped before?"

"Yes, I have, at college, and you have to remember, that I rarely receive any interest from men – I'm not a lovely thing like you. Well, I really thought this chap was the one, you know. We were friends for about two years and we got on well – then it became something more. Anyway, we went out for about six months, and then he ran off with someone an awful lot prettier. I think he was embarrassed. He was better looking than me, you see. I think they're married now. I was devastated at the time – I lost a really good friend you see, as well as a boyfriend."

"Did you ... were you ... I mean did you?"

"'Close but no cigar' – I never even managed that. But I can imagine what it must be like. When you are intimate, you put your trust in someone, don't you? You trust them not to laugh at your underwear, or your teen bra ..." Jemima smiled, and then her face clouded over again, and another big tear oozed out of her eye.

"I did trust him. I really did," sighed Jemima.

"I know you did," I said, giving her a pat.

When I left to go back to my room, Jemima was a lot calmer. She was tucked up in bed, hugging her pillow. As I left she said sleepily,

"By the way, what has a cigar got to do with it?"

A day or two later I wandered into the postgrad. and admin. tea room, and everyone stopped talking. A dropped-brick moment. A tumbleweed moment. Sally, Christian and Rosy looked up from the corner where they were huddled. Christian was looking very amused; Sally and Rosy were looking annoyed. I overheard Rosy say,

"That's just bloody typical ..." and then there was silence.

"Oh dear," I said, as I put the kettle on. "I smell a rat. Would you like me to leave?"

"We were just discussing your non-trip to Vancouver," said Christian, grinning.

"Oh?" I said.

"I'm sure it's just a mistake, Christian," said Sally, giving Christian a Paddington stare.

"It's just that Sally is supposed to be getting the plane tickets for the conference in Canada, and apparently you're not on the list," continued Christian with satisfaction.

"I'm sure it's an oversight," persisted Sally.

"Oh come on," Rosy joined in. "Irene did exactly the same thing to Jenny – you know – that conference in Nice." The kettle started to boil and the water vapour scalded my hand, because I was still holding onto the handle.

"Ouch!" I exclaimed. "Oh well," I continued, putting my hand under the cold water tap, "to be perfectly honest, I'm not very surprised. Irene has never said that I would go."

"Well, I think it's mean," concluded Rosy. Sally remained diplomatically quiet.

I didn't stay in the tea room. I was not unduly upset. I had made no assumptions about who would be going to Canada. It would have been interesting, of course, and it seemed a little unfair, given that the work being presented was essentially what I had been doing for the last six months. But when all was said and done, I was only the monkey – it was what I was paid to be.

In compensation, the next few weeks afforded me some amusement. Being in possession of this information, I was able to wind Irene up a little every time I saw her. She would have to get the results from me: I held all the cards. It began as we met briefly in the corridor one day,

"Oh Ellinora, you'll be delighted to know that we had the abstract accepted for the Vancouver conference."

"Yes, I know, Sally told me," I said.

"Ah, yes, splendid, Sally – yes, I, I er told her to pass it on. I've been so busy, you see. Well, anyway, we obviously need to think about what material we should present. Perhaps you might draft something out?"

"Do you want me to stick to the abstract we submitted?" I said, "Because that might be difficult. The results so far are rather different to the ones suggested."

"Dear Ellinora," said Irene with a pitying look, "so much to learn. Sixth rule of academe: what you put in the conference abstract doesn't matter." A little later Irene said,

"We do need to have that chat about the conference paper. Let's have a meeting next week, and you can show me what you've got."

"Are we all going?" I asked, innocently.

"I, er, I've yet to decide that, Ellinora. Obviously plane fares are pricey to the West Coast. We do have only a limited budget. Must dash – important meeting!"

After I had taken her through the work and my ideas on how to present it, I said,

"It would be great to have a dry run of this. Perhaps we could do it one lunchtime in the seminar room. You know – get some informal feedback from the department. I always find that useful." She replied,

"Oh, I think this is probably all I need at the moment, Ellinora. Oh, is that the time – I've got a train to catch."

A month later, I decided it was time for the finale. When I next saw Irene I said,

"Would it be possible to go through the talk today? I like to be well rehearsed. Or perhaps you will want to do it on your own. Either way, you probably want me to double check the facts and figures. Incidentally, I thought I'd take a few days off after the conference if that's OK. You know, look around Vancouver. I might even pop over to the Rockies. I ought to let Sally know so she can sort out the ticket."

Irene smiled, and morphed her face into a suitably regretful, but not guilty, expression.

"Oh, Ellinora, I suppose I ought to have told you before. We didn't actually budget for four people to attend an overseas conference in the grant application. Terry, Max and myself have no choice but to go, but it means that on this occasion, we can't take you. I'm so sorry. It was Terry's doing – I told him at the time the travel budget was too small – especially with his back. I do hope you don't mind. We'll do a good job, don't you worry, and of course, you can count the conference on your CV – you will be credited in the proceedings. Now I must go, I'm meeting Max for lunch." She swiftly extracted herself from our conversation, too cowardly to witness the potential emotional reaction. She need not have worried. I merely shrugged and went to the Union canteen to find something large and sugary (preferably with a raspberry jam centre) to immerse myself in.

23

PERFIDY

The Fraser River Hotel shuttle returned from the airport laden with another batch of delegates for the International Workplace and Productivity Meeting. Grace had set up a desk in the hotel foyer so that they could register straight away. She had four hundred conference bags behind the desk, all bearing Amity Action's logo. This was a revealing time. The true character of delegates would be exposed in their choice of casual clothing, deprived as they were of anonymous suits and ties by the fear of plane-generated wrinkles.

It was late afternoon when Alec Tramane walked in. After their telephone conversation, Grace had scoured her records for his name, but couldn't see him anywhere. In fact, he had been put firmly to the back of her mind as she dealt with the inevitable hiccups of registration: fussy academics, lost key cards, misplaced luggage. When she saw him approaching, she was taken aback, and found herself blushing. He waited patiently as she dealt with a rather vague professor who had (apparently) drunk a lot in transit to help him counter his fear of flying.

"Hi Grace," said Tramane, after she had passed her charge to a responsible bell-hop, "how are you?"

"Busy," she replied, attempting to remain calm. "I'm sorry, sir, but I don't recall a Mr Tramane on my books."

"That's because 'Mr Tramane' is not on your books. Try Dr James Ross, Docklands Institute for Work and Social Life Research, London."

"Docklands, eh? Very fishy. Yes, it appears we have your reservation. You'll be in room 604; that's on the sixth floor. The elevator is to your right. Here is your pack. We will be holding complimentary drinks in the Black Bear Suite at seven this evening, if you would care to join us." She gave him her professional smile.

"Do you have a break from this soon?" said Tramane, ignoring her attempt to dismiss him.

"I'm expecting another crowd from a European flight in ten minutes. After they're sorted I'll be free for an hour."

"Are you willing to spend that hour with me?"

"I suppose there's no harm in it," she said wearily. "You couldn't make me any more annoyed if you tried."

"I'll see you in my room then, in about half an hour?"

"I'll meet you in the bar," replied Grace firmly. "Let's deal with this on neutral territory." Tramane smiled.

"In the bar it is then. I'll look forward to it."

'Charming as ever', thought Grace as Tramane turned and walked serenely to the elevator. Her mind was prevented from wandering by the arrival of an elegant English woman. She was accompanied by two male colleagues, one highly scented and slightly crumpled; the other, handsome, lupine and dressed in black.

"Dr Irene Spatchcock," said the woman as she reached the desk, smiling briefly, "and Professor Terry Spigot and Dr Max Snoode, University of Hardnox."

"Ah, Dr Spatchcock," said Grace, raising her eyebrows, "welcome to Vancouver." She consulted her list. "You'll be in room 402; Dr Snoode is in room 447, and Professor Spigot, 415 – all on the fourth floor. Here are your packs. The elevator is to the right. We will be holding complimentary drinks in the Black Bear Suite at seven this evening, if you would care to join us."

"Thank you so much," said Irene. "Now, I don't suppose you could type these up and pop them onto acetates for me, could you? We've been so hectic these last few days." She flourished a handwritten pile of notes. "We'll need them for our presentation tomorrow."

Grace smiled coldly.

"I'm Grace Lefavarie. I'm in charge of things here. We do offer secretarial help. After five, this desk will become a help desk. If you would like to come back then, there will be several staff members who can provide computing facilities and help with audio-visuals."

"Oh Ms Lefavarie," said Irene, her eyes lighting up. "I'm so sorry! What with you sitting there looking so pretty, I thought you must ... Oh never mind. I'll drop these off in a bit then." She wrinkled her nose apologetically and walked over to the elevator, with a peremptory, "Come on, you two."

Half an hour later, Alec Tramane sauntered over as Grace was tidying up a few odds and ends.

"You look as if you need a drink," he said.

"You could say that," she said. "Your friends from Hardnox are here, by the way."

"Are they now."

"And what do they know you as?" asked Grace sarcastically.

"Ross," said Tramane.

"And what are you going to tell Jack when he appears? I'll expect you to be wearing your name badge, you know."

"Actually, I've mislaid my name badge. In any case, I'll cross that bridge when I come to it."

"That should be interesting."

"There's something I need you to do for me," said Tramane.

"Yes?"

"Can you change my room?"

"Oh, and what's the problem? Is the telephone bugged? Is there a microphone in your chandelier?"

"As a matter of fact, there is," said Tramane, "but I don't expect you to believe me."

"Good, because I don't."

"Perhaps you'd like me to show you?"

"We'll change your room," said Grace. "I've heard of young ladies being lured up to gentlemen's rooms to see their etchings, but not their bugs." She walked over to the reception desk.

"Harry, I'm afraid Mr, er Dr Ross has a problem with his room, number 604. Do you have another free?"

"We could swap him with another delegate, Ms Lefavarie," said the man behind the desk. "May I enquire as to the problem?" Grace leant over the desk and whispered. Harry smiled and said, "Of course we can accommodate Dr Ross's needs. Would room 204 be more suitable?" Grace nodded and turned to Alec,

"There you go, Dr Ross, room 204."

"What were you whispering about?" asked Alec. He looked serious.

"I had to give him a reason as to why you didn't like room 604."

"And what did you tell him?"

"I told him you were an eccentric Englishman who suffers from vertigo, and did he have something a little nearer the ground."

"Oh," said Alec.

"Come on then, buy me a lemonade." They walked into the hotel bar, which was down some steps from the foyer. It was dark and luxurious, with velvety, secretive booths. When they were sitting, Grace said, "Before you start, I need to know exactly who I'm speaking to: Dr Ross, the mad inventor, or Mr Tramane, the mad creation of Dr Ross? Or is it the other way round?"

"My name is Alec Tramane. Dr Ross is one of my pseudonyms."

"Oh, we're talking multiple aliases now, are we? More and more fascinating."

"Grace, be serious, will you?"

"You mean you have something serious to say to me?" said Grace, feigning surprise.

"I do," replied Tramane.

"Go on then," said Grace, resignedly. "And if you spin me one more lie, I guarantee at the very least you'll go upstairs with a sugary drink down your very classy tie. And I'm not joking, Alec, this isn't idle flirtation. I've been worried sick on and off ever since I last saw you. It's affecting me and my work. You've undermined me. You've made me question everything around me. I've never felt so insecure."

"I'm very sorry to have put you through all this, Grace, truly I am," said Tramane. "I know you don't believe me but I do care about you. I meet many people," he cleared his throat, "many women in my line of work, but you are special to me. I've been thinking about you a great deal."

"And now I suppose you expect me to sigh and say 'Oh Mr Tramane!' Please, Alec, there's no need to soften me up. I'm not an idiot. Just get what you want to say over with." Tramane looked a little despondent.

"OK then, if that's the way you feel, I'll tell you what I know. I *do* work for the British Secret Service. Dr Zuserain Nexus *is* under suspicion. He's pouring money into research, working with some of the most intelligent scientists in the world. The work they do is overtly as clean as a whistle – bona fide research, and that's what the majority of those working for him believe they are doing. But we know he's broken the rules occasionally. We've been monitoring his activity and the movement of ingredients and materials. The R&D Facility on Vancouver Island is developing something much more powerful than health supplements. He's had biochemists, pharmacologists and even a neuroscientist out there."

Grace listened, shaking her head.
"This is ridiculous! It all sounds completely over the top; completely double-oh-seven. These things don't happen in reality."

"Regrettably they do, Grace, and it's people like me who stop people like you from ever hearing about them."

"Well, why don't you just arrest Nexus, then?"

"We're waiting for the right time. We need a body of evidence."

"But what has all this got to do with Amity Action and me? We fund our own projects – they are nothing to do with Dr Nexus or Praefortica."

"But have you funded them really? Where does Amity Action get its funds? Donations? You and Jack were more than happy to try and charm some money out of me."

"We vet our donors carefully," replied Grace indignantly.

"Jack vets your donors," corrected Tramane.

"Jack is a sweet man," said Grace defensively. "I really can't believe he can be part of all this."

"According to Amity's annual reports, donations have substantially increased since Jack has been in post."

"He works very hard."

"At least two substantial donations within the last two years have come from companies that we have been able to link, one way or another, to Zuserain Nexus."

"But the projects we fund are about human relations and communication. Why would Nexus want to involve us in whatever he is doing?"

"That was our thinking. We were very curious about this link Nexus was forging with Amity Action. But think about it – you've met the man. What is he into?"

"I don't know – I suppose he had a slightly unhealthy interest in control."

"Exactly. We think he's been covertly testing something – we're not sure what – but I think I've seen what it can do. The researcher at Hardnox – Ellie Frumpp – she showed me the most peculiar transcripts from their study. They were perfectly normal, then suddenly changed, as if people were being influenced by something external."

"Are you saying Terry Spigot is working for Zuserain Nexus?"

"I'm not sure who at Hardnox it is yet, but I have my suspicions."

"But why would he do this – it would put his whole reputation on the line?"

"Well, there's always money straight up, of course. But perhaps this is more to do with enhancing than destroying a reputation."

"What do you mean?"

"What are academics judged by, Grace? What do they and their institutions really want?"

"Freedom to study?"

"Project grants? Publications? Kudos? Nexus can arrange *all* of that. Not just money, but the whole academic dream. It's his reward. People agree to work with him on his experiments. Jack ensures they get funding for a cover project. Not only that – Jack ensures they get to conferences and they get publications. It's part of the deal. I bet Hardnox is not the only place. I only wish I could have had more than a glance at your rejections. So many of your projects are about people, Grace, and getting people to do things or say things – to work better together. It would be the perfect testing ground for something that can change the way people think, or behave, or simply what they say."

"But why would Nexus want to do that?"

"Being able to control what people say could have a serious impact on, I don't know, delicate negotiations, politics?"

"Are you 100% certain about all this?"

"No," said Alec honestly, "but it's a theory that fits the facts and we are beginning to get some decent intelligence. I'm here to find out more. We believe Nexus will be coming here to the conference, perhaps to meet up with his beneficiaries."

"Well, he wasn't on my list," said Grace.

"Neither was I," replied Alec. They were silent for a minute.

"Look, Alec, I've heard what you have to say," said Grace. "I'll keep my eyes open, but you must understand that you are implicating an organisation within which I have worked very happily for two years. I have friends and loyalties here. I've known you for a much shorter period of time. Unless you are absolutely sure ... I'll have to think this through carefully." She got up. "Thank you for the drink."

"Well, I'll see you this evening then, at the introductory get-together."

"Yes, I daresay you will. I'm looking forward to your identity crisis."

Grace had booked herself a room at the hotel. She went there to contemplate, feeling slightly guilty that she had not mentioned the other six projects about which she and Jack had disagreed, and the strange file concerning the payments. The payments in particular would fit Alec's theory perfectly. But that was it, wasn't it? It was all just a theory.

Grace would have to perform again that evening: Jack would expect her to be gracious and charming. She had subconsciously picked the red dress for this purpose. As she looked at it lying on the bed, she wished she had brought another. All this trouble had started the last time she had worn it.

At half past six Grace was just putting on some make-up in the bathroom when she heard some raised voices coming from next door. She had made a mental note of the delegates on each side of her. She shared this particular wall with Dr Max Snoode of the University of Hardnox. The voices were muffled, and although her inclination was to try and ignore them, the link to Hardnox invited her curiosity. Her room had a little balcony, and the first thing she did was open the French windows. She could see from there that the curtains were drawn and the lights were on, but noises from the street made listening difficult. She went back to the bathroom, and tried the old trick of holding a glass up to the wall. A Canadian male was talking to an English man. He was saying,

"Well, you've got another publication now. We'll be asking you to contribute to the journal on the basis of what your group present at the conference. But it's going to have to be better than the abstract. It helps, you know, if we can accept the paper on merit."

"I didn't write the abstract, and in any case, it's a bit difficult when what you ask us to do produces unusable data."

"I thought the whole point was that there were other data you could draw upon for the study."

"There were, but I couldn't just remove the tapes – Irene would have noticed."

"I can't believe you didn't keep the data to yourself – you took an incredible risk!"

"I got it back in the end – the researcher had hardly looked at it. She was more concerned with the quantity she had to get through."

"Well, whatever – but for goodness sake, make the paper a good one." There was a pause. "What about your biochemist friend? I assume he got the revised formula to Praefortica by the deadline."

"Absolutely. Should do the trick."

"Well, that's a relief at least." The conversation ended. Grace opened her door very slightly – just as Jack D'Oretz left room 447. She took a step back, and as she did so a draft from her open windows caused the door to click shut. Grace walked unsteadily to the bed and sat down. She went through what she had heard. There was no mistaking the content and every bit of it reinforced Alec's hypothesis. Selected conference papers were to be put together in a journal special edition *after* the event. No decisions had been made on the content as yet, but from what she had heard, Jack was giving a slot away to Max Snoode based only on the abstract. Then there were the comments about the quality of the work!

It was ten to seven. Jack was no doubt in a hurry to get to the function. He was supposed to be welcoming everyone. Was there time to get to Alec? Did she have enough now to tell him what she knew? She could stop at Tramane's room on the way down. She made her way to the elevator and got out on the second floor. The corridor was empty. Just as she got to room 204, the door opened, and a woman's voice said,

"Goodbye, darling. I hope you enjoyed my little surprise."

Grace stopped in her tracks. This was possibly the last thing she expected. Alec had a woman in his room! Not only that, the shoulder strap of her very attractive dress had slipped sexily off her shoulder, and as she moved snakily into the corridor, she adjusted her zip. As she turned to face Grace, the two of them physically started. They looked at each other for what seemed like minutes, before Sorrel Surrido came forward, proffering her hand.

"Grace. How are you?"

"I, er, I'm fine. I don't remember seeing your name on my register." Grace looked at Sorrel's hand for a second, and shook it, beginning to wonder why she bothered with a delegate list at all.

"Oh, Jack said I could come – last minute thing. Were you, er, were you heading somewhere in particular?"

"I, er, no, er downstairs. I was just …"

"Come on then," said Sorrel, "let's go down together."

24

MS BLOFELD

I rene Spatchcock is sitting behind a desk in a large minimalist office, with a white cat on her lap. She is plotting to take over the world. Her shoes contain daggers. She has at her side a man named 'Mad' Max Snoode. He has bleached blonde hair, a European accent, and a penchant for explosives. Irene bears a grudge against the academic world. A year ago she had a grant proposal turned down, and two papers rejected. This has not happened before. Despite her celebrated beauty and her networking skills, a promotion is not forthcoming. She faces a full stop at Research Grade 2. She will reach sixty-five and be a bitter and twisted old woman still on the same pay scale. She will not let this happen. She has enlisted the notorious talents of 'Mad' Max Snoode to ensure her future in academe. She is plotting to deactivate her rival researchers in one fell swoop. She has planted a *monstrous stink bomb* in the Fraser River Hotel.

"How could the world think it would survive without me?" she questions Snoode. "My insights into worker satisfaction have revolutionised management practices." She gasps and a confused frown flickers across her face, distorting its perfect symmetry. "Why, just yesterday I heard that sales at Middle Waddling Mini Mart are at an all-time high." The cat leaves her lap with a soft thud and saunters over to Snoode, who is reclining on a large bean bag. He reaches forward to stroke the cat. She hisses, her tail thickens, her back arches. She is a bad tempered cat. Snoode recoils.

"The world cannot survive without you, Irene," he murmurs. "In approximately half an hour, they will be clamouring for your perfumed presence." He stands up and walks towards Irene. He massages her neck, and bends to kiss it, lingering by her right ear before he does so. The cat mews enviously. As Snoode lifts his head, a small red light appears on the top of Irene's desk.

"Camera number three!" she exclaims. "It appears that we have an intruder." She flicks a switch on her desk with her long, perfect fingernails. There is a whirring and a shifting of mahogany before a monitor is revealed. A man in a dinner jacket has entered through a window. He is creeping furtively along a corridor. Another ping of nail against plastic,

"Why, Dr Ross, we have been expecting you." She is speaking down a microphone, which has emerged like a fruiting body from her desk top. The man on the monitor stops and looks around. "Second on the left, Dr Ross, I'll have your drink ready for you. Oh, and Dr

Ross," she adds coolly, "leave your gun with Tarquin and Christian on the door."

James Ross has reached the door. He is met by two men. One of them has sticky tape around his glasses. Beside Ross he looks small and puny. He enjoys the power he has over this man. He opens his mouth with contempt.

"This is neither the time nor the place for a computer joke, Christian," preaches Irene down the microphone. Christian looks at the camera angrily, but closes his mouth, frisking Ross roughly before escorting him through the door.

Irene stands to greet James Ross. She is wearing white. Her shoulders are bare, her underwear is clean.

"Well, Dr Ross, what can I do for you?" She lifts her leg onto a chair, exposing a perfect thigh with the hint of a suspender at the top of it.

"I know what you're doing, Spatchcock. You'll never get away with it," says Ross, his pale grey-green eyes narrow and fierce.

"Oh, let's not talk shop, Dr Ross. Why don't we talk about *us*."

"I don't think we have anything to say on that subject, do you?"

'Mad' Max Snoode has moved away from the desk. He is jealous. He does not like James Ross.

"Do you want me to dispose of this troublesome agent, Irene? It would give me great pleasure, I assure you."

"Of course you may, Max darling, but first, I think we have a little unfinished business." She walks towards Ross seductively. "Can't I interest you in a little rest and relaxation before you go, James?"

"I would rather take up your friend's kind offer, Spatchcock." She is offended, and turns away from him. Her face hardens.

"In that case, Ross, I shall detain you no longer. Max," Irene snaps her fingers, "you may deal with him as you wish. But I want you to know, Dr Ross, that you have failed in your mission. The smell of academe will never be the same again. My dear friend Max has planted a *monstrous stink bomb* in the Fraser River Hotel. It is due to go off in exactly twenty minutes and fifteen seconds. Take him away, Max."

But as Max comes forward to grasp Ross by the arm, Ross turns and throws him over his shoulder. A fight ensues. The cat mews. Max has a hard stomach and does not feel Ross's punches, but Ross is deft and nimble. He throws Max against the wall. Irene looks on impassively. She knows there are two men on the door who will stop Ross, but in a moment he has leapt out of the window behind the desk, crashing through the glass. He falls an implausible distance into a tight cluster of four large, square parasols below. They cradle him, then part with kaleidoscopic synchrony, and he plops into a seat opposite a mature, but handsome woman in dark glasses. Ross adjusts his jacket, and with his perfect English accent says,

"My apologies, Madam." The woman remains cool and crosses her legs.

"I ordered a White Russian," she says in a gravelly voice.

"I thought you might prefer a Sloe Screw. Shall we say tonight, at 8.30?" The woman nods her assent, a mild smile plays upon her lips. Ross kisses her gloved hand before running out into the street to where his car is parked. Behind him is the clatter of Tarquin and Christian. They emerge from the hotel brandishing guns and run down the street after Ross. Failing to reach him, they flag down a car. The driver is evicted cruelly. He gets up from the road and shakes his fist.

Back at the hotel, Irene looks at her watch: ten minutes to go. She looks self-assured. Ross will never get to the hotel in time. Meanwhile, an exciting car chase is occurring: market stalls are being upset, people are running ahead of the screeching vehicles. There is a procession in one street: a marching band with sousaphones and trumpets; there are also majorettes. The road is blocked. Ross's car hurtles towards them. They are unaware of him. He is looking behind to see where his pursuers are. Suddenly he sees them: young, innocent girls, celebrating, happy. He has to do something. He swerves violently to the right down a side street; his car grazes the corner of a building. There are sparks.

He's temporarily lost his tail, but above him he hears the sinister whomp of helicopter blades. He must conceal himself. He finds a back street which leads to a fly-over by the waterfront; he takes the low road and pauses. He can still hear the whomp of the blades, and in the distance above the hubbub of the city, he can hear the screeching of a car in pursuit. He drives onto a new section of road, but discovers that this road is under construction. The road is being lifted up by a crane; higher and higher he rises! The man in the crane doesn't realise.

Ross stops the car. Below him, the diminished city carries on. For everyone in it, this is just an ordinary day. And then the helicopter is there in the sky, blades threatening, armaments glistening, a hovering bird of prey ready to strike. The man in the crane sees the situation. He is gesticulating wildly! The helicopter opens fire – rat-tat-tat-tat! Little pieces of new tarmac ping off the road. Ross revs the car. He has no choice. He drives, nought to a hundred in seven seconds. He launches the car off the section of road. For a few moments he flies in the sky. All is silent. Then CRUMP, he lands on the roof of a nearby hotel: it is the Fraser River Hotel. He has landed on the helipad.

Ross has four minutes. He leaps out of the car and finds a door. It leads to a narrow staircase. He flings himself down the stairs. The helicopter has landed behind him. He is being pursued by more gunmen. Far below in the foyer, Tarquin and Christian have arrived. They have rushed past reception. The young man on the desk did not have a chance to apprehend them. They still carry guns. Guests move nervously out of their way. Women scream.

Ross is being fired at by the helicopter crew. He slides down the banisters and reaches the fifteenth floor. The elevator has arrived. A respectable gentleman is emerging from it.

"Excuse me, sir," says Ross pushing past him, "I've got a *monstrous stink bomb* to defuse." The man shrugs and walks on. Ross is in the elevator. It's going down, but people press the buttons and it keeps stopping. Ross is frustrated. Sweat appears on his forehead. He gets out at level ten. He finds a service lift and gets in. He presses a knob and down he goes to the kitchen on the ground floor. He clambers out into the steam. The chef looks surprised. Ross stops to taste a risotto on a plate.

"A little truffle oil perhaps?" he says, cocking his eyebrow in amusement at the bewildered chef who cries,

"*Sacré bleu! Y*ou are right, *Monsieur!*"

The *monstrous stink bomb* is ticking. There are thirty seconds to go, tick tock tick tock. Tarquin and Christian look at their watches. They cannot see Ross. They know the device is due to go off. Christian looks uncertain, but just then they hear a crack and Ross bursts into the room where they are standing. He kicks the guns out of their hands, one foot to each gun.

"Where's the *monstrous stink bomb*, you bastards!" he shouts. "It's too late for you, as well, unless you tell me!" Christian still looks uncertain, the moisture on his forehead is unfurling the sticky tape on his glasses. Tarquin is plainly a maniac with no regard for his own life. He charges at Ross who swiftly out-manoeuvres him. He knocks himself unconscious against the wall. Christian shouts,

"It's in the conference hall, under the stage. Remember to tell the police I helped!"

But Ross isn't listening. He charges into the hall. The room is darkened. He can hear people snoring. A bearded man with an infra-red pointer is speaking quietly to his slide. It is a complicated slide with much writing. The writing is too small. Ross charges down the aisle. The chairperson awakes, and stands up. Just then the helicopter crew arrive. They are waving their guns around. The audience rustles in a wave before panic takes hold. People are rushing everywhere. The chairperson declares a recess, and that drinks will be served in the restaurant, but no-one is listening.

Ross reaches the stage. He crawls underneath it. The helicopter crew has arrived. They grab Ross's legs but he kicks himself free. They try to shoot at him but it is dark under the stage and they cannot see him. They crash in after him. Ross has reached the *monstrous stink bomb*. He must defuse it. The dial says ten seconds to go, nine ... One of the helicopter crew has caught up with him. They struggle ... eight seconds ... Ross disarms him. They are punching each other ... seven seconds ... one down, one to go. The second man is trying to strangle Ross. Ross frees himself and knocks the man out ... five seconds ...

Ross looks at the device. He recognises the system. He must cut the wires ... three seconds ... He feels in his pocket for his pliers ... two seconds ... where are his pliers? One second ... Damn, he left his mini tool kit in the car ... the timer clunks to zero ... surely he can get out of this?!

"Oh bugger," says Ross.

I was awoken by a loud noise outside. It sounded like a bomb going off, but in fact it was a car in need of a service. The room was filled with the stink of rotten vegetables, sautéd in engine oil; I had forgotten to top up the U-bend again. My dream was unsatisfactory, and I closed my eyes to try and put it right. The tool kit had surely just slipped out during the final struggle. James would have found it on the floor ...

... James finds the tool kit on the floor. One second to go. Clip clip. The *monstrous stink bomb* is defused. It reads zero zero zero. A bit contrived, but I was loath to let Irene win. She, Terry and Max had flown off to Vancouver the day before.

Well, fancy that. I had been dreaming about James Ross. I noted that I did not feature. This was no surprise, but I was disappointed that even my subconscious recognised my limitations.

25

ACADEMIC CHIT-CHAT

A gaggle of academics swarmed around the drinks table as Grace and Sorrel arrived in the Black Bear Suite. Armed with name badges, they were populating the air with introductions. Groups were forming of old friends, regulars on the conference circuit. Enthusiastic postgraduates were lining up behind eminent professors for earnest discussions of plans and professional positions.

But Grace was oblivious to this. Sorrel had excused herself, having fetched Grace a glass of wine and subsequently failing to engage her in any meaningful conversation. Grace stood with her drink at a dangerous angle, numb to the chatter around her, and the imminent staining of her dress. She may have been greeted by familiar faces; she may have responded appropriately. She would never remember. Sorrel

Surrido! In Alec's room! What did this mean? How could this possibly fit with anything? Was Alec working with Nexus? Quite apart from shattering the picture of orderly conspiracy that had been forming in her head, Grace was dumbstruck by Alec's betrayal. He had said she was special. She thought that he really did care for her! And now he was with Sorrel! She had called him 'darling'!

It was at least ten minutes before Grace became properly aware of where she was, and what she was supposed to be doing. She took a draught of wine to steady her nerves and began to register the people around her. She spotted Irene Spatchcock, smoothly moving from person to person, trying to expend energy only on those with money to spare. Her small black dress was both a help and a hindrance in this. Grace was relieved: at least she would not be the centre of attention today. Terry Spigot, his flies partially undone, was chatting with animation to the barman, who was trying to retain his unruffled demeanour, despite having to dodge Spigot's flailing arms. Grace thought she heard the word 'bollard'. Jack was circulating, but was looking anxious. In fact, he seemed to be avoiding her. There was no sign of Alec Tramane.

"Ms Lefavarie?" She was interrupted by Max Snoode, who was looking slick in a stylish dark green suit and a white, collarless shirt. "I believe you are responsible for organising this impressive event."

"That's right. I had the pleasure of sorting out the programme and managing the venue, yes."

"I'm so pleased you chose to accept our little offering." Grace said nothing. Snoode was a curious creature. He was not an imposing man, but he was attractive. His face, vaguely piratical, was decorated with a sheen of carefully groomed gnathic dark hair. His eyes were shrewd and penetrating, and he made no attempt to conceal his sexual interest in her.

"It's certainly a pleasure to be here in Vancouver," he continued. "Perhaps I can get you another drink?" Grace looked at her glass, which was empty.

"Yes, I think I need another drink," she said absently. He returned shortly.

"I expect this has all been a bit exhausting for you."

"You could say that," replied Grace. She smiled faintly, and found herself fascinated by a small piece of blue fluff caught in Snoode's designer stubble. He was pleased to see her looking at him so intently.

"I'd like to see a bit more of Vancouver. Perhaps you could show me around?"

"Pardon?" said Grace.

"Perhaps I could take you out after this – you could show me a few of the night spots?"

"Anything's possible," she said noncommittally. He nodded, satisfied.

"Later, then." He raised his glass and, noting the approach of Jack D'Oretz, moved on. Jack had finally come over to greet her. He did not look happy, and his words of praise lacked their usual sincerity.

"Great job, Grace – really very well done."

"Thanks," said Grace blankly. She could not think of anything else to say, and excused herself when they were joined by an effusive Spatchcock. It was all too much.

Jet lag or hunger got the better of the party by about nine, and delegates began to disappear in groups to find restaurants, or to have an early night. Tramane had not appeared all evening. Grace did not even try to guess where he might be – he was placeless; his affiliations a confused compass. There was now no one in whom she could confide. She had no idea of anything anymore. She left the scattered diehards in the Black Bear Suite, and went back to her room. Ordinarily she would have gone out with Jack and some of the other delegates. She knew that she should, but just could not face it. She sat on the bed defeated.

There was a tap on the window outside. Grace's first response was one of curiosity, but then she had a little pang of fear. She got up and peered through a crack in the curtain. It was Alec Tramane. She stared at him for a second as he motioned to her to open the window. She shook her head, and let the curtain fall back over the pane. He knocked again, and she could hear him saying urgently,

"Open the window, Grace!"

There was no avoiding him. She let him in. He stumbled heavily into the room, his usual poise awry. It was then that she noticed that his head had been bleeding.

"Are you OK?" she said, her anger temporarily side-tracked. This man was like a wretched roller coaster. He made her like him, then hate him, then like him, then hate him and now he was coming up trumps with an injury to make her feel guilty and sympathetic, just when she had consigned him to her love-rat bin. He looked at her, and held his finger to his lips.

"What?" she said, snappily. He steadied himself, then produced a little gadget from his pocket and plugged it into some earphones. He walked round the room – it seemed to be guiding him. Grace rolled her eyes and crossed her arms. But then he went to the telephone and displayed a small disc on the bottom. He set off again and found another behind a picture, and another in the lampshade. He came towards Grace, still indicating that she should remain quiet, and leaned forward. He put his mouth to her ear and said,

"We've got to get out of here."

"But your head ..."

"I'm OK," he whispered, "follow me."

"But ... but I'm angry with you!" said Grace quietly, "we need to talk." He looked at her quizzically,

"Not now," he said softly, and beckoned her to the balcony. Grace put on her coat, hung her bag across her shoulder and body and went out onto the balcony after Tramane.

"Can't we go out of the door and take the elevator like normal people?" said Grace worriedly, peering down at the road beneath.

"Not at the moment," whispered Alec. "We'll take the fire escape over there." He indicated a metal staircase, but in order to reach it they would have to move across two other balconies via a narrow ledge. Tramane withdrew what looked like a gun from his jacket, which caused Grace momentary alarm, but it turned out to be some gadget which fired a rope across to the fire escape with a soft clang. Alec fastened the near end of the rope to the balcony. Grace hitched up her dress indelicately, and moved gingerly after him. With the rope to hold onto, the clamber was not as bad as it first appeared.

Once on solid ground, they caught a cab to a restaurant in a quiet part of town, where Alec went to the washroom to tidy himself up. When they were finally sitting together in a booth, food and wine in front of them, Alec said,

"So why are you angry with me? I thought you weren't going to let me in."

"I wasn't going to," said Grace stubbornly. Although their flight had created a hiatus in her mood, it had re-emerged: big, ugly, green. In some ways the delay, combined with the irritation she was feeling towards Tramane's flamboyant 'Look, I'm a spy' routine, had increased her pent-up frustration with him.

"Whyever not?" he asked innocently.

"Because I'm completely confused again!" she retorted angrily.

"Women!" he exclaimed, shaking his head, amused.

"Don't you 'women' me!" she said furiously, attracting the attention of the couple on a table nearby. "This is all your fault! I, I came to tell you some things, and … well what was Sorrel Surrido doing in your room; why was she calling you 'darling,' for goodness sake?! After all that 'you're special to me' crap!"

"You saw her in my room?" Alec looked put out.

"Yes I did – and it was quite clear what she had been doing with you!" The lady on the next table looked at her partner sadly and shook her head. Alec lowered his voice.

"I was just doing my job, Grace. I had reason to believe she was an associate of Nexus. I had to see if I could find out more."

"Well, she does work for Nexus," said Grace, still angry. "I would have told you that had you asked me. And might I enquire as to how you went about finding out more, eh?"

"By talking to her."

"And the rest!"

"It's something I had to do, Grace. I did not enjoy it, and it meant nothing."

"You're a bloody tart, that's what you are! You'll do anything to get your precious information!"

"Shh, be quiet – people are looking."

Grace was accumulating sympathy from the women around her, and her plight resonated. Little arguments were spattering hotly here and there like mudpots in Yellowstone. Respectable suitors tried hopelessly to distance themselves from the fickleness of their sex apparently revealing itself in the nearby narrative.

"I don't care," replied Grace, although she dropped her voice, conscious of the ripples she was creating around her.

"I can understand how you feel, but really, it was nothing," he said earnestly.

"Nothing! Just like I mean nothing!"

"That's not true," replied Tramane, quietly.

"Pull the other one …"

"If you must know, I regret it. I regret it because I didn't get anything from her, and she set me up."

"Well, as I see your regret does not extend to even thinking for a minute about how I would feel about what you did with her, hooray for Sorrel!"

"She sent in two heavies to get rid of me," said Alec. Grace paused.

"What? They tried to *kill* you?" Her sarcasm disappeared.

"Well, at least put me out of action. It was quite a fight."

"What … what did you do?"

"I dealt with them."

"You mean you ...!" Grace was aghast. She had visions of a blood-spattered bedroom and grisly national headlines.

"I didn't kill them," said Tramane, laughing. "I dispatched them – bum's rush. I have a choice of martial arts at my disposal. Hadn't you guessed?"

Grace thought for a moment, the full weight of recent events dispelling her personal feelings. She took a deep breath.

"I saw Sorrel because I came to your room to tell you some things ..." she began. She told Alec about the file on Janus's computer disk, about the other abstracts, about her growing distrust of Jack's judgement, about the overheard conversation. "One thing's for sure," she concluded, "you can't stay at the Fraser River Hotel tonight."

"Maybe, but I'll certainly be attending the conference tomorrow."

"Surely not!"

"It's all part of the game, Grace. Don't worry, I can look after myself. To be perfectly honest, I'm not too happy about you staying at the Fraser River. We should find another hotel, and you should stay away from the conference."

"Don't be so hypocritical and don't be so silly," said Grace. "It will collapse in chaos tomorrow without me."

"Well, if you must be there, I'll be close by, even if you can't see me," said Alec. "We should go somewhere else tonight."

"OK then," said Grace, "if you insist. I do see some logic in it. I don't suppose I'll be missed now. It's quite late. We could go to my place."

"That would be too obvious." Grace thought for a moment.

"I know a small place we can stay in Kitsilano Beach. I'd better check they've got some space." When she returned from the telephone, they finished their dinner. It was raining. They arrived at the bed and breakfast just after eleven thirty. Grace had booked separate rooms.

26

GRAD. SCHOOL HUMOUR?

Grace arrived at the Fraser River Hotel next morning in time to hear Jack's address. She had organised the conference into a mixture of plenary sessions, parallel presentations and workshops. There were a few 'early bird' slots for those desperate enough to want to discuss work during breakfast. The main lecture theatre was full when she arrived so Grace sat near the back.

Jack welcomed the delegates and hoped that the conference would be stimulating and interesting. He talked a little about Amity Action and its objectives. After a while, Grace became aware that someone was looking at her and when she turned she saw Sorrel Surrido two or three rows behind her. Sorrel smiled, and Grace nodded. During the coffee break, Sorrel came over to her. She was wearing a jacket with rather prominent shoulder pads and a large brooch in the shape of a rose; its metallic brutality did not do justice to the real thing. The jacket emphasised the slimness of her waist and Grace was cross with herself as a sliver of envy ran through her.

"Good morning. How are you today?"

"Oh, I'm fine, thank you," replied Grace, shortly, suddenly conscious of the inappropriateness of her attire. Sorrel would surely remember the dress from the evening before.

"You looked a bit tired yesterday. Still, it was an exhausting day for all of us. All that travelling ..."

"And socialising ..."

"Yes – meeting new people – it takes it out of you. They seem to be a good crowd though. You've not seen Dr Ross from London, have you? He promised me one of his papers."

"I think I know who you mean, and no, I haven't seen him. Perhaps he's worn out as well. Excuse me, what's that?" Grace removed a piece of blue fluff from Sorrel's hair.

"Oh thank you," said Sorrel, "it must be from the towel in my room."

"Hope you enjoy the day," said Grace impassively. She made a mental note that blue fluff was plainly an indicator of a villain.

Grace knew the programme backwards, and had decided beforehand which sessions she would like to attend. She had made some adjustments in the light of recent events and had included the presentations from all the abstracts she had rejected, and Jack had wanted, including the Hardnox team offering. The latter delight, however, would not occur until the afternoon. In the meantime she was interested in a paper from a doctoral student from the States, which was being held in the Black Bear Suite, so she made her way there. She noticed Alec talking to a delegate from Spain. He caught her eye and smiled.

There were only about fifteen people in the room. A doctoral presentation was obviously viewed as unimportant by the majority of the delegates. The person giving the paper, a nervous-looking young woman, was sitting on the edge of her seat next to the professor chairing the session. Grace felt for the speaker. It might well be her first paper at an international conference – a completely nerve-wracking experience. She would have a dry mouth now, and Grace could see her taking deep breaths in an attempt to remain calm. Grace thought back to her own initiation into this strange world. At least this person did not have Ronald Tweezer in the chair. Her pensée was interrupted by an overpowering smell, and she turned to see Professor Terry Spigot taking the seat next to her. He peered conspicuously at her breasts, but it transpired he was simply trying to read her name badge.

"Ah, if it isn't Miss Grace Lefavarie. So pleased to meet you – Terry Spigot, University of Hardnox. So glad we have a special relationship with Amity, absolutely marvellous. This should be a bit of a laugh," he nodded towards the podium.

"I'm sure it will be very informative."

"Doctoral students, eh? Wouldn't have got a trip to Vancouver in my day. Still, mustn't knock the girl before I've heard her …"

"No, indeed," replied Grace. She restrained her impulse to 'educate' Spigot on his description of the woman, conscious that the chairperson was trying to get people's attention.

"Looks damn cocky though, doesn't she?"

"Actually she looks very nervous."

"It's all a front – she's still at the age where she thinks she can change the world. She'll grow out of that, eh?"

"Shh," said Grace. She was becoming aware that Spigot's ruminations were more and more public as the murmuring around them died down. The chairperson was peering towards them with mild disapproval.

"If we could have some quiet now, please. I would like to stick to the timetable. I'm very pleased to introduce Deanna Drumlin from Bright Canyon University. She will be talking to us today about 'The role of team-based production in workplace satisfaction,' which forms the basis of her doctoral thesis. Deanna." The woman got to her feet slowly and walked to the lectern. She cleared her throat.

"I would like to talk to you today about, er, team-based production and its role in er workplace satisfaction ..." It was always difficult to know whether the chairperson would speak your title, and not easy to adapt a talk on the hoof. The woman paused and looked nervously at the professor, conscious that she had just repeated what he had said. He smiled encouragingly.

"We already know that," whispered Spigot into Grace's ear, chuckling. Grace ignored him.

"I thought I would begin by telling you a little about the study site ..."

"How original," said Spigot.

If Grace had thought she could move without upsetting the woman presenting, she would have done.

As it was, she felt compelled to stay put. The professor glanced over in her direction again.

"Shhh," said Grace, firmly. The woman presenting spoke clearly but monotonously. She was obviously reading from a script, but what she was saying was sensible and interesting. She had some slides which described everything effectively, and as she came to the results section she was gaining in confidence and beginning to move her hands about a little, deviating slightly from her notes and lifting her head to view the audience. She was evidently committed to the study. As she completed the results, Terry Spigot put up his hand. The chairperson looked slightly annoyed, and indicated with his expression that questions ought to wait until the end of the session, but Spigot was too obtuse and started wiggling his fingers.

"Excuse me," he said at last. The woman was taken aback and stopped abruptly.

"If we could wait until the end before we have questions ..." said the professor.

"It won't take a moment," said Terry. "I was merely wondering whether the young lady had considered bolstering the qualitative element to her work. She has probably heard of the 15th century Italian poet and clockmaker, Virago Innocenti? He believed that to move from a mere 'dream' to a better 'reality', one must change the dream to reality by climbing the 'gripless face'. I have discussed his ideas in the context of phenomenology in Spigot, 1995. To climb the face one must have a mutual understanding of the 'better place' and here, communication and respect for all concerned with the process are obviously paramount. Rather than opting for traditional notions of outcome, i.e.

satisfaction, would it not be more revealing to examine process-oriented concepts encapsulating organisational change – ideally those which could be elicited using the Spigot Sympathetic Interrogation Technique? I'd be very happy to supply the original paper describing this approach, which was published in 1991, to much acclaim I might say, in the *Quarterly Qualitative Methodological Review.*"

"I, er ..." the woman did not know how to handle the question. You could see her face transform itself from one of confidence when she had been speaking, to confusion at being interrupted, to blankness at her lack of understanding of Spigot's question, to blind panic as silence fell upon the room and all eyes turned to her for a response. "I, er ..." she repeated. The chairperson, noting her discomfort, said,

"I think we should let Deanna finish her presentation first, then perhaps we can discuss some of these issues. Deanna, do continue."

"I, er," stuttered the woman. She turned to look at her notes but her increase in confidence prior to interruption had meant that she had strayed from them, and she did not know where she was.

"You were concluding the results and moving onto the discussion," said the professor, beginning to lose patience.

"I, er ..." the woman continued to flounder. She dropped her notes on the floor, and had to bend down to pick them up, trying desperately to identify where exactly she was. Standing up, she began to regain composure. After about thirty seconds of silence, which felt like a millennium, she began again, reading from the script.

"My results indicate an association between team-based production methods and increased satisfaction ..." But somehow the interest she had raised had evaporated. Perhaps it was the prospect of having to discuss Spigot's absurd comment at the end of the presentation, but she spoke quickly and shakily. Before she was finished the professor interrupted her with,

"One minute to go," at which point, Ms Drumlin looked as if she was going to cry. Instead of completing her discussion, she moved onto the conclusions and finished not with a bang but a whimper. Grace imagined the summarising quotation she would have chosen – the finale, and felt deeply sorry for her.

"Well, that was a bit of a rush," whispered Spigot, picking his nose. Grace did not respond.

"We have a minute only for questions," said the chairperson rather crossly. Spigot raised his hand. The professor kindly ignored him, in preference to another person who, no doubt taking pity, asked a simple methodological question that Ms Drumlin answered quietly, but without difficulty.

"What a nerve," protested Spigot to Grace. As Deanna Drumlin stood down, it was obvious that she was upset with her performance. As the next speaker stood up, Spigot crept along the aisle and sat behind her. As the second speaker started, he began to whisper to the woman. She was evidently torn between trying to defend her work against Spigot's incomprehensible criticism and not wishing to upset the chairperson who looked angrily at them. Every time she tried to ignore Spigot or put him off by saying,

"I'll speak to you afterwards," he would continue to talk. The man who was speaking was being distracted, and kept looking at the chairperson for help. Eventually Ms Drumlin got up and walked quickly out of the room, pulling her hair across her face, and snuffling slightly. Although she must have felt that the whole world was looking at her, the majority did not notice. Grace felt compelled to leave quietly after her, and found her in the washroom weeping. When Grace came in, she darted into one of the cubicles.

"It's all right," said Grace. "Listen, I know you're crying, I've come to provide you with a shoulder." Deanna Drumlin emerged, and burst into a new frenzy of tears. Between each gasp, Grace learnt how she had spent weeks writing the presentation, how she had timed it to perfection, how she knew it was a good study, how important it was for her to make a good impression and what was the Spigot Sympathetic Interrogation Technique anyway? When she had stopped, Grace told Deanna about her London presentation, and between occasional remnant sobs, she began to smile at the story.

"Believe me," said Grace, "you did a very good job. Most of the people in the room would have been on your side. It was a stupid, unnecessary interruption and very few people were looking at you when you left the room." Thus comforted, Deanna gratefully accompanied Grace in search of a cup of tea. As they went into the room where drinks were being served, a man came up to Deanna and said that he thought that her study was very good. They struck up a conversation and Grace left them chatting.

"And I thought espionage was a bit rough." Alec appeared behind her.

"Spigot is a complete idiot!" exclaimed Grace in exasperation, and then more calmly, "shouldn't you be out of sight?"

"We're pretty well concealed here, I think." He led her under some stairs.

"Have you learnt anything?" asked Grace.

"Only that I'm happy with my vocation," joked Tramane. "Nexus is due in town this afternoon. One of our operatives intercepted a fax."

"You don't think he's planning anything for the conference?" queried Grace anxiously.

"I doubt it. We think he's just coming to meet D'Oretz and some of the people who have been working for him through Amity Action. Anyway, I need to be in the right place when he appears."

"Your best bet is probably to shadow Max Snoode."

"I daresay you are right. I'll see you later."

The next session Grace wished to attend was a workshop in one of the small seminar rooms. Unfortunately she found Snoode lurking in the corridor outside.

"I missed you last night," he said, seedily. "Did you get my note?"

"No."

"I slipped it under the door."

"It must have gone under the carpet."

"Very *Tess of the D'Urbervilles.*"

"I'm sorry, I didn't see it."

"Well, I was merely following up on your promise of a date. What about tonight?"

"I'm afraid I'm too busy – it's the conference dinner."

"Tomorrow then. I can promise you an amusing time." He lowered his voice. "I'm no Angel."

"I'm sorry, Dr Snoode, I really can't spare the time." He was remarkably immune to the usual hints, but eventually settled for a 'rain check'. The workshop consisted of a debate about the relative merits of qualitative and quantitative data in research studies, and it proved to be lively, and, with the odd exception, civilised.

During the buffet lunch, Grace felt obliged to chat to a few delegates, but she kept scanning the room for Nexus.

"Put the PhD girl back in her place." Terry Spigot's aftershave mingled unpleasantly with the savoury odours of lunch and Grace turned to find the man with a plate piled obscenely high with food in one hand and a glass of orange juice held precariously in the other. He flapped around for a few seconds looking for somewhere to put his drink before commencing a tirade about what he had said to Deanna Drumlin before she had made her escape. As he said the word 'SpIT,' a small chunk of pastry from a recently demolished mushroom vol-au-vent was propelled from his mouth. Its trajectory was sufficiently close to her own plate for Grace to feel she no longer wanted her lunch. Luckily, she was saved from further flying fodder by Sorrel Surrido who interrupted them politely, saying she was keen to speak with Terry and Irene Spatchcock about the Spigot method. Terry's eyes lit up with the prospect of further SpITting and guided Sorrel to the coffee where Irene was conversing earnestly with a representative of a US funding board. Grace saw Irene shake Sorrel by the hand and the three of them headed for some chairs in the corner of the room.

Terry, Irene and Max were due to give their presentation just after lunch. Grace was in the mood to heckle, but knew she would have to control herself. She entered the room just as people were settling down and the chairperson rose to her feet.

"I'm very pleased to introduce a paper by Professor Terry Spigot and Drs Irene Spatchcock, Max Snoode and Ellinora Frumpp from the University of Hardnox in the UK. I believe Professor Spigot and Dr Spatchcock are doing the honours today." Terry stood up and, peering over his small spectacles, began his talk with the aid of an OHP slide of a clockface.

"I am sure you are all familiar with the works of the 15th century Italian poet and clockmaker, Virago Innocenti. He said: 'We are two realms: one is a limp and unsprung coil; it is oblivion! To reach the second we must climb, insensible, the gripless face, through mainspring, verge and foliot. With good grace, a mechanism and a bell, we make dream reality.'" He paused for dramatic effect. "Innocenti encapsulates the philosophy of the Spigot method: the changing of dream to reality, the climbing of the 'gripless face'." He paused again.

"Actually, I'm not quite sure how Innocenti relates to SpIT but he sounds very grand and exotic, doesn't he?" There were a few muffled laughs. "To continue! Through my novel technique (actually it's not *that* novel if I'm honest, more second hand) we are able to tap into people's experiences and opinions unhampered by reticence." He looked slightly cross as someone raised their hand to ask a question and said, "Might I request that we save comments and questions to the end?"

The chairperson caught the eye of the questioner and nodded,

"Perhaps we could take this, if it is just a point of clarification?" Grace turned round to see who was asking the question: it was Sorrel.

"You said the technique was not novel, Professor Spigot, and yet in the original paper published in 1991, in the *Quarterly Qualitative Methodological Review*, you claimed the work was novel. Can I therefore ask how you first came up with the idea of SpIT?"

"Well, I pinched it, of course," he said without hesitation. "It's all a bit vague now, but there was some doctoral student – I was his external examiner; anyway, bloody good idea – so I failed him and pinched it." There was a distinct murmur among the audience. Grace looked at Spigot, who seemed surprised at what he had said, but showed no sign of retracting his confession. Irene Spatchcock looked shocked. The chairperson said,

"Well, I think maybe this is something we could discuss later, but Professor Spigot, for now, perhaps you should continue with your paper?"

"Yes, of course," he said, a little confused, "of course. Well we used the method to elicit views on work satisfaction in a variety of settings. Well I say 'we' but in fact the focus groups were conducted by Irene here and my colleague Max Snoode. I'm not much of a researcher myself, you see, I just like to feel important. Actually what I really want is a parking space with a retractable bollard ..."

Irene stood up hurriedly and said,

"Well thank you Terry, over to me I think." She looked at her notes and read, "Sympathy begins at home. The Hardnox research team believes in the values knitted into the Spigot Sympathetic Interrogation Technique, and that is why the work we undertake is not only successfully co-operative, but a genuine pleasure. For us, the word 'sympathy' is not lip service, but a true reflection of the ideals we promote and the methods we use ourselves." She stopped, a slightly sceptical look on her face, before laughing a little nervously, "Actually that's not strictly true – I'm a hopelessly unsympathetic person!" There was another murmur in the audience and the chairperson looked rather irritated. "Um," said Irene, collecting her thoughts, "as Terry has indicated, Max Snoode and myself conducted thirty focus groups with staff based on a maximum variation sample of workplaces – size, public, private etc.. As you can see from this slide," Grace noted a typo, "following detailed thematic analysis, a number of specific areas have emerged which we have now incorporated into our survey instrument …" She paused again and laughed, "Well again – that's not true either because our researcher – who's a bit of a nitty-gritty fuss-pot – took such a long time over the qualitative stuff, she's not quite finished the details yet. We didn't give her much time, to be honest. I guess I should just say that this is fairly broad brush stuff with some probable rather than definitive items for inclusion in the questionnaire at present."

She then continued in a superficial way to talk through her list of 'broad brush' themes and 'probable items'. She ended with,

"I suppose it was a little sneaky of me to imply that we had the finished product in our abstract – but then we all know abstracts don't get accepted without results!" The chairperson was understandably disinclined to allow the Hardnox team any questions and she speedily moved on to the next presentation which went ahead with no apparent anomalies. Irene and Terry left the room somewhat sheepishly, but Grace saw them both drinking tea a little later, laughing with delegates. Spigot was gorging himself on chocolate cake and she could hear him saying,

"Did you see Irene's face? Well of course – we did it all as a bit of a dare! We've not lost our grad. school humour!"

Grace found Tramane under the stairs.

"Did you see the Hardnox presentation?" she asked.

"Yes, I did. In any other circumstances I would have found the whole thing most amusing. What is their take on it?"

"They are passing it off as a 'youthful prank'."

"It reminded me of Ellie Frumpp's transcripts," said Tramane. "People being very direct."

"It sounded to me as if they were just telling the truth."

"I think this is Nexus at work."

"Actually, they were with Sorrel Surrido just before the talk. Maybe she gave them something."

"Hmmm. Quite possible." Alec thought for a moment. "You don't happen to be recording the presentations, do you?"

"Yes, we are – follow me," said Grace. They went into the recording room, which stood between the two main conference rooms. The tape recorders were still running, so Grace stopped the one from her session, rewound it and played it back for a few seconds. Alec raised his eyebrows.

"We'll need to take this tape."

"Yes, of course," said Grace. She was just putting it into her pocket when the door opened behind them. The reflex reaction of both Grace and Alec was to dash for the door on the other side of the room, which exited onto the mezzanine level overlooking the foyer. They left the hotel and went to a small coffee shop nearby to talk. Alec had a small tape recorder, and they listened to the whole presentation again.

"Ironic really," said Alec, "researchers being experimented on. Look, I don't think you should go back to the conference, Grace. This is all getting a little disturbing."

"But it's the conference dinner tonight. I can't miss that. I'm supposed to be hosting our guest speaker. Talking of whom, look at the time. I've got to go, Alec."

27

BIT OF A BALLS-UP

Jack had said that he would meet Grace in her room at seven fifteen. She had not been up there all day, but needed to change. Her red dress was looking a little droopy. She replaced it with a long blue one, and a black decorative jacket. She found the note which Max had put under her door. It read: 'Dropped round to follow up on our little conversation. Disappointed but not despondent. Another time perhaps.' She screwed it up and threw it in the bin. Jack arrived promptly, and asked how her day had gone. He looked ill at ease. Nothing out of the ordinary nowadays, reflected Grace – she was getting used to Jack's twitchiness.

"Fine," she replied.

"Did you notice anything abnormal? I believe there was some talk about one of the presentations."

"I heard it was all a joke," she said simply. Jack seemed pleased with her response.

"We have a change of guest speaker," he said. "I tried to find you to tell you, but you were nowhere to be seen." He looked at her closely.

"Is everything all right, Grace?"

"Of course it is. I'm so sorry you've had this last minute hassle. I should have been here to sort it out for you."

"It's not a problem, really. I've got a replacement."

"Who?" asked Grace.

"Dr Zuserain Nexus. You know, the chap from Praefortica. He was visiting Vancouver today anyway, and what with our new arrangement with his company, he seemed the perfect person. I think it's very important to have someone actually working in business."

"I, er, yes of course. How fortunate, er, that he should be here."

"He speaks very highly of you. He was most impressed when you met."

"I got the feeling he didn't like functions," said Grace.

"I heard about his exclusive dinner with you," smiled Jack. "He wanted to get to know you personally. He's very particular about who works closely with him."

"I thought perhaps he was some sort of recluse."

"It's just his way. I went through the same rigmarole. He's not averse to a crowd, I can assure you."

The conference dinner was to be held in the ballroom at the hotel: a remarkable affair adjacent to the bar, with long mirrored walls and three chandeliers. The room had been laid out beautifully with small flower arrangements on each table. Delegates had been left to sort themselves out into a seating arrangement and it was interesting to see the natural groupings which had formed. The few remaining unallied people had to slot in where there were spaces, to the slight disapprobation of established cliques and clans.

Jack and Grace waited at main reception for Nexus. He arrived in a black, chauffeur-driven sedan, Jack obsequiously emerging from the hotel to open the door. Nexus was wearing his dinner jacket. His moustache and beard were neatly trimmed; his face was calm and controlled. He greeted Grace with the expected courtesy, glancing only briefly and efficiently into her eyes, before allowing Jack to escort him down the steps to the ballroom.

The conference dinner had been planned carefully. Grace had negotiated a balance between quality and price with the hotel and the food and wine were plentiful. By the time Jack stood up, at the top table, to introduce the speaker, the atmosphere was jovial and welcoming. It would be easy to please the crowd tonight. Grace noticed that Nexus had abstained from drinking. He probably enjoyed having everyone around him at a lesser level of consciousness. Jack was a little overboard in his introduction. There was something rather nauseating in his deference to Nexus. She was not sure why Jack was like that – was it respect, or fear?

"Ladies and gentlemen," began Jack, "as you know, we have a tradition at the IWaPM of inviting pioneers of workforce initiatives to come and tell us a few of their secrets." There was a ripple of amusement. "Tonight, it gives me immense pleasure to introduce to you a truly awesome businessman; an entrepreneur who, whilst modest and private about his involvement, is, in fact, the man behind the success of Praefortica, Dr Zuserain

Nexus. Dr Nexus, as some of you will know, has, for the last year or so, been working in close collaboration with Amity Action, and from next year will honour us by allowing Amity to co-ordinate the training for his organisation. Prior to Praefortica, Dr Nexus ran a string of small food technology companies in a number of countries in the Asia-Pacific region. For the last five years, he has flattered us by setting up his main business here in Canada. Praefortica has been quoted in the press as being 'in the top ten companies worldwide with the most promise' last year, and their work, currently being undertaken in the field of supplements and wellbeing, has been heralded as some of the most innovative and exciting seen in years. Dr Nexus."

Zuserain Nexus got to his feet with casual elegance.

"Ladies and gentlemen. Thank you for your kind welcome, and thank you, Jack, for a most flattering introduction. As a modern businessman, it is my philosophy never to make anyone do what they do not want to do. The art of running a business, for me at least, is to ensure that I have a happy, productive workforce. There are different ways of making a workforce productive. Some businesses, and I might say, the old-fashioned ones, tend towards a regime of confrontation and punishment. Myself, I prefer bribery."
A murmur of laughter.

"Of course, bribery is an offence, so I should really explain my methods before Jack notifies the local police force." More laughter. "Maybe 'conditioning' is a better word, or 'control'. You have all heard of Mr Pavlov's dogs?" A few quizzical looks, a little nervous shuffling. "I jest," added Nexus. A collective feeling of relief, muffled tittering. "If only it were that easy. A productive workforce will only exist where there is trust, honour and sincerity. The term 'control' is to us pejorative: it is negative, it feels oppressive; it is the opposite of freedom. And yet if we can institute the necessary controls to ensure a healthy business, whilst retaining the loyalty and happiness of our employees, we have the perfect scenario: a recipe for the flexibility and agility required to respond to the assault course that is the business world today.

"How can we do this? By involving the workforce in the design and implementation of our control mechanisms; by making them part of the whole business process; by listening to them, negotiating and compromising; above all, by providing them with an incentive to work well.

"I like the methods endorsed by Amity Action, which has organised this conference. The courses that they have helped us to set up at Praefortica have increased our output by 15% in the last year. My employees are instructed in how to communicate effectively, in how to assert themselves, in how to value, and feel confident enough to contribute, their own brilliant ideas to enhance the business (and believe me, they are quite astonishingly brilliant). We have a relationship based on symbiosis – mutualism: whilst the company 'controls' its employees," Nexus motioned the inverted commas with his fingers, "the employees most certainly control the company. Our workforce shares the company's successes and failures. When we succeed, they are motivated by their rewards: bonuses, pay rises. When we fail, they are motivated by their genuine desire to see the company do better, and, of course, the lack of a bonus or a pay rise." Laughter.

"Ownership and shared responsibility are the keys. This conference gives us all the opportunity to learn from the successes and failures of our attempts to nurture and maintain good workplace practices. I would like to end by proposing a toast to all of you, who are developing better and better ways for us to work together for economic prosperity. To all of you!"

The delegates raised champagne flutes, which been surreptitiously distributed during the speech. Jack got up and thanked Dr Nexus, and the dinner resumed as if a restart button had been pressed, with clinking, scraping and conversation. From where Grace sat, further down the table, she observed Jack and Nexus chatting quite amicably, when suddenly she noticed the former blanch in response to something that Nexus had said. Jack stopped talking and looked distraught. Nexus said something else to him, and dabbed his serviette genteelly to his lips. Jack looked helpless, and although obviously conscious of his public situation, appeared to be pleading. At this point, Grace was distracted by the entrance of Alec Tramane, who came into the room and settled himself at one of the tables. Looking back up her own table, she could tell that Nexus had also seen him. He frowned, and leant over to Jack, nodding in Grace's direction. Jack looked upset, and came over to her.

"Grace," he said, attempting to smile. "Dr Nexus has to go now. I wonder if you would be so good as to escort him to the door; sort out his coat, and car."

"OK," replied Grace, "I hope he's had a good evening."

"Oh, yes, very pleasant," said Jack. Grace got up. He added, "I'm sorry, Grace ..."

"Sorry for what?"

"Er, I'm sorry to, er, trouble you with this."

"It's not a problem, Jack, honestly. I'll be back in a minute."

"Er, yes," said Jack, returning quickly to his seat. Grace felt a pang of anxiety at the prospect of being alone with Nexus again, made worse by Jack's evident unease. She couldn't help thinking that something was afoot. She went to Dr Nexus. Among the delegates, Grace could see Alec Tramane watching her acutely. He was looking very concerned.

"My dear Grace," said Nexus, standing up, "it is so kind of you to see me off the premises. I have told Jack that I am more than able to manage this on my own, but he insists."

"Really, it's no trouble," said Grace. Nexus looked relaxed, and emanated the generosity of spirit she had felt when he showed her round the factory. It made her feel a little better. He offered her his arm, which she took with a smile, and he led her out of the room. As she passed through the door, Grace glanced at Alec, and she was surprised to see that he had stood up with a look of alarm on his face. She vaguely noted that he looked hemmed in; it was almost as if the tables had re-jigged themselves magically to block him.

Grace and Nexus walked up the stairs to the main reception area.

"I'll get your car to come round to the front," she said.

"You are very kind, Grace," replied Nexus, "but I can see that my car is already at the door. I'll just need my coat." He smiled warmly.

"Oh, yes! I'll just get it then. Were you given a tab?" Nexus handed over the small, red, plastic disc, which

Grace took to the cloakroom: the number on it was 13. She was handed a heavy, woollen overcoat, which she took back to reception. Nexus was no longer there. Thinking that he had probably gone out to the car, she left the foyer and saw his large black sedan parked on the right. Nexus was chatting to the chauffeur. He turned and waved at her. She brought the coat down the steps to him.

"Thank you," he said. "And now, I'm afraid I must insist that you accompany me."

"I beg your pardon?" said Grace, half-smiling.

"Get in the car, Miss Lefavarie."

"I'm afraid I'm expected back in the hotel," said Grace, backing away. But the chauffeur was behind her and took her arms.

"Will you please let go. What is all this about?"

"I have reason to believe that you have been keeping poor company," said Nexus, "and I suspect that he has been leading you astray."

Before she could do anything else, Grace heard a sharp hiss and felt a light mist on her face. Bemused, she vaguely acknowledged that Nexus was holding a small canister, which he had clearly discharged. Her last memories were of the sign saying 'Fraser River Hotel,' which blurred and exploded into a thousand particles of light in her mind.

28

THE FIENDISH PLAN

Grace opened her eyes. She was in a room. It was dark, but the glow from under the door produced a modicum of illumination: a slice of light that dusted the floor tentatively. She could make out various horizontals, verticals and the odd curve – a black and white Kandinsky. Gradually, the shapes took on meaning. She could see a chair, a desk. She felt the bed beneath her, the softness of the mattress, the freshness of the linen. Grace put her hand to her head, then propped herself up. She had a slight headache. What on earth had happened? Where was she?

Grace registered what looked like a lamp on a bedside table next to her. Feeling for the switch, she turned it on. The brightness paralysed her for a moment, and she shut her eyes, opening them intermittently until she had accustomed herself to the new light level. The room was comfortable and well furnished. It was prettily decorated – feminine.

She had been lying on a single bed with a floral duvet, still wearing her blue dress and black jacket. The carpet was soft and pink; curtains matched the bed cover. A dressing table stood on the other side of the room, and she rose to her feet slowly and looked at herself in the mirror. She didn't look too bad. Her make-up was a bit smudged, and it had crept into the usually invisible lines on her face, making her look older. She noticed the reflection of a door in the corner of the room and turning to investigate, found an en suite bathroom.

Five minutes later, Grace was feeling more normal, but now she was properly awake, she felt increasingly panicky. What had happened? How had she got there? She had to find out where she was and what was going on. A set of curtains in the room concealed a pair of shutters, which explained the darkness. Struggling briefly with the latch, she opened them and immediately recognised Vancouver Island. 'Nexus!' she thought to herself and some vague memory from the conference dinner infiltrated her brain. She had taken him his coat and then? It was a blank. This must be Praefortica's set-up near Chesterman Beach! The place Alec had come to the year before. Grace stared at the inhospitable, grey sea for a moment; its familiarity brought no comfort.

The bedroom door was unlocked. There seemed no point in trying to conceal herself as the door, presumably, had been left open on purpose. No doubt she would be where Zuserain Nexus wanted her in a matter of minutes. Outside the bedroom was a landing, which looked down into a wooden floored hallway. The place had the look and feel of an immense log cabin.

There was little sign of habitation on this floor, so Grace made her way downstairs via a grandiose staircase.

Now she could hear voices. Guided by the sound, she came to a door, where she listened briefly, and taking a deep breath, knocked loudly. There was a pause from inside the room. Uninvited, she opened the door. Nexus was sitting on a large leather sofa having a tête à tête with Sorrel Surrido. The latter moved away from Nexus as Grace came in.

"Forgive the intrusion," said Grace, "but I'm looking for an explanation."

"Ah, my dear Grace," said Nexus, rising to greet her. "Welcome to my little hideaway. How good of you to join us. Congratulations on a most fruitful conference. You will be pleased to know that the last day was a great success, despite your absence. How are you feeling after all your hard work?"

"Confused," she replied. "What am I doing here?"

"Let me pour you a coffee. I know how fond you are of it – and you will find this an excellent brew." As he did so, Grace looked at Sorrel, who nodded to her coldly.

"You know my colleague, Sorrel Surrido, of course," said Nexus, having observed their chilly pleasantry. "She has been instrumental in Praefortica's recent successes."

"I can imagine," replied Grace, sarcastically, accepting the cup of coffee which Nexus brought to her. "It's not got anything in it, I hope?"

"Of course not. I do apologise for whisking you away from the climax of your event, but I assure you, no harm has come to you. Ah, and here is your friend Jack D'Oretz." Grace looked up in surprise as Jack came into the room. He looked at her briefly, then averted his eyes. Turning to Nexus he said,

"It's all arranged. The presidential press conference is the day after tomorrow in Washington. All the major papers will be there. The helicopter will take Sorrel back to Vancouver this evening. Her flight to DC is booked."

"Jack?" queried Grace, but he did not reply.

"You deserve an explanation, my dear Grace," said Nexus. "Our mutual friend Jack has been helping me out." He paused and nodded at D'Oretz. "We have been making such progress! For the last three years I have been funding research into the development of what I would like to call my cure for hypocrisy and corruption: 'Tell It How It Is'. Humourists might call it 'TIHII', and it has certainly furnished me with much amusement. Most of my work has been quite above board, although regrettably the later trials have required a small bending of the rules. Luckily Jack has been most successful in aiding me with these by providing a few far-sighted scientists not averse to a little subterfuge for remarkably little in the way of reward. Such vanity! I used to think money could buy anything. But, it appears in the intellectual world of academic research, grants, conference papers and publications are the main currency."

"I don't understand," said Grace, frowning.

"We've been testing TIHII on people involved with some of your projects, Grace," said Nexus, "for which I thank you. The early trials involved spicing up refreshments; more recently we have developed a more effective formula that can be delivered by aerosol. It is a harmless substance, but creates a brief window in which

305

recipients recognise and retract dishonest statements as they flow from the mouth."

"Our projects! But that's awful! Jack?" Again she turned to D'Oretz, whose eyes were cast to the ground.

"Of course, you must be aware of our latest experiment, which went without a flaw. Our new dispensing device, so cunningly disguised as a very attractive feminine accessory, worked very successfully – what a classic! A squirting rose! And as a bonus we revealed a truth or two to the world at large about Professor Terrence Spigot and his colleague, although I doubt the consequences will amount to much. It will be different, however, when we execute our plan the day after tomorrow. President Fairgood will be given the gift of honesty for a few important moments, and I think he will tell us all enough to ensure calls for his impeachment and replacement. It is my desire to lead the most powerful country on Earth, my dear Grace, and I now have the ability to remove anyone who stands in my way."

"You want to be President of the United States!"

"I have brave and admirable plans for a society led by an honest and ethical man."

"You consider yourself honest and ethical?" exclaimed Grace. "Do you think you would stand up to scrutiny yourself, under the influence of your so-called 'cure' for even a moment?!"

"I will never have the pleasure. Nor should I have to. My objectives are pure, noble and right; the end justifies the means. I am on a stratum above the common human. I am the composer and the conductor – *they* are my instruments – my orchestra. Together we will play the most harmonious symphony of life." Nexus had become uncharacteristically animated and he paused to take a deep breath before continuing calmly. "It is unfortunate that you acquired the record of our final test. I would be grateful for the tape, Grace."

"What tape?"

"Please don't try my patience. You must surely know by now that I cannot tolerate deceit." Grace thought for a second. Was there any point continuing with her charade?

"I don't have it," she said decisively.

"Then I suspect our friend Mr Alec Tramane has?" Grace said nothing. "It is of little importance," continued Nexus. "No doubt he will pay us a visit before too long, and we can determine its whereabouts from him then. It is a great pity that you became entangled with that tiresome agent. But perhaps I will be lenient with you. You have many talents. Not least a great beauty and a charming way with people. You could be most useful to me if you chose to join my election campaign. The rewards would be great, both in terms of finance and power. And you would be joining a worthy venture." Grace shook her head with incredulity,

"And what if I decline?"

"That would be a sad day for both of us, Grace. You are but one person; I have a duty to millions. And now I think this meeting has progressed far enough. I am sure you are in need of further refreshment, and time to contemplate my offer. Allow me to arrange for some food to be sent to your room."

"I'm not hungry," said Grace stubbornly.

"Oh, I think you are," said Nexus. He turned and pulled a cord that hung from the ceiling. "You will be shown to your room. Ah Mr Janus – thank you for coming. I am sure you will enjoy escorting Miss Lefavarie back to her room. And this time I think we shall lock the door." Sevi Janus had walked into the room, his gait muscle-bound and robotic.

"Sevi!" cried Grace but he did not look at her.

"It would indeed give me pleasure," he said with a sneer, nodding to Nexus. "I think we've all had enough of her majesty the Ice Queen's antics. Not so high and mighty now, eh?"

"Sevi, we should talk," Grace said breathlessly as Janus pushed her back up the stairs and into her room.

"I think you missed your window," he said with a grimace and shut the door. After a while he brought her some food,

"We're all out of ice cream I'm afraid," he laughed and left. Alone again, Grace sat on the bed, playing with her fork.

There was not a lot that Grace could do. She rapidly ascertained that whilst the windows and shutters could be opened, she was on at least the third floor of the building, with a drop onto rocks and no convenient drainpipes, balconies or fire escapes. After Janus brought her more food later in the day, she discovered that he was immutable. Any interest he may have had for her had been crushed by her disdain for him, and he was relishing the power he now had over her.

In the late afternoon, she heard voices outside, and the door was opened. Jack came in.

"Hello, Grace," he said guiltily.

"I really don't know what you expect me to say to you," she replied.

"Look, I'm sorry."

"You're sorry!" she exclaimed, "sorry!" She threw her hands in the air in disbelief. It was the first opportunity to vent her frustration and unhappiness, and the vehemence of this reaction took her by surprise.

"I can explain," began Jack, "this is not what I wanted."

"What did you want then, Jack? I have been working with you for two years now, and I have always looked up to you. I respected you, I trusted you. And now I find …" she could barely locate the words. "Now I find you are rotten through! I can only assume you have done this for your own material gain. I saw the special file on Sevi Janus's computer disk. I know what it is about now. Those were payments, from Nexus to you and to those reviewers, for accepting useless projects and lousy abstracts. How long has this been going on, for goodness sake?!"

Jack sat down wearily in an armchair. "I thought you knew something," he said, sadly. "Tramane got to you, huh?"

"Got to me! Sure, he tried very hard to 'get to me' and for months I supported you in the face of his suspicions. I could not conceive of your being a bad guy!" She paused, relenting a little. "I thought we were friends, Jack."

"I couldn't tell you about this," said Jack. "It's been a gradual process. It's been creeping up on me. I had no choice."

"What do you mean, you had no choice? You chose to accept his money. You chose to work with Nexus!"

"I did not have a choice," repeated Jack. The pretty floral design on the chair was at odds with Jack's pale and sweating face. "Nexus never gives you choices. He got a hold on me, Grace. I made a mistake and he's been exploiting it ever since."

"What do you mean?"

"The mistake was accepting a donation from him. It was all above board, but ..." he found it difficult to continue, "I took the money for myself. I needed it. It was too easy. I intended to repay it. Nexus found out – I think he may have set me up. If Amity knew, they would sack me."

"You're being melodramatic," said Grace, unsympathetically. "You still had the choice. I don't know what your personal circumstances are, Jack, because you always keep them to yourself, but if you'd talked I am sure that someone would have listened."

"No," said Jack, "and in any case, the situation was quickly compounded. Nexus knew my frailties. He planted Janus in the organisation. That made the regular donations to Amity Action easy, and gradually, more and more conditions crept in. I couldn't stop. My successes were always down to him. At first it was just one or two projects, and then ... then it got out of hand."

"I should have known something was up a long time ago," said Grace. "We used to agree on everything."

"I know," said Jack, with a small sigh. They sat in silence for a moment, Grace fuming at Jack's weakness.

"What now?" she said.

"I don't know what now," said Jack. "I'm afraid."

"Afraid?"

"Afraid for you, Grace. Nexus can't let you go. You know too much. He's been planning this for years. It's his reason for existence – he's a zealot. You must join his campaign."

"You must be joking – he's obviously a maniac."

"In that case, Miss Lefavarie, you will not leave alive." Nexus entered the room. "Such a pity," he continued, "I rather hoped that Jack could talk you round. Our cause is a worthy one. But for now, you'd better come with me; I believe you have a visitor."

29

THE DENOUEMENT

Nexus led both Grace and Jack to a large, minimalist office, where he took his seat behind a desk. Janus followed them in and stood beside him; two other men remained outside the door.

"Look," said Nexus with satisfaction, pointing to a small red light flashing on top of his desk. "Camera number three. Mr Tramane always takes the most contorted routes into my establishments." Nexus flicked a switch next to his chair. There was a whirring and a shifting of mahogany before a monitor was revealed. Tramane was wearing his black night gear. He was creeping furtively along a corridor. Nexus reached for another switch, and spoke down a microphone that had emerged like a fruiting body from the desk top.

"Why, Mr Tramane, we have been expecting you." Tramane stopped and looked around. Spotting the camera, he glanced up at it, shrugged and waved. "Second on the left, Mr Tramane. Oh, and Mr Tramane," added Nexus coolly, "please leave your gun with the boys at the door." The camera followed as Alec was accosted by the two men outside the office. One of them clearly had a power complex, but Alec remained calm.

Nexus stood to greet him,

"Well, Mr Tramane, what can I do for you?"

"I know what you're up to, Nexus, and so do a large number of other powerful people. You've reached the end of the road."

"Oh, I don't think so," replied Nexus. "You are so very tiresome, Mr Tramane. I knew as soon as Jack reported your visit to Amity Action that you would prove a thorn in my side. But this will be the last time, because you won't be leaving here alive. Perhaps you would be so kind as to hand over the conference tape."

"I don't have it with me."

"That is a shame, but it does not matter. You and my dear guest Miss Lefavarie here are the only people standing in my way. The only question left for me to resolve now is how to dispose of you both."

"I don't think that's a subject you'll need to worry about," said Tramane. "I have considerable back-up, and we have enough evidence to put you away for a long time. I bugged this building months ago."

"Such bravado! Believe me, I know you have come alone – we have an intricate surveillance system, and as for bugs, we have highly sensitive instruments here and I know you left nothing following your unwelcome visit last year. I will have the pleasure of dealing with you as I please." He snapped his fingers and Janus came forward.

"Mr Janus, perhaps you would escort Mr Tramane to the cellar." Nexus turned to Grace.

"Such a shame, Grace, that you had to get mixed up in all this. Let me give you one last chance, my dear. I can assure you that my tactics will be merely to expose the faults of my political rivals. Anything revealed will be the truth, and, with only a little coaxing, the truth by their own admission."

"Your tactics so far have involved unethical research, blackmail and what now? Murder? I doubt the people you hope to embarrass into resignation could beat that, for all their petty hypocrisies and adulteries. What gives you the right to put yourself above them?"

Nexus gave Grace a sad look, and took her by the arm.

"Perhaps you would like to accompany us, Mr D'Oretz?" Jack said nothing but followed as Janus grasped Tramane by the shoulder. The latter tried to break free and there ensued a brief fight, but Nexus summoned the two men from outside and Tramane was overwhelmed.

As they stumbled along the corridor, and down a flight of stairs, Nexus said,

"Of course, the 'cellar' is a bit of a euphemism. As I'm sure Miss Lefavarie is aware, the Pacific here is something of an animal. When this complex was being built, we took advantage of an offering from Nature. She generously furnished us with a small underground room which floods with the tide. I've always wondered how best to utilise it. Now, at last, its purpose is clear to me."

Grace looked at Tramane, who smiled at her confidently. She felt disinclined to confidence herself and made a brief attempt to break free from Nexus, who gripped her even harder.

"Jack?" she said as they reached a metal hatch in the ground, surrounded by damp rock – the 'door' of the 'cellar'. He said nothing and did not look at her.

"Farewell, Mr Tramane," Nexus said, "and Miss Lefavarie, it's been a pleasure." He kissed Grace's hand, "you have about twenty minutes." Janus lifted up the hatch and guided them roughly inside. They had to descend a ladder to the floor, which was already under a foot of water. The large metal hatch was closed, and Alec and Grace could hear bolts being drawn across it. The room was really a cave, somewhere beneath the shore. The only light was supplied by a circle of fortified glass in the ceiling – an optional viewing point for macabre theatrics? The walls were wet and barnacled and Grace could see a few sea anemones closed in on themselves like blobs of jelly.

"Alec?" she said, wide-eyed; she could visibly see the water rising.

"It's OK Grace, don't worry. I've got the gadgets. We'll be out of here in no time." Alec pulled the clothing away from his top half, exposing a flat, criss-cross of belts with discreet pockets, within which nestled an assortment of objects. He had climbed to the top of the ladder again, and was pushing at the door. He then peered at his equipment, and started fiddling with the hatch. After a few minutes, during which Alec seemed to be fumbling through his kit, the water had reached Grace's hips. She looked up at him anxiously, shivering with cold.

"Is everything all right? Are you making any progress?" After a pause Alec said,

"Bugger!" and jumped down into the water, which was now at their waists. "Look, you'll have to stand on the ladder, the water's rising too quickly. I need to have a look around. The water's coming in from somewhere; we may be able to get out the same way."

"But what about your gadgets?"

"The explosive – it must have fallen out of my belt."

"What!" exclaimed Grace. "We'll not get out then! We're trapped!"

"Calm down, I've been in these situations before. Just stay put!"

Grace stepped up onto the bottom of the ladder, bewildered. Alec ducked down under the water, which seemed to be coming in more quickly now. Grace retreated up the struts. Tramane popped out of the water with a gasp and a shudder.

"Anything?" said Grace, panicking.

"Not yet," Tramane said, taking another deep breath and ducking down again. Grace cast her eyes around desperately. She was wet through and it was as if the water was pressing into her, confining her, infusing stiffness into her. She could not take in the fact that these could be her last few minutes. She felt she should be thinking of something profound, running through her misdeeds, or praying, but all she did was look at one of the green anemones unravelling in the water beside her. She found herself wondering how long it could survive in the dry: a lot longer than she could survive in the cold and wet, she concluded. Tramane reappeared, almost banging his head on the roof of the cave. Grace searched his face for some good news but he didn't even look at her. She noted the trace of fear that had entered his eyes, and knew that all was lost.

"Alec," she said gently, and pulled him towards her.

"I haven't the time, Grace, I must carry on looking."

"There is no way out," she said, suddenly calm.

"I must look." Their eyes met for a second before he went under again. The water was now lapping under Grace's chin, and she grazed her cheek against the hatch. As she shut her eyes, waiting for the water to enter her nostrils, she felt the metal give way above her. Looking up, she saw Jack, on his knees, reaching for her.

"I, I can't let you die Grace," he said. "I, I love you …" She was momentarily stunned by this last-minute reprieve and did not register what he had said.

"Alec!" she exclaimed. "We must wait for Alec!" But Jack leant down, scooped her out of the water, slammed the hatch shut, bolted it and started to push her quickly along the corridor.

"Wait!" she said. "Leave the hatch open!"

"If I leave it, they'll know you've escaped. I have to shut it!"

"No, you can't!" Grace broke free and went back to the hatch. Yanking at the bolts, she managed to pull the heavy metal slab up a few centimetres. Jack helped her lift it open. The water was right at the top. She stepped back onto the ladder and made her way down it, Jack urging her to hurry up. She was numb to the cold, spurred on into the swirling ocean by her determination to find Tramane. She opened her eyes under the water, but it was too dark and cloudy to see anything. The prospect of her surviving this event without Alec had not crossed her mind, so the concept of his loss had not been part of her thinking. But now it came upon her in a flood of misery. She went back under, but could see nothing.

When she emerged, Jack said,

"That's it. We're going. It's too late for him now. If he were alive, Grace, he'd have appeared by now. I can hear Janus. The tide is up. He's been instructed to check on things." He slammed the great metal door shut at last, wrenching the bolts across it, fighting off Grace. He grabbed her and pulled her along the dark corridor and into a side room. He listened at the door until he was sure Janus had come and gone. Grace was in a state of shock.

"He's dead," she whispered, when Jack moved his ear from the door. "I can't believe it. He's gone!" She slumped onto the floor, but Jack was urging her on.

"We've got thirty minutes, Grace, before Sorrel leaves. We have to stop her. We have to blow up the helicopter or something."

"He's dead!" repeated Grace, tragically.

"Come on! You'll have time for him later. We've got to get this sorted!"

"And why now, exactly? To appease your conscience?"

"Please, Grace. I need your help," Jack was in earnest. "Come on. Look, I found this. It might be what we need!" Grace looked at what he was holding. It appeared to be a small explosive device.

"Where did you find that?" she said suspiciously.

"Tramane had it," he explained. "He dropped it when he was fighting Janus."

"He was looking for that to get us out of the cellar!" said Grace furiously.

"Please come on, Grace," urged Jack. He hauled her up the stairs they had descended less than an hour before.

"Well, now you have it, do you know how to use it?" asked Grace.

"Of course not. Do you?"

"What do you think?" replied Grace impatiently. The two of them moved along the wooden corridors, pausing and hiding from time to time as necessary. Jack seemed to know where he was going.

"The helicopter," he declared, "it's in here." They darted through a metal door, and Jack pushed Grace to the ground behind some large oil drums. Peering through a gap, they could see Sevi Janus checking the machine. There was no-one else around.

"Perhaps we could cause a diversion," said Grace.

"Couldn't you try and charm him – I'm sure he has a thing for you."

"*Had* a thing for me, I'm afraid – definitely past tense. And 'hell hath no fury like a *man* scorned'."

Their vacillation was brought to an abrupt halt by an explosion nearby.

"What's that?!" exclaimed Grace, throwing herself closer to the floor, which smelt of oil. A siren sounded and red lights started to flash on the walls. Janus had reached into the helicopter and was wielding a large and efficient-looking machine gun but before he had a chance to use it, he was pushed to the ground by a swarm of armed men in black. Grace and Jack remained pinned to the floor.

The initial fracas finished, instructions were shouted and some of the men came towards the door. They were surprised to find Jack and Grace on the ground, and for a moment, the two of them were surrounded by gun nozzles at every conceivable angle.

"Look, we're the good guys!" shouted Grace. "Don't shoot! Don't shoot!" The men were cautious, frisking them as they lay on the ground. Jack volunteered the explosive quickly, keen to be rid of it; then they were hoisted roughly to their feet.

"This way," said one of the men, and pushed them quickly out of a large hole in the wall. "Keep your heads low," he commanded, as they were shunted out into the cold evening air.

Fifty minutes later, Grace was sitting in an armoured truck, covered in a blanket. From where she sat, she had a perfect view of the storming of Nexus's headquarters. The wooden dwelling sat adjacent to several large modern buildings – probably his laboratories. People were streaming out of the buildings. As they did so, they were pushed to the ground at gunpoint. The whole place was burning, with clods of fire reaching up into the darkening sky, creating a furnace-like glow carried high and wide by the ocean's spray.

Having been identified, Grace had been escorted to the truck out of harm's way. Jack had been taken elsewhere. His eyes had met Grace's briefly before he was marshalled away and he had looked strangely at her, a mix of relief and – she was not sure what.

"How're you doing, Miss?" A young man climbed into the truck and handed her some chocolate. "We're just about finished here. I've been told to take you to the nearest town. You can stay there overnight. We'll have to debrief you tomorrow though – so no slipping back to Vancouver."

"Of course not," said Grace, trying to smile. "Is there any sign? Did you find ..."

"'fraid not, Miss," said the man solemnly. "These things happen, you know; part of the job ..."

"Did you get Nexus?"

"Unsure as yet. Tricky customer, that one. I get a bit sick of these lunatics ... second one this year and it's only May. I tell you, they always slip through your fingers – escape pods, underwater passages ... sneaky bastards." He started up the engine, and Grace leant back in her seat and let her face vibrate gently against the chilled window pane.

It took just ten minutes to get to Tofino, and Grace found herself back at the Orca Hotel. Perhaps if the man had known of what had passed there before, he would have checked her in elsewhere, out of kindness. A little later, as she stood in the heat of the shower, the shocked and frozen state she had been in during the last two hours thawed, and she began to cry, her tears mingling with the drops all around. Encouraged by the surrounding wall of sound from the falling water, Grace placed her hands over her face and let out a cry, slid slowly down the wall and crouched over the plug hole, sobbing. It was all over – but he was gone.

When Grace awoke, it was still dark. She glanced over to the bed-side table. The red glow of the clock told her that it was half past two. As she emerged from unconsciousness, the soft, sweet blanket of oblivion lifted, leaving beneath the acute pain of her current reality. She wished she could sleep again, but the sheer exhaustion that had permitted her rest when she had finally made it to bed was gone, replaced by a dull thumping sorrow in her chest and limbs: Alec was dead.

But why had she awoken? Could she hear something? She strained her ears: nothing, apart from the gentle swish of the sea outside. She sat up, and switched on the light, shading her eyes at first from the brightness. She looked around the room, then got out of bed. Picking up a hotel robe and wrapping it around her, she moved towards the window. As she did so, she heard a gentle tapping. She pulled back the curtains but could see nothing. She opened the glazed door and a cold blast of air came into the room. She peered out: nothing. She was about to shut the door when a hand grasped hers.

"What the fuck …!"

"Whoa!" came a familiar voice. "I thought I was getting better at this!" Alec Tramane was standing on the balcony.

"Alec!" she exclaimed, her mouth dropping open in disbelief. "Alec, you're alive! Come in, come in! This is wonderful!" She grabbed him, lugged him over the threshold, and hugged him tightly to her at the first opportunity.

"A better reception than last time," he said wryly.

"Where have you been? What happened?!" She embraced him again. "Here, sit down." He did as he was bidden. He was soaking wet and shivering, and his hair was dishevelled and spattered with mud and seaweed.

"You look beaten," said Grace, at last getting a chance to survey him more rationally. She moved a stray piece of kelp from his ear. "Can I get you something?"

"I wouldn't mind a drink," he said jovially. "A scotch would be just fine."

"You must be frozen," said Grace, touching her hand to his face. She went to the mini-bar and got him a whisky. "Come on," she said impatiently, as she handed

322

him the drink, and a blanket from the cupboard, "tell me what happened."

"I found the way the sea got in," he said, smiling. "Came back for you, but you were nowhere. It was a squeeze but I got out; had a quick swim; came out somewhere beyond the beach; wandered a little in that famous temperate rainforest of yours. By the time I got back to Chesterman Beach the fun and games were well and truly over. The lads told me where you were. I came right over."

"So you really did have back-up then," said Grace, beaming.

"Nexus was wrong and I'm not that stupid. I knew they'd got you, Grace, and we had enough to go on. I was just going in for a recce. The men had instructions to come if I wasn't back in an hour."

"Have they got Nexus?"

"No, not yet. They might find him."

"Did they stop Sorrel Surrido from leaving?"

"Yes, she's in custody."

"You know that Jack rescued me," Grace said.

"I know, and for that I'm exceedingly grateful. It might help him. These last hours have been a nightmare. I didn't have time to look for you properly. I thought you were dead. I couldn't believe I'd let you down."

"You didn't let me down," said Grace pulling him to her and kissing him. "You know, you really need a shower," she said laughing, as the cold salt water seeped through her robe. Tramane smiled, stood up and offered her his hand.

"Would you care to join me?"

"Oh Mr Tramane!" she said, "I'd be delighted."

The next morning, Grace and Alec had a large and hot breakfast sent up to the room. The two of them were due to meet up with Alec's team later that morning. Alec had assured Grace that her debriefing would be a gentle affair. They would then head back to Vancouver.

"Will all this business be on the news?" Grace asked Alec as her eyes fell upon the radio on the bedside table.

"In some form or other," he replied. "Actually, that reminds me. What did you do with that tape from the conference cassette deck."

"It's behind the gutter downpipe on the balcony outside my room at the Fraser River. I hope it's still there."

"I'll get the lads to check it out," said Alec. "Come to think of it, I'd quite like a copy. I have a friend I'd like to share it with. And now to more important matters: an English breakfast in bed!" Alec stuck his fork into a large chunk of grilled sausage, which fizzed and exuded a trickle of fat. He chomped on it mercilessly.

"I think this is the first time I've seen you eat in an ungentlemanly fashion. I knew you were a dinosaur, but I wasn't sure until now that you were such a voracious carnivore."

"Well, I thought you found my gentlemanly behaviour patronising," he replied, smiling.

"I think we established the difference between civility and condescension," she retorted, giving him a prod.

"Are you saying this is an uncivil sausage?"

Grace laughed. "On the contrary, it looks very civil, and this feels very civilised." She lay back on the bed and stretched.

"What do you think of Nexus's plan, Alec – I mean, if he was just going to tell the world the truth about our politicians, was that really such a bad thing?"

"Telling people the truth is undoubtedly a good thing – although sometimes there is a time and a place for it. But Nexus's plan was never about the truth – it was about the acquisition of power. We've seen it all before. Can you really imagine a President Nexus? He would have been a despot! Nexus is a hypocritical, unethical criminal. You told him so rather eloquently yourself."

"But for his plan to work, wouldn't every political rival have to have a skeleton in their cupboard?"

"Do you think he would simply stop his campaign in the face of a squeaky clean candidate? No way! I wouldn't rate the chances of anyone opposing him, however angelic their track record."

"What do you think will happen to the current President? Nexus clearly had something on him."

"Oh I daresay that will be looked into – although it wouldn't surprise me if the people who need to know already do. As I said – there is sometimes a time and a place ..."

Grace rolled over and looked at Alec playfully.

"Well, you foiled Nexus's evil plan, anyway – I guess that makes you a hero," she laughed.

"Perhaps," replied Tramane seriously, "but not always for you. In our business we say the end justifies the means, and as a result we often leave a wake of upset behind us. To do my job, I need to be emotionally cold. I am a good agent, but I'm afraid that makes me a challenging lover. Grace, you have broken through my shell and I think I'm falling in love with you, but I am who I am, and I do what I do. I don't know where we are headed."

"Oh Alec," said Grace, kissing him gently, "let's just wait and see, shall we? Here, have another civil sausage."

30

DR HERMANN PEEWIT

D r Irene Spatchcock breezed into the DoA full of post-conference exuberance. It was almost June and she was already wearing her summer wardrobe[27] – today a flattering green dress, a white linen jacket[28] and a pair of elegant sandals with tapered heels.

"Oh, Ellinora," Irene said dreamily. "If only you'd been there! So many delightful, and, dare I say it, useful people. I must have made at least a dozen influential contacts."

"How was the presentation?" I said, more out of politeness than interest.

---

[27] Frumpp's Fashion Tip Number 20: forget casting clouts after May is out. The shedding of clothing is never to be recommended even in the hottest of seasons.

[28] Frumpp's Fashion Tip Number 21: you have to choose between wearing white linen and eating. For me, the decision is easy.

"Well, we had a bit of a shaky start for some reason, but on the whole it went well. I'm pretty sure I made a good impression. Terry was OK too," she added as an afterthought, "although I wish he'd stop rattling on about Virago Innocenti. It's incomprehensible nonsense. If he quotes that man again, I shall go mad."

"Actually Virago Innocenti was a woman," I said, "and the quote is about early alarm clocks. It comes from the poem, 'An ode to the chiming hour'. I looked it up."

"Oh Ellinora – ever the pedant," tutted Irene, shaking her head. "Now back to business. You'll be pleased to know I'm trying to get another team meeting sorted. Unfortunately Max seems to have disappeared. I've not seen him since we got back. His secretary is being most evasive."

A flicker of suspicion, or was it sadness, scuttled across her face. "If he doesn't appear soon, we'll just have to meet without him."

"That's fine by me," I said. I had made good progress in the absence of my team-mates. The data from the twenty focus groups were more than enough, and I had managed to put together a draft questionnaire.

Shortly after coffee break, I had a visit from Professor Tweezer.

"Ah, young Flop," he began, "need to borrow the tapes and transcripts from the *WImpI* project. Got some people interested in having a peep at them: nothing important."

"Fine," I said. "Max has the original tapes for the ten focus groups he was going to analyse, but I have copies of them. I'm not sure whether he ever did that work. He's never given me any results."

"I'll take what you've got, Flop – I am sure they'll still be useful. You'll have them back shortly." I had a rummage around and gave him some files and a box of tapes.

"Thank you, Flop!" he said jovially and left. I made no further enquiries as to why he needed them. Tweezer was, after all, a law unto himself. He left them in my pigeon-hole a fortnight later, a yellow sticky note attached with the message, 'Much appreciated, Flop!'

I had tried to stop fantasising about Dr James Ross since I had last seen him at the course. Despite my very great satisfaction at our parting as friends, my imagination had decided to latch upon him as an object of infatuation. After all, we had made no plans to keep in touch, and the assurance that we would never meet again allowed my unruly mind to wander and indulge. Without the reality of his presence, I was able to misrepresent our relationship quite delightfully in my daydreams. *The Best of James Bond* merely fuelled my fantasy. I had taken to driving around the countryside on rainy weekends to get my fix. I know it is unhealthy.

I was rather shocked, therefore, when a small padded envelope arrived for me at the DoA, with 'Docklands Institute for Work and Social Life Research' on the front. Sally detected my blush, and smiled sweetly. I took it hungrily back to my room, immediately feeling quite silly, indeed guilty, about my recent musings upon James's perfect bod.

Ripping the envelope open with little ceremony, I found a tape, and a brief note, 'Believe it or not, you've helped make the world a safer place. Hey, who's the monkey now? James'. Quite inscrutable, and I couldn't wait to play it. Luckily, I'd brought my car to work that day (Boffin of the car parks was on holiday). I was tempted to take a circuit round the one-way system rather than work, and was just contemplating this when there was a cautious knock at my door.

"Come in," I said. Nothing happened, so I got up and opened it. Outside was a tall, thin man with a very interesting face. His eyes were a nutty brown, quite close together, large and endearing. His hair was also brown and ruffled, rather like mine ('through a hedge backwards'). His nose was long and crooked but this added a humour and even a sexiness to his face. He was scruffy but not smelly, and held in his hands something glittery, which he offered to me.

"Bulldog clips," he said.

"Bulldog clips?" I repeated.

"Bulldog clips," he said again. "I think you need some."

"Well, yes, I do actually." I had been looking for some for the boards we were using for the first pilot of the questionnaire. I picked one out of his hand.

"They are very pretty," I said. And they were – unlike any other bulldog clips I had seen. They were iridescent, and reflected all the colours of the rainbow. The man seemed pleased.

"Would you like to come in?" I said.

"Could I?" the man responded.

"Yes, if you like." He moved timidly forward, and I ushered him into Rosy's chair.

"You see, bulldog clips convey a very particular psychology among the different paper fastening technologies that exist. They are impermanent, like paper clips, but much, much more substantial, more chunky, more robust," he said.

"I see," I replied.

"Unlike staples," he added.

"Indeed," I said. "Er, could I ask who you are?"

"Oh," said the man nervously, twiddling his fingers. "I'm Hermann Peewit. I, I, er work in the Annex, on, er, paper fastening technologies, PFT. It's er interesting …"

"I'm sure it is," I said. "I'm Ellie Frumpp."

"I know," said Hermann. "I've been sharing my stationery with you. I thought I should. I, er, wanted to …"

"So you're my secret supplier of paper clips and treasury tags!" I had tackled Sally on this subject, and she had denied all knowledge of my rather attractive office accessories. She was both curious and envious that I had somehow thwarted the bureaucracy of UCLOG. "Well, thank you very much!" A pause. More finger fiddling.

"A drink sometime perhaps?" queried Hermann, the words jerky, dragging their feet.

"I'd like that very much," I said.

"Tonight maybe?"

"Tonight would be grand."

"Pig and Trough, Bloort Street?"

"No," I said, firmly. "The Jaunty Scholar, Park Road."

"Seven o'clock?"

"I'll be there!"

With that, Hermann Peewit got up, a look of excitement playing on his unusual face. He paused at the door, and raised his hand before leaving – it was large and cartoonish (although, I hasten to add, had the full complement of digits). Overall, he was *very* sweet.

That evening I felt positively happy; a light-heartedness I had not experienced in several months. I

331

had a date! A strange date, perhaps, but not unattractive in a rangy sort of way. It would mean I would miss part of *Reality Crescent*, but that did not seem to matter. Marjorie and Derek were temporarily reconciled, brought together by the disappearance of Twinkletoes, who, weary of their shenanigans, had escaped to Abergavenny with Lady Honoria Twiglet's diamond. The police had never found it; the bird was a clever little thing. I pondered what I should wear. Perhaps tonight it DID matter.

Jemima popped in for some camomile and was very excited on my behalf. She and I were now firm friends. Having got to know her better, I had discovered that she did, in fact, have a mischievous sense of humour, although it was usually caged with apology. She was beginning to emerge from her Snoode-induced sadness, and had even hazarded a date with a postgrad. she met at church.

I had brought James's tape home with me, and, too pre-occupied with my impending tryst, decided to keep it for a rainy day. I put it carefully on a shelf next to my other tapes. My attention was drawn to the great variety of music I actually had. Maybe it was time to give *The Best of James Bond* a rest.

ACKNOWLEDGEMENTS AND REFERENCES

Alec Tramane shares similarities with 'secret agents' generally and James Bond specifically (for example, his cover company, 'Amatheia Exports', is an intentional reference to Bond's cover 'Universal Exports'), but he is not a replica – Bond would not give Ellie Frumpp the time of day! Ellie Frumpp's fantasies relate to her love of the *James Bond* books, films and music and Grace Lefavarie, who in many ways finds herself in a world not dissimilar to Ellie's dreams, recognizes her role as a 'Bond girl'. In addition, the Canadian storyline broadly (and knowingly) follows 'Bondian' lines. Inevitably, therefore, there are references and allusions to 'James Bond', the character, and *James Bond* media in this book.

I would therefore like to gratefully acknowledge the influence of the following: the *James Bond* books of Ian Fleming (Jonathan Cape: London); the *James Bond* films, almost all of which were produced by, or with, EON

Productions (for complete details, however, please see the *Internet Movie Database* – www.imdb.com); and *The Best of James Bond: 30ᵗʰ Anniversary Collection* (EMI, 1992).

A number of specific references to Bond books, films and music (see above for sources) are made. These are as follows: the 'unforgettable melody from Monty Norman' is, of course, the *James Bond Theme* (Monty Norman Orchestra), first used in *Dr No* (1962); 'Dr No' is the eponymous villain in the *Bond* book (1958) and film (1962) *Dr No*; the song, 'The Man with the Golden Gun' was written by John Barry and Don Black for the film of that name (1974), and was sung by Lulu; 'Little Nellie' is a direct reference to the small helicopter James Bond uses in the film *You Only Live Twice* (1967); 'Ms Blofeld' is obviously inspired by 'Ernst Stavro Blofeld', the most significant villain in the *Bond* series, who makes a number of appearances in both the books and the films; Irene Spatchcock's shoes containing 'daggers' is a reference to Rosa Klebb, a character in the book (1957) and film (1963) *From Russia With Love*. Two *Bond* films are specifically mentioned in the text, namely *Goldfinger* (1964) and *GoldenEye* (1995). 'Felix Leiter' and 'Xenia Onatopp' are characters in *Goldfinger* (although Leiter appears in other books and films) and *GoldenEye* respectively.

References are made to other films. These are as follows (refs. *IMDb*): *Waterworld* (1995), Universal Pictures, Gordon Company, Davis Entertainment, Licht/ Mueller Film Corporation; *The Terminator* (1984), Hemdale, Pacific Western, Euro Film Funding, Cinema '84/ Greenberg Brothers Partnership; *Terminator 2* (1991), Carolco Pictures, Pacific Western, Lightstorm

334

Entertainment, Canal+, T2 Productions; *The Great Escape* (1963), The Mirisch Company, Alpha.

Other references are as follows (refs. *Wikipedia, IMDb*): 'Romulan attire', 'James T. Kirk', 'warp progress' and 'Beta Quadrant' refer to the TV Series *Star Trek: The Next Generation* (1987-1994; Paramount Television) and *Star Trek* (1966-1969; Desilu Productions, Norway Corporation, Paramount Television); 'Room 1.01' is a reference to 'Room 101' in *Nineteen Eighty-Four* by George Orwell (1949), various publishers; the 'Queen of the Night' is a character in Mozart's *The Magic Flute* (1791); 'Nature, red in tooth and claw' is a quote from *In Memorium*, by Alfred Lord Tennyson (1849); 'Jane and Peter and Pat the dog' is a reference to the characters in the *Key Words Reading Scheme* (1964-1967, with later updates), Ladybird Books: London; 'Everybody Wants to Rule the World' by Tears for Fears (1985) is from the album *Songs from the Big Chair*, Phonogram; 'One Step Beyond' by Madness (1979) is from the album *One Step Beyond*, Stiff Records; 'Paddington stare' is, of course, from Michael Bond's *Paddington Bear* series (1958-2018), HarperCollins; Grace makes a reference to *Strange Case of Dr Jekyll and Mr Hyde* (1886) by Robert Louis Stevenson, various publishers; *Tess of the D'Urbervilles* is by Thomas Hardy (1892), various publishers; Grace paraphrases the William Congreve quote from *The Mourning Bride* (1697), 'Nor hell a fury like a woman scorned,' commonly quoted as 'Hell hath no fury like a woman scorned'.

James Chapman (1999) *Licence to Thrill: A Cultural History of the James Bond Films*. I.B.Tauris Publishers: London, provided interesting reading and useful information which helped in the writing of *Ellie Frumpp Pee Aitch Dee*.

Last, but not least, I would like to acknowledge the following for their comments, help and encouragement: Michael and Kathleen; Andrew and Lynda; Deborah; Andy; and, with special thanks, Suzy.

CPSIA information can be obtained
at www.ICGtesting.com
Printed in the USA
LVHW081312250220
648153LV00015B/702